Other books by the author:

The Other Door, stories
The Soft Room, novel
Journey to Bom Goody, novel

The Made-up
Man

Karen Heuler

Livingston Press
The University of West Alabama

Copyright © 2011 Karen Heuler
All rights reserved, including electronic text
isbn 13: 978-1-60489-080-8 library binding
isbn 13: 978-1-60489-081-5 trade paper
Library of Congress Control Number 2011931226
Printed on acid-free paper.
Printed in the United States of America by
United Graphics
Hardcover binding by: Heckman Bindery
Typesetting and page layout: Joe Taylor
Proofreading: Joe Taylor, Stephanie Camille Murray,
Connie James, Brittney Ivy, Tricia Taylor,
Schuyler Bishop, Dannielle Harvey, Robert Sims
Cover layout: Joe Taylor
Cover art: David Fratkin

first edition
6 5 4 3 3 2 1

The Made-up Man

E'en hell hath its peculiar laws.

Faust, Part I

Chapter 1

$\mathcal{T}$here are three things a woman should take for granted: looks will fade, men will stray, and wishes are worthless without actions.

But learning this is the result of experience, and experience takes too long. At 35, Alyson Salky was still young enough to have confidence in her looks and in the fidelity of her boyfriend, and to think there was time to get what she wanted—well, she might not even know *everything* she wanted (occasionally she had a twinge about babies—possibly more than a twinge; but Peter didn't want kids and really, wasn't Peter better than a kid? More fun? Not so demanding?). She was happy, and therefore confident. She loved the feel of Peter's body beneath his shirt when she pulled him close for a hug, the roughness of his chin, the nimble flexibility of his body, his half-lidded sex look, the way his face burst into laughter, his roaming curiosity, his wit. "I love you because you love me," he'd say, and wink. And laugh. And grab her with one arm like she was his moll in an old Hollywood film. When she was with him she felt smart and funny—hell, she *was* smart and funny, and that kind of hard-core bliss was her due, and inviolable.

So there she was, a good job, a great boyfriend, a fine dog, some really great girlfriends—when that magazine came out with the article stating that a woman over 40 stood a better chance of being killed by a terrorist than getting married.

"Do we want to get married?" she asked her co-worker, Anna. They were turning into good friends.

Anna's mouth got unhappy. "Sometimes, yes," she said. "Sometimes we want to get married. Especially if we want to have kids. And I want to have kids." She raised her eyebrows significantly to Alyson, who shrugged.

"I'm already complete," Alyson said. "I have everything I want."

Who needed to be married, anyway, in this day and age? What did marriage bring to the table? A woman could get everything she needed under her own steam—career, love, fulfillment, self-respect! Statistics could be manipulated to prove any point; everyone knew that, so who could say if that statement was even true?

She had no interest in marriage, not a bit. Anna was just in a bad mood.

But she wasn't; she was happy and lucky and safe and in charge.

Until all of it fell apart, the day she saw Peter get into a cab with her best friend Maggie. She stood on the sidewalk, stunned, watching with a clarity of vision that was almost supernatural. She saw them get in the back seat and fuse—that was it; they fused into one organism, their heads their arms their mouths coming together like two drops of water irresistibly combining.

The cab was gone, with its unicellular monster in the back; yet the picture throbbed in her mind as if constantly refreshed: Maggie got in, then Peter got in, closing the door. Peter leaned forward to give the address to the driver, then he turned to Maggie and fell back against the seat and smoothly draped himself around her as she draped around him and they were indelibly lit up through the cab's rear window, as if a spotlight shone on them, or the burst from some sly terrorist's bomb.

Everyone kept walking and she did too, but she didn't turn in to Peter's studio to surprise him for lunch, of course; that surprise had been tossed on its head. Instead, she walked back to her own job, skipping lunch altogether, walking hard to try to get her heart to match the rhythm of her feet instead of racketing around like a roulette ball. A fire engine blared its alarm as it made its way up the avenue, and the scream of its siren merely served as the soundtrack for the image in her head: Peter turning to Maggie, Maggie turning to him, the vanishing perspective of the two of them, together.

*S*he got back to the office and walked past Anna with a wave, shutting her door, saying vaguely that she was under deadline. But in fact she spent the afternoon trying to find a way of making that scenario innocent. Despite her determination and imagination, there was none. Anna tapped on her door before leaving for the day, asking, "Feel like a drink?"

"That's not what I feel like," Alyson said under her breath, then shook her head no. "I'm behind on the schedule for the meeting." Anna nodded (meetings ruled them both) and left. Alyson moved some papers around on her desk (she certainly would end up being behind schedule) and tried to come up with a plan. She had no room for any other thoughts but thoughts about Peter, and the only way she could move forward was to do something about it. She could already feel the corrosion of his betrayal eating at her; there was nothing to do but face it.

He had been working late a lot; she had trusted him. She went home with dread in her heart, not even noticing the frenzied welcome she always got from Dingo, their dog, though she picked up his leash, clipped him in, and took him outside. Every thought was about Peter. Dingo went about his doggie business, subdued.

When Peter finally came home late he was surprised to see her still dressed and waiting for him. He was just about to stride across the room when she said, "I know about you and Maggie."

He stopped, frowned, his eyes shifted to the window opposite, to the doorway to the left, to the wall to the right. He leaned back a little. He started to say something and then stopped and thought some more. "Okay," he said finally. "Good." He still stood in the same spot.

In fact, he smiled. "I've been feeling terrible about it. I'm glad you know. It's a relief."

Her mind was double-tripping around what he'd said. Was it a relief because he felt guilty and would apologize and get it over? Relief because he really didn't want to betray her and now it was open for discussion? Why would he be relieved unless he felt he had a way out, a way to fix it? Her mind seemed to have wrapped its arms around itself; it wasn't going to expose anything. "What are you relieved about?" she asked finally.

The dog moved in between the two of them, halting with a low whine and sitting facing Peter.

Peter cleared his throat and said, almost theatrically, "I can't live here anymore, I can't. I didn't know how to say it, to tell you. Maggie and I feel awful. But I don't love you, Alyson. I've tried and—and, no. I can't force myself to, you know. It's no good." He had even managed to have a tear well up on that—on how he had tried to love her, and no, he couldn't.

"*Tried* to love me," she said, hoping to shame him.

"Yes." He nodded. "I didn't want to hurt you. So I tried. And I couldn't."

"But you *said* you loved me—"

"I said what I believed; also what I wanted to believe. Don't throw it in my face, Alyson. I'd give my left arm to make this better somehow."

And it went on from there: she pleaded, she accused, he stood there deflecting. She cried and he came over and hugged her and she sank into him, thinking there was a reprieve, but he pulled away and said he had to leave. She asked why, he told her, and it went on for a while until he took some shirts and things in a hastily packed bag and left.

And where did he go? she thought bitterly. To Maggie. Whom she now hated even more than she hated Peter who—despite it all—she still loved. Her head was chattering. She thought she would lie down at least until she could control the violent movements in her head and in her heart.

Dingo was hiding under the bed. His snout peeked out, and his sad brown eyes followed her as she stood in the doorway, then walked away, and then walked in again. She saw him, pulled him out, and hugged him, not noticing it was too tight. He groaned. "Poor Dingo! What will we do? He's gone!" The dog licked her face, a frown between his eyes,

Karen Heuler

and she let him go and began to pace again.

She passed a mirror and saw herself—gray eyes, medium brown hair to her waist. Peter liked to braid her hair, the two of them had braided it together, braiding the braids, toying with her hair as they lay in bed. He had pulled it, he had stroked it, lifted it, brushed it, parted it. It had coiled around her head like a snake, he had said he loved it.

She found a pair of scissors, coiled the hair around her fist, and chopped it off, bunch after bunch, laying it out on the dresser like an animal pelt. She found a box in the closet and rolled the hair up nicely in one of the styles she wore, put it into the box and wrapped it. Gift wrap. In times like this, drama was called for. How many years did that hair represent? The same number of years she'd spent with Peter? She figured it was pretty close.

That made her feel better, briefly, just briefly, and she looked around the room and saw all the heaps of things—his things, the room would look bare without his half—and another wave of distress washed over her. What next?

She despaired at the unfairness of it all. He could move on, he could always move on, a man could always find a woman, but what would she do—loyal, loving, trusting—a goddamn idiot who didn't see it coming?

How long before she could find someone she could love and believe in again? Was that even possible? Peter had been the one, she'd wrapped herself around him, she'd made a cocoon out of him. Where could she start over, in a city where all the women were single and all the men were married? That was how Maggie had characterized it, and Maggie should know, the whore, how could Peter fall for her? Sure it was funny, listening to Maggie's endless parade of lousy lovers (when had Maggie stopped talking about them? How had Alyson failed to notice?).

She hit her forehead with her fist, as if to get a stuck movie reel going again. She didn't want to get stalled on this, she couldn't get stalled on this. If that was the end of the picture, that was the end of the show. One minute she wanted to die, the next she just wanted to kill him. No, her. Impossible to let them get away with it.

She was filled with a kind of relentless energy. The dog began to whine and she stopped, briefly, to pet him and give him a biscuit. He left you too, poor thing, she thought. And then she started cutting up Peter's clothes, cutting off the heels of his socks, the toes of his shoes, until the fun went out of it, finally, and she sat on the floor, the dog beside her, worried and pulling at her with his paw.

She jumped up and ran outside, stopping once she hit the front door to consider her next move. The Vulture was at the bottom of the five front steps, shifting from leg to leg. He lived on the first floor and was always hanging around the garbage cans. He moved back, his eyes cast down, as he usually did. Alyson had once tried to say hello to him and he had winced.

He was skinny, long matchstick legs hidden by loose, wrinkled jeans that highlighted his thinness. He wore an old stained peacoat and a ski cap pulled down nearly to his eyebrows. Peter had nicknamed him the Vulture because he thought he picked through the garbage for food. Old meat, fruit rinds, containers with a lick of sour cream in them. She tucked her head down and turned her eyes away as she passed.

He went out of her mind immediately. She paced up and down the streets, finally ending up in a bar where she ordered a glass of wine. White wine. A single woman in a bar with a glass of white wine. No wonder Anna had suggested a drink: it was hard to go it alone. Alyson's hands began to sweat. She looked around. Couples, leaning into each other. A few men alone, but they were too old, hacking coughers, half-lidded drunkards, men tensed over their shot glasses and glancing furtively at her. Dismissing her? She looked in the mirror behind the bar and saw her hair. It looked like a child had cut it. It made her thick eyebrows seem even thicker, overshadowing her gray eyes. Her mouth looked swollen. Her face was haphazard.

She gulped her wine and left the change on the bar. In the mirror she saw a neon sign, and her eyes caught it again as she left. There, across the street: Madame Hope, Fortuneteller. In red and yellow and green.

She had to know her future. She had to know there was something ahead of her that would break open like a fruit. "This future she tells me will be my future," Alyson thought. She looked in through the window. An empty room, two folding chairs, a small round table with a deck of Tarot cards, an unlit candle and a palmistry chart. She could just make out a doorway with bead curtains. Alyson knocked on the front door, waited, and knocked again. A black dog slightly bigger than a spaniel shuffled through the curtains and stood facing her, a very old dog who bared his teeth but made no sound.

Alyson was about to knock again when the curtains parted and a face peered out. The beads rippled and knocked against themselves like a cloud of insects.

The gypsy looked very ordinary. A plain square face, low forehead, hair dyed ash blonde and pulled back behind her ears. A line of dark roots edged the part like a black scar. She smiled gently, but more as if her lips had settled that way than as if she meant it. She wore a cotton print dress and an oversize cardigan sweater. She was chewing something.

"Don't worry about the time," the fortuneteller said, opening the door. "Come in." Alyson realized with a start that it must be midnight; one of the churches nearby was beginning to toll.

"Sit, sit," the gypsy urged, waving her hands at the chairs. She eyed the dog. "Go inside," the gypsy ordered. The dog stared her down, growling faintly. "I said go in." The dog turned grudgingly, looking over his shoulder at Alyson, and walked insultingly slowly. The curtains continued to click even after his black shabby tail had disappeared inside.

"That dog doesn't love me the way a dog should," Madam Hope sighed, settling herself down in a folding chair. "And he won't go away, either; he'll live forever just to make a point. He never forgave me, you know," she said, lowering her voice conspiratorially. "He's been like that ever since I had his balls cut off. But what could I do? He was jumping everything, humping away, the customers weren't safe. In a continual rut. I thought his hormones were stuck or something, but

they tell me all males are like that. Wanting to plug everything in sight."
She laughed tolerantly. "He stares at me and I know what he's thinking.
Someday he hopes to get even. But I don't think so." She shook her
head. "I don't think so at all. Do you have a dog?" Alyson nodded.
"I knew it. You can always tell. People who have dogs expect a certain
amount of order. People with cats—well, cats are the devil's familiar,
aren't they? Sly creatures."

Alyson nodded, but she wasn't really listening.

"Well," the gypsy said, eyeing her, "let's get down to business, shall
we? Tarot reading is twenty dollars, palm reading is ten dollars each
hand. Spells are extra, though candles come at a bargain rate this time
of year." She winked. "The crop is in." Alyson looked at her blankly.
"Tallow candles, dear. Made from animal fat. There's been a large kill
this year and the fat was cheap. I have my sources."

"No candles," Alyson said hastily. Her eyes were darting quickly
around the room. There seemed to be a few bones lying in a corner—
something slender and white, at least, with knobs on the end, like
thighbones. She remembered reading about animal sacrifices, horrible
cults with goats bleating, their throats cut. "Don't do this to yourself,"
she thought. "Don't be suggestible. Take it at face value." She went over
the prices the gypsy had named. They seemed a bit high. "What if I only
have one hand read?" she asked.

"You can," the gypsy nodded. "People do." She looked a little bored.
"Your right hand contains all the influences at work right now; your left
hand holds the future. The sinister hand, you know. From the Latin."

"I don't know Latin."

"I used to speak it. Sinister, left hand. Dexter, right hand. If you're
right-handed you're dexterous, get it?" Her eyes crinkled in amusement.
She reached into her pocket and brought out a peppermint. It went
into her mouth like a mouse down a hole. Alyson had to drag her eyes
away from the chomping jaw.

"I know all the forces around me now," Alyson murmured. "I need
to know the future."

"I'm very good at futures," Madame Hope said smugly. "You could say future's my specialty. And I don't mince words. Good or bad, I'll tell you. Though, to be honest, I don't see that many good ones. People don't take care of their left hands."

"I do," Alyson said, "I take care of my hands."

"Good for you, then," the gypsy said, patting her "Yes, pretty hands. Soft and white. Long nails, too, how do you manage? Beautiful polish, not everyone can carry it off, hey? Stops this side of being garish. I like that. But that's all dressing, so to speak." She stroked Alyson's hand lovingly. "Let's see what's on the other side." Her head bent down, she bit her lip in concentration, running her forefinger over the lines, back and forth, tickling Alyson, who straightened her back to remain immobile, refusing to twitch.

The gypsy drew her breath in and said, "Well, I guess it depends on what you're looking for."

"I want normal things," Alyson whispered. "To love and be loved forever."

"Forever?" She laughed. "I don't see a forever in this hand."

"For the rest of my life. As much of forever as I have."

Madame Hope chewed her lip. "Husband, house, babies?"

Alyson nodded, feeling herself cave in. "And love. Don't forget love."

The gypsy scraped her nail into the palm of Alyson's hand. "No husband," she said. "No house."

"Love?"

Madame Hope closed Alyson's hand into a fist. "What do they say? It's better to have loved and lost than never to have loved at all?"

"Bullshit," Alyson hissed.

"Probably, but they say it anyway. Maybe it doesn't apply to you. But as to your future—a lot of it depends on what kind of choices you make. If you continue along these lines—that's what I see, you know, what your future is *at present*. As if you were to take a drive and go exactly where you'd planned, no detours. Well, *that* future is pretty shallow. A lot of waiting around and eating yourself up with spite. In fact, you lose just about everything. Mind you, I don't know exactly what 'everything' is. That's your business. But it's a one-track line. You'll live a long time, if that matters, and I don't see why it should, I think we're talking about quality, aren't we? Amazing about these long lifelines. They go to conservative, dried-up people, as a rule. Sometimes to crazies. Unfortunately, lifelines have nothing to do with lines of the mind or the heart. You can live to be a hundred and have your mind stop dead at ten. Not lovely. Your mind is all right, but your heart line stops right here—see it? like a car crash. Only one survivor, not two."

"You're telling me my life is empty?" Alyson was aghast.

"Empty. That's a comparative term, isn't it? You could have a career if you set your mind on it. Become a minor something-or-other, that kind of thing. You could feel important, a lot of people do, as long as there's someone to boss around. But as for the rest of it," she cocked an eyebrow, "I read this article a while ago, about women over forty. Not many get married, you know. Very depressing, if that's what you're after. In fact, it said—"

"I read the article," Alyson interrupted. "I don't want to hear."

"There are probably more terrorists around than you think."

Alyson shook her head, blinking hard. "I don't want to sleep alone for the rest of my life."

"Oh, if that's all that's bothering you!" She made a sound like she was shooing chickens, and her eyes were laughing. "No one has to sleep alone in a town like this, not even if you're eighty. I can help you with that all right, and I don't mean candles, why go for candles when you can have the real thing? I thought you were talking about love." She seemed to be laughing to herself, still enjoying Alyson's innocent despair as she plumped another mint into her mouth.

"I was," Alyson answered. "I was talking about love."

"Think about it some more. After all, what's love? It's a figment of your imagination. Read the reports. Love dies. Everything dies. People change their minds. They don't know what they want."

"I do," Alyson said, exasperated. "And I can't have it."

"Think it through," the gypsy chided. "Look at it all a different way. There are things you *can* have."

Alyson shook her head. "I don't want anything I can have now."

"Ah," Madame Hope growled. "Self-pity. Useless. You can't get anything when you're weak. It's no use at all. Think it through. Find out what you can get, and let me know." She winked at Alyson broadly, and her head moved close. "I can help you, you know. I can do a lot. I know my business inside and out. You'd be surprised." She nodded forcefully, like a dog thumping its tail. "There are more things on earth than you dream of."

"Or less," Alyson said, reaching into her pocket for a crumpled ten-dollar bill. "Much less." The woman was impossible, she thought, but there was some relief in feeling irritated, rather than miserable.

Chapter 2

Alyson had done a number of things in her life. She had worked in a bookstore, in a boutique, in an art gallery, for a broker, as an administrative assistant, anything that came along and only until it lost her interest. But almost two years earlier Peter had mentioned buying a house, and Alyson suddenly embraced the idea of permanence. She wanted a job she could stick with.

She saw an ad for an editorial assistant for a new magazine. She had done that once before, she was qualified. After she got the job, she was pleased to find that most of the other employees were women. Chums, she thought eagerly. Her former friends had drifted away to other states—some geographically, some psychologically.

The hierarchy was male, of course—publisher, editor, managing editor—but the little slots were filled with women, women who worked hard, long hours, who made the coffee and typed the letters, made the phone calls asking for favors, who licked the envelopes and made sure the right things got to the right messengers. Even then, a dozen years before the 21st century, women were cheap labor. Smile at them, tell them how important they are, how much their work is appreciated. Women drink that up, greedy for any indication that they matter.

Every single one of them considered feminism a done deal, in spirit if not in practice. The name of the magazine was *Adventure*, and for the first six months at least, the women imagined themselves on all sorts of harrowing trips, rising above obstacles, winning the prizes, while the men looked serious and talked about money, ad rates, printing costs and blow-in cards.

All, that is, except Anna, the office manager, who figured everything out before anyone else did, who said firmly, and a little too often, that she had no illusions left. She narrowed her hazel eyes when she said it; she meant business. She was the only one who referred to her position as a career. To everyone else it was a job—with any luck, a fun job. But after two years of working together, they knew each office personality a little too well to be surprised, or at least Alyson had thought so, until Anna invited her out to lunch some weeks after that damned article came out and told her she was going for artificial insemination.

"There's so little time left, to get everything done," she'd said. "It's bad enough I haven't managed to get my career on track, but I can't afford to wait any longer for a family. And as for finding a husband and father—this is New York. Mention babies and all the men go limp. You can't count on them, except by default. There's plenty of sperm to be had. Why not? They've got so much of it, they can be big spenders. And there are no emotional or financial repercussions that way. It's just a drop in somebody else's bucket as far as they're concerned. Men hate cause and effect. This way they get away easily." She paused. "I've thought about it a lot. I've saved the money. The health plan covers pregnancy and birth, and I've heard of a good nursery. I know, it sounds like surrogate parenthood both ways, doesn't it?" She rolled her eyes. "But I want this baby." She hugged her stomach as if it already bloomed.

For a moment—baby talk could be infectious—Alyson had pictured herself pregnant; who knew, maybe someday Peter would change his mind.

Now, of course, she had no baby and no Peter, either. The cloth of her life had frayed in all directions.

The gypsy's nasty predictions had not made the rest of the night any easier. Alyson walked herself into exhaustion. It was cold and misty; the street lamps seemed to pour out light in concentric splinters of glass. When she finally turned home again she saw a man standing in the front of the building, his back turned to her. For a split second, she thought it was Peter, but it was the Vulture again—or still. He saw her, twitched, and scurried away down the street.

Back in the apartment, sitting in a chair with all the lights on, she fell asleep for a few hours, only to wake with a start and the terrible sense that she'd been condemned.

Then it was morning, and she went to work.

No one gave her an inch more than necessary on the subway. No one even noticed her swollen eyes or hunched shoulders. Work was suddenly desirable as a comforter—familiar faces, something to *do*—and a distraction. She also wanted someone to tell her that Peter would come to his senses and that none of this was true in the long-term sense.

"What happened to your *hair*?" Anna cried when Alyson got to the office. Anna's hair was very fine and thin and even though it gathered around her face softly, she had often wished for Alyson's hair. Then she noticed the look on Alyson's face and added, "My God, what's happened?"

The central office was basically one large room where most of the staff sat: Anna, who was the office manager; the publisher's secretary; the bookkeeper; and all of circulation. Little rooms radiated off the hub—advertising, art and production, editorial, and the largest room with the best view, the publisher's, who was rarely there at all.

A few female faces turned up at Anna's question, and looked at her attentively. Alyson waved Anna to follow her into the small side office she shared with the editor-in-chief, who also was rarely there.

"Peter's left me,'" Alyson said, closing the door. It was the first time she'd said it, and it sounded awful. She looked at Anna, hoping she could do something about it.

"Oh, Al, I'm so sorry." Anna looked appalled, but also, Alyson thought, slightly relieved. It's hard, when you're a single woman determined to have a child on your own, to look at women in couples, and not feel cheated. It was better to have everyone else in the same boat as you.

Anna always called Alyson "Al." It had started as a joke one day, one of the first times the women began to comment on the obvious class divisions in the office. The men, when they showed up, came in late, had a meeting, went out to a business lunch, spent the afternoon on the telephone, and left early. This meant that the women had to work even harder, creating reports, tracking down prices, and relaying various messages from one man to another.

Clare, from production, had been particularly annoyed one day when all the decision-makers had failed to return from lunch. She had a schedule to meet, and no one to sign any papers. She could make decisions as well as anyone; but her decisions, somehow, were always contradicted by the production manager—or the editor-in-chief, or the publisher. This was true even when they agreed with her.

It was getting late and Clare knew she would be blamed for missing the deadline. Everyone knew that would happen. Clare, aggrieved, began to saunter through the office, pretending she was one of the bosses. She also called anyone in pants by a male name. Alyson became Al, Terry in accounting became Tom. Anyone in skirts was addressed as "dear." This tickled Anna, who had worn a dress that day. She called Alyson Al from then on. This got to the publisher somehow—Anna claimed she knew it was his secretary—and the first issue's masthead listed Alyson as Al and Terry as Tom. Pierre, the publisher, in a nice little speech on the day the magazines were distributed, apologized for not remembering to inform them. "Things kept coming up," he said. The magazine obviously had a largely male readership, he explained, and it just didn't look good to have all those female names on the masthead, so he had used their nicknames. This, he thought, was easier than replacing them with men. He grinned boyishly to show that he was kidding, but there was no doubting the annoyed rustling of papers and the general crossing of knees that greeted his joke.

Terry quit shortly afterwards, to be replaced by a real man; and Alyson remained Al. Pierre had apologized to her privately, sweetly, so she hadn't found a way of getting angry or confrontational, as Anna had urged. Instead, she was just Al.

"What happened?" Anna asked, hovering close to Alyson.

"He was rehearsing yesterday," Alyson said, keeping her voice even by an immense act of will. "I thought I'd go over and surprise him.

"I was across the street when I saw he was outside. Obviously waiting. I wondered how he knew I was coming. Then I saw Maggie hurrying towards him."

"Maggie? The one who works in an ad agency?"

"I've known her for ten years," Alyson said bitterly. "And for ten years she's always been a flirt. I should have noticed that."

Anna knit her brow and decided not to question this statement. It obviously represented some more elaborate thought. She tried to look deeply sympathetic.

"I saw them," Alyson said, closing her eyes and holding her breath. She breathed out; her eyes opened. "They left in a cab together. In a clinch in a cab together. It wasn't a professional meeting."

Anna was busy supplying all the visual elements—Alyson reeling back in horror; the illicit lovers tearing off each other's clothes in a cab (probably not, but interesting), a trip to a cheap hotel (unnecessary, really; no doubt Maggie had a splendid rent-controlled apartment). She thought, quite possibly, it had not been terribly cinematic. All the traumas in her own life had come limping in, cliché-ridden, Grade B. No one ever got the dialogue right. Everyone fell back on what they'd said before, in other events, that had safely gotten them out the door. Al's abbreviated rendering was perhaps more workable. It left so much to the imagination.

"I waited at home," Alyson said. "I looked at his things. I told myself that he lived there, with me. That seemed like a fact, at the time, very solid and reassuring, like gravity. I read somewhere that gravity's not the fact they thought it was, either," she said vaguely. "It's some other fact, though its effect is the same. Still, somebody got it wrong."

"Newton," Anna murmured.

"Newton. Peter came home late. I blurted it out, that I'd seen them, and he just stood there with his jacket on. I kept waiting for him to take his jacket off, to sit down or at least look like he wanted to stay. His eyes were very bright. He has incredible blue eyes, like the Caribbean. The most beautiful blue eyes." Alyson shuddered. "He said maybe it was good that I'd found out. Maggie was very upset, he said. And he felt horrible. I sat there and waited for him to stop looking like that like a man with an announcement. He didn't even pet the dog, who was staring at him all the time. Peter was the one who wanted the dog, after all. He shouldn't just ignore it like that."

"The dog's not important," Anna said gently.

"He is to me. I love that dog. He loves me like a dog should," she said thoughtfully, hearing a mental echo.

"Peter," Anna prompted.

"He said he loved Maggie. He said they hadn't known how to tell me. He said he was leaving me and moving in with Maggie. I used to think she was a little selfish, you know, even when I liked her. I don't think I'm a good judge of people."

"You're a good judge of people. Good enough."

"Then how did I get so much so wrong? I never even noticed he didn't love me."

"Maybe he's just a good liar."

"Maybe I'm just a good dupe."

"He left?"

"He left. He took some clothes, enough for a few days. I started yelling, I think. Once I saw he meant it, I told him to get out. I wanted to hurt him; I didn't know that was impossible. I just made it even easier. I told him I never wanted to see him again, that he could come get his things while I was at work so I didn't have to see him again. I called him names, like a child. He looked embarrassed for me. And then he left."

Anna waited briefly for more of the story. When none came, she said, "So he's getting his things out today?"

"Today." She rested her eyes on Anna, having told her story. Would Anna come up with the solution?

"And what will you do?"

That terrible question. "I don't know."

Anna chewed the inside of her mouth for a moment. "Maybe it's for the best. He would have left sooner or later, you know. I mean, he didn't have much loyalty; at least you know that now. Now you can get on with your life. It's always best to know where you stand." She finished up by sounding almost angry; and she was. The words, even as she said them, sounded shabby and worn.

"Get on with my life," Alyson repeated.

"Of course. You can do anything you want now! You're free again."

Alyson's eyes slipped away from Anna's face and traveled down to her own hands. "I wouldn't call this freedom."

"Of course not, it's too soon. You need time to get over it. At least there are no children." She bit her lip instantly; that was always a sore point for the woman after a breakup. God! How she wished she could think of the right thing to say. "I'm sorry. I wish it hadn't happened. I wish everyone loved everyone else forever." She caught her breath. "But they don't."

"I can see that," Alyson said heavily.

"I've got to get to work, Al. Pierre wants to go over the budget for supplies."

"I'm all right, then," Alyson said faintly.

"That's good. We'll talk later," Anna answered, scuttling out the door and heading for her desk. The budget wasn't urgent and she knew it; she couldn't stand another moment listening to herself blunder.

Pierre didn't show up at all that day, but Alyson didn't notice; she wasn't noticing much. She typed a few answers to queries on article ideas; she sent out some galley proofs; she looked at the layouts and suggested one story be moved. It took her so long to follow through on any of this—consecutive thinking seemed to be damaged in some way—that these jobs filled the day.

She took the subway home, telling herself that maybe, after all, Peter had changed his mind, that he would be there, shame-faced but there. She would hold her head high; she would forgive.

Karen Heuler

Her heart racketed behind her ribs, she turned the key in the lock. The door opened and the small hallway was empty; the boxes were gone.

It was seconds before she realized that Dingo wasn't at her feet. She looked for him, he was nowhere. She panicked; her first thoughts were that he had gotten out somehow; had gotten away and was lost. Then she saw that his leash was gone and his bowl and his food were gone; a single piece of kibble sat on the kitchen floor.

Bastard, she thought; kidnapper, murderer. She ran to the living room, lunging for the phone. She dialed Maggie's number quickly, before she could change her mind.

Maggie answered, and Alyson heard Maggie's hand muffle the phone as she passed it to Peter. "So he has to be warned that I'm calling," Alyson thought bitterly. As soon as he got on the line, she asked, "Did you take Dingo?"

"I left a note on the counter. Didn't you see it?"

"I was too busy looking for him. What right do you have to take the dog?"

"You never wanted a dog. You wanted a cat."

"And you just *took* him?" she yelled. "You don't even discuss it, you don't ask how I feel about it, you take what you want and that's it? He's as much my dog as he is yours." ·

"He's my dog," Peter said firmly. "I signed the papers for him. You never said you wanted him."

"You never said *you* wanted him! Well, I do want him, he's mine, you can't take everything away from me! Give him back!" She paced back and forth, to the limit of the cord and back.

"Alyson, be reasonable. I'll get you another dog if you want, but Dingo's mine. I even named him, remember?"

"No, you didn't, *we* did. Together. We got him together, we named him together, and you betrayed us both. You walked out. You left. You don't deserve him. Liar! You're a liar! And a thief! You're killing me!" she screamed.

"I've never heard you like this," Peter complained. "Calm down.

Look, maybe we can work something out—"

"Never! Bring him back! How can you walk out like I don't exist? How can you leave? And take the dog too? You've become a monster; you don't know what you're doing!"

"Look, I can't talk to you right now. Do you want to meet for lunch tomorrow? We can talk about the dog. I'm sorry, Alyson, really I am. I just assumed you'd expect me to take him."

She stopped pacing abruptly. "You want to get together to discuss the dog?" she asked. "Is that all you want to talk about?" Hope tickled her ear.

"Maybe I can explain things to you," he said, dropping his voice.

"Do you want to come back?" she whispered.

"God, Alyson," he said quickly. "That's not what I meant. The answer to that question is no, anyway. I just feel I owe you an explanation."

"I know the explanation," she jumped in, shaking with anger. "You've got a hole where your heart should be. Keep the dog! Keep everything! I never want to hear you or see you again. I hope you die." She hung up.

The phone stayed silent, and the silence spread.

She caught her breath and slammed out the door. Liar and thief! He couldn't stop taking things away from her! She flew along the streets again, along the avenues with pale thin trees bending into the streetlights. She jammed her hands into her pockets and felt a piece of paper. Ticket stubs from a movie she had gone to with Peter. She threw them into the air. She paused in the light from a store window and started going through her purse. Anything with Peter's writing on it she threw into the wind. He'd given her the wallet! She emptied it out and threw it in the gutter, stamping on it for good measure. She picked up speed and pulled things out, throwing them in the air as she found them, scowling, nodding.

She walked until she was tired and then headed home. Her feet moved her past her own building. She realized she should eat, and she walked around the block to an all-night Greek diner.

Karen Heuler

The light hurt her eyes, and the number of surfaces. She ordered pale foods—mashed potatoes, creamed corn, a glass of milk. The potatoes were made from a mix. She picked listlessly at her food, not liking it. Two tables across the way, a woman was eating her dinner. Her baby, about a year old, lay asleep in a carrier on the seat beside her. The child's head had fallen slightly to the side, so Alyson could see its soft hair, its closed eyes, its parted lips. Why wasn't the baby in its own bed by now, covered with a pink or blue blanket, warm and safe and smelling of powder?

She was so absorbed in imagining the smooth pink skin, the tiny hands, that it came as a shock when a voice at her shoulder said, "Do you want that baby?" She looked up and saw Madame Hope smiling at her indulgently. "You can have that baby. If you really want it. Do you mind if I sit down?" She sat without waiting for Alyson's reply, sliding into the seat opposite her. "I'm so glad I ran into you."

Alyson was taken aback, but some sense of politeness kept her from leaving or telling the gypsy she preferred to be alone. Instead, she merely watched her in astonishment.

"Aren't you going to eat that?" Madame Hope asked. When Alyson shook her head, she took the plate and began to finish the food. The gypsy scooped the food together in clumps, tucking it quickly into her mouth. "Waste not, want not," she chided.

In the bright light her skin was a golden color, as if tanned. The blonde dye of her hair was getting dull, and the dark roots bothered Alyson. She liked casual looks, she did not like sloppiness.

"Of course it's a girl baby. Maybe you don't want a girl baby? Maybe you'd rather have a boy?"

"No. I'd want a girl," Alyson answered unwillingly.

"Then how about that one? You know you don't want the bother of pregnancy. This one's already packaged, it's ready to go."

"It belongs to someone," Alyson pointed out.

The gypsy shrugged. "A quibble. An annoyance. It wouldn't stand in your way. Do you want it?"

"No."

The gypsy nodded. She took up a piece of flat white bread and buttered it. "They're getting awfully close to being able to decide what sex a baby will be, you know. Not just find out, I mean. Soon you'll be able to *choose*." She wiped her mouth with a paper napkin and crumbled it into a ball. "So what do you think will happen? They'll choose boys!" Her eyes glittered. "Still the premium sex, you know. Oh yes, when science offers a choice, we'll end up with a whole generation that's mostly boys. No stuffing little girls behind a bush or going through three or four pregnancies until you get a boy—oh no! Right you go, here you are, a son and a cigar!" She chortled. "But they'll grow up, you know, and then what? Not enough women. Who'll keep the place running? So what will the next generation be? Girls! And so on and so on. It's downright comical!"

"But why did you ask me if I wanted that child?" Alyson said finally, finding it a little hard to keep up with the gypsy's change of direction.

"Well, you don't know until you ask, do you?"

"But what if I'd said yes?"

"You'd have it, wouldn't you?"

This was getting annoying. "Just by saying yes, you mean? Just say what I want and I get it, even if it belongs to someone else?"

Madame Hope laughed. "You're talking legally, aren't you? I happen to know that child is abused. The mother is a junkie." Alyson's eyes strayed to the baby. "What? It looks clean and comfortable? You think the miserable of the earth never look clean and comfortable? You go merely by surfaces?"

"You could be making this up."

"Why should I? What would I gain? Come, come," she said impatiently. "Which is it, then? You don't believe children are abused, or you don't believe someone close to you would abuse a child?"

"I don't even know her."

"She's sitting ten feet away. She's in your circle."

"But you can't just take someone's child on suspicion of cruelty."

"Oh, so you want proof. We're not talking legality, then, or even morality. As long as you don't see it, it doesn't exist. As long as she hurts that child *in private*, you don't have to worry? Is that it?"

"I don't *know* that she hurts anything. I don't know her."

"Oh, but I do. I know all about her. In the abstract and in the particular. The baby will be dead within a year."

"Why don't you take her, then? Since you're the one who knows?"

"Be your conscience? I like that! You don't want to see what's unpleasant. And you don't want to do anything risky, even if it's necessary. So you think it would be immoral to take a child away from a bad mother?"

"No. No, I wouldn't think it's immoral. But there are laws about it. You can't act on suspicions."

"But the laws fail, don't they? At least sometimes? So if the law didn't have enough proof, even if it were true, then it would be okay—moral, even—to let that child die?"

"Of course not. But this is speculation. I don't know any of it."

"That's the point. You would do the right thing, then. You'd let the child die?"

Alyson shook her head, which felt like it had been whiplashed by the gypsy's observations. "Not if I knew. No. If I knew for a certainty, I think I would take the child."

"You *think* you would?"

"How can I know?"

"You might let it die, then?"

"No," Alyson said, getting annoyed. "No. I wouldn't. I'd take the child."

"From a mother that society has declared innocent?" the gypsy asked craftily.

Alyson looked at her in disgust. "You just told me she wasn't."

"Well, you can't take my word for it." The gypsy drummed her fingers. "So morality is an individual decision. You would kidnap a child because it was morally right, even though theft is morally wrong. Interesting."

Alyson sighed. "It all depends, doesn't it? I don't know what I'd do, really."

The gypsy said softly, "Personally, I think you'd let the child die. It wouldn't require any decision. Any other course of action would." Her eyes looked comfortably at Alyson, bright and serene.

"I don't know," Alyson sighed. She was tired of this. "I'm too tired to think right now. I just want to go home."

"Poor thing," the gypsy said practically. "You *look* tired. You live around here? I've just moved into the neighborhood myself." She looked around. "I think I'll do very well here. Lots of potential. They have stores that sell nothing but rocks, you know. Minerals with sacred properties. Definitely my kind of neighborhood. What street are you on?"

Alyson was spilling out change for a tip. The gypsy watched the change pile up, and Alyson left a quarter more than she'd planned. "Seventh Street."

"I'm on Sixth. But you know that already. You must stop in again. We'll have tea." She beamed at Alyson, and Alyson felt suddenly sympathetic. Maybe the woman was lonely. Maybe that explained things.

"Any good bars around here?" the gypsy whispered as they walked together out the door. "You know what I mean." She winked and pinched Alyson's arm.

Looking for a man, Alyson thought with revulsion, and at her age! Was that what her own life would be? She had to repress a shudder.

Chapter 3

*W*ithout Dingo and Peter, Alyson only had her job, and she started defining herself in relation to it: how necessary was she; what could she do with it, where would it lead? And, since Peter was no longer contributing his half of the rent, was it time for a raise? She would have had no trouble asking for a raise with Peter around, but now she was afraid of losing the job. Not just by asking for a raise, no, but because she might feel obligated to quit if it were refused. Defiance was beginning to creep in: defiance, self-righteousness, even fury—though she was careful to keep herself in check.

"I don't know what's going on here," Anna warned her in the middle of the week, "but the big boys are rumbling."

"In what way?"

"Phone calls. Messages. Code words. Something's up."

"How can you tell?" Alyson asked dismissively. "They're always doing that."

"They're both in," Anna said with significance.

That caught Alyson by surprise. The publisher, Pierre, came in early, when he came in at all, but Mickey, the editor-in-chief, liked to come in right before lunch. He was a food-oriented man, partly, Alyson guessed, out of nervousness. His ties were always stained, he had ketchup on his cuff and mustard in his lap. Alyson had once watched, fascinated, as he dipped a chocolate cupcake into a pile of mayonnaise on his plate. He chewed with his mouth open. He always took candy out of the candy dishes put out by the advertising department—eating automatically until someone called him in to a meeting.

Alyson walked into her office, which she shared with Mickey and the consultant managing editor, who came in rarely and called all the women "kiddo" instead of learning their names.

Mickey held a cup of coffee and a donut. He had already spilled coffee on his jacket. "You look different," he said, wiping powdered sugar off his lapel. His belly bulged a little over his pants, but he looked cheerful and friendly, like a large, benevolent pet.

"My hair," Alyson said.

"Oh yeah. Looks good."

"How come you're in so early?"

Mickey suddenly looked uneasy. "We're having a meeting." He finished the last of his donut. "About the issue."

"No one told me," Alyson said, immediately panicking. She was the one who presented the basic lineup for the issues, summarizing queries and submissions, following through on assignments. The meetings were sporadic, but she always got some notice. She swept through her desk, organizing the papers and hastily beginning to draw up lists. "This is crazy," she moaned. "What time is the meeting? I'm not prepared."

"As soon as Pierre's ready. Don't worry about the lists too much. This is informal."

Alyson looked at him, her eyes narrowing. She was beginning to recognize the accents of guilt. "Something's going on," she muttered, "and I don't like it." She appealed to Mickey's sense of fair play. "I do all the work and I'm treated like temporary help. We've got to talk about this, Mickey." She shook her head as if her hair were in her eyes. "Something has to change around here." She put a threatening tone in her voice. With Mickey it was easy; his eyes shifted back and forth guiltily; he sipped his coffee.

Anna appeared in the doorway. "Pierre wants you both in his office." She caught Alyson's glance and raised her eyebrows.

Alyson figured out what the eyebrows meant when she got to Pierre's

Karen Heuler

office. A strange man sat to the right of Pierre's desk. She hesitated for a split second, expecting the man either to leave or to be introduced to her. Neither happened. She sat down.

Pierre was in a cheerful mood. "Let's get this issue settled," he said agreeably. "What's our lead story?"

Mickey looked at her. It was a good thing she was ready.

"Fire and explosion in a chemical plant," she said. "First person narrative."

Pierre nodded. "Good. Sexy. Good photos?"

"Photos of fires are all pretty much the same," Mickey said, clearing his throat. "Smoke, flames, hoses. But they'll do."

"Blow it up. Make it into a spread. Let it bleed off the pages." He looked at the stranger, who was leaning forward in his seat, hands clasped. "What else?"

"Mountain climbing. A woman, aged 63."

"No more women. We did one last issue. Let's give it a rest."

"Now Pierre—" Mickey began, looking uneasily at Alyson, who lowered her head.

"This is not political, Mickey; purely business. I have nothing against women. We all know our readership is male. Let's keep track of that."

"The only other hobby story we have about a man is a tightrope walker," Alyson said.

"Gay," Mickey said. "No way you can hide it unless you go strictly without photographs." He had discussed this with Alyson weeks ago. He liked the piece; he was sure Pierre wouldn't.

"Out," said Pierre. "Who's getting these stories, anyway?"

"We're going with what comes in over the transom, Pierre. We don't have the staff to go out searching—"

"Don't give me excuses, Mickey. Make some calls, line something up. Everybody knows somebody who does something exciting. I could give you five by the end of the day."

"I'll find something," Alyson said quickly.

"What else?"

Alyson consulted her list. "Report on a death in a survivalists' camp, a calendar of drag-car racing; survival guide to desert tours. . . ."

"Two survival themes? One goes. Keep the death story."

"The survival guide was our health section," she said weakly. "The only other thing we have is on tick fever."

"Play it up, but don't make it local."

"I don't like the tick fever story," Mickey said. "It's too late in the year, anyway. Ticks die in winter."

"A good story never dies. Besides, they'll be back in the spring. How many cases per year?" Pierre asked Alyson.

"I don't remember, but I'll..."

"If it's over a thousand, go with it. People respond to a thousand. How much do we have in-house?"

"Everything except what we dropped."

"How are we set up for the next issue?"

"Nothing much yet. I've got some queries that look interesting. I'll be sending letters this week."

"On spec, remember; give them the bit about a small, struggling magazine."

"I'll give them the bit," Alyson repeated coldly. Pierre and the stranger kept looking at each other, checking each other's expression. There was some understanding between them; it was obvious.

"We have to build a better backlog," Pierre said.

"I'm doing the best I can," Alyson answered. She was not, she decided, going to behave as if she were an underling. "I'm doing all the proofreading and fitting as it is. I've got a stack of mail on my desk and I still make the deadlines."

"We all know you're doing a great job." Pierre grinned at her personally, and she felt, briefly, that he *did* understand, that he took it all into account. But then he continued. "We're growing and we can't expect one person to be able to handle it all." He cleared his throat. "This is Eliot Edwards. He'll be taking quite a load off your shoulders; I'm sure we'll all find it easier going from now on."

Alyson's mouth dropped open. Eliot was nodding at her in a smug sort of way, radiating goodwill and competence through his striped shirt and snugly fitting suit. He personified forty years of sleek feeding and constant personal attention. Short dark hair, a well-clipped mustache and a light tan smoothed over the slight beginning of jowls and a double chin. Alyson hated him immediately.

"What's his title?" Alyson asked rudely, speaking to Pierre.

The smile was turned off; he frowned slightly. "Senior editor," he answered.

"You hired someone *over* me?" she asked. "After all I've done?" The months of hard work swept over her.

"You're an editorial assistant," Pierre pointed out. "There's no need to hire someone *under* you."

Alyson's mouth clamped shut. Pierre turned deliberately to Eliot, whose eyes had watched Alyson's face with a wary expression as if he'd caught the first scent of a problem.

Alyson got up abruptly and turned blindly to the door. Mickey followed her. "Don't get upset," he whispered as soon as they were outside. "This might work out, really. And there's a raise in it for you. I was going to tell you before the meeting. I never got around to it." He followed her to the editorial office. She closed the door once they were inside.

"What's his background?" Alyson asked. She felt cold and trapped. She knew perfectly well that it was pointless to take it out on Mickey. He was nice but ineffective; he wasn't the one who'd hired Eliot.

"He's written a book. He's Pierre's friend."

"And he's got a prick," Alyson breathed. "All the boys together."

"That's not true," Mickey said, frowning.

"Then tell me why I didn't get a promotion, and why you hired above me. That puts me in my place, doesn't it? That tells me that no matter what I did so far, it wasn't good enough. Right? Did I get the message? You didn't take me seriously." She was trying, desperately, to keep her voice under control but she was afraid she had a quaver. A damned female quaver.

"I didn't even know you took it seriously."

"Well, I do."

"Since when?" Mickey asked. "You never mentioned it before."

"Like you never mentioned you were hiring someone over me. You could have warned me." She glared at Mickey.

"Pierre barely talked to *me* about it," he answered. By the look on his face, Alyson could see this was true. "You know Pierre. Once he makes up his mind, it has to be done immediately."

Alyson nodded; she did know Pierre. In fact, if she'd had any intentions of becoming a full editor, she should have gone to Pierre. She could see that now. Dealing with Mickey was easier, so she'd never gone to Pierre for anything. But the real game was with Pierre.

"You're telling me I got what I deserved," she said flatly.

"Who gets what they deserve? No one I know. It isn't like it's terrible, is it? You never said you wanted anything different, and this isn't so bad." He looked at her appealingly. "When you put it in context."

"Ah yes, context," Alyson said without conviction.

"After all, you've got your personal life, that's more important. You know this magazine isn't the whole world for you."

"Really?" she asked bitterly. "But this *is* all there is."

"I thought you were living with someone?"

Alyson felt her throat tighten. "I was. Past tense."

She felt the minute pass as Mickey mulled it over. "Do you want to talk about it? We could get some lunch—maybe a drink?"

She looked at him suspiciously. He'd never suggested going out together before, when he knew she was living with someone. "Fair game, is that it? An easy mark?"

His face got red. "I said lunch. It was perfectly innocent. We could even bring someone along, if you want." He opened the door, went to the desk outside and got some candy, which he chewed thoughtfully as he returned. She felt insulted by it. What was his game?

"Thanks." She turned away from him, looking for a paper she could pick up.

"What's that mean?"

"That means no lunch."

He sighed. "I just want you to remember. I'm your friend. However it seems."

"You just told me I didn't get the job. Because I didn't want it badly enough."

He nodded

"Tell me. I work hard. Let's just pretend, for a moment, that I was a man who worked as hard as I do. Let's pretend. Would Pierre have done the same thing?" She looked at him intently. "This question is for my information only."

"How do I know what Pierre would do?"

"You can guess. I can guess. Pierre knows how far he can count on people, he knows what they're worth. There are a million like me, aren't there? Hard workers, asking very little. That's important. Women like me get the work done. They make your life easy. They don't pull tricks; they don't have tantrums; they keep the office going. And whatever else, you know you need to keep the office going. We're a category. Few demands. And when there *are* demands, you can bulldoze us, right? We don't fight. It's the truth, we don't fight. We know it and you know it. There's no negotiation necessary. You can step over me and I'll make sure my back is clean. It's how I was born. A rock-hard spine. That's fine. That's okay." She stood up, leaning on her desk, her hands grasping the edge. "But I want you to know something. I found it out, I know all about it now. I know I'm not serious. I've never been serious. It's how I got where I am today. With nothing. You're right, I won't fight it, any of it. I never played baseball, I jumped rope. I wait for the next one to tap my shoulder and push me out." She sat down, shaking violently. "It's how I was raised. I'm a woman. I wait."

Mickey backed out the doorway. "I'm sorry," he said, "I only meant lunch."

Chapter 4

𝒜lyson was definitely catching on: no lover, no dog, no promotion. And yet she suddenly felt almost electrified by misfortune, as if she were being pushed past some boundary. She didn't know what the boundary was, but she was tired of being herself, of feeling the same feelings, hour after hour. Couldn't she be someone entirely different, with a better attitude, more determination, no looking back, no regrets?

Apparently not.

She missed Peter with a sharp intensity; but more to the point, she realized she hated Maggie, and the hatred grew day by day. Men, after all, were hardly responsible for their actions; they lived in a sort of alternate universe where moral laws were skewed. All over the world, they behaved without fear of consequence. Face it, there would be no wars if there were no men. That put the responsibility on Maggie's shoulders, who had betrayed a friend, who had taken another woman's man—and who knew it was wrong. All women know that's wrong, and even if so many of them end up involved with married men, it's still true. They rarely succeed in detaching the men from their marriages, and when they do, it's the wife who's suspected of inadequacy, and the mistress of being a siren. The husband is merely a heel. And the movies make heels into heroes.

Which only goes to show how much easier men have it. One couple hears of another couple's breakup: to the woman it's a warning, to the man it's a promise. That's how hormones work.

*A*nna went on a Tuesday to the fertility clinic for her "shot," as she called it. A little army of sperm in a glass tube. It was very much like a Pap test, she claimed, and a lot better than some of the sex she'd had lately. "At least they were careful not to hurt my feelings," she said. She had gone to the clinic in the morning, and was only a little late for work. She hummed all day, and Alyson resented it. Of course, Alyson thought, I wish her all the luck in the world. But not too much luck, she thought; leave some for me.

She admired Anna. She was at least decisive: she knew what she wanted to accomplish and she set out to get it. Anna was strong; perhaps Alyson would be as strong someday. Until then she went home to an empty apartment and sat on her sofa with no one beside her, trying to picture herself as firm-jawed, open-eyed, glaring, a woman with a serious tread. And then, on a Friday night, the phone rang.

Alyson leaped for it.

There was a moment before the caller said anything. Alyson thought she heard a stealthy gasp for air and then Anna quavered, "Al? Can you come over? Something's happened."

"Of course," Alyson said, instantly alert to the strain in Anna's voice. "What's wrong?"

Again Anna hesitated, pulling her voice together. "I've been raped."

"Yes," Alyson said. "I'll be right there," and she grabbed her coat and hailed a cab, the streetlights whipping past the car like a carnival as she raced uptown to the East 30's, to Anna's apartment, keeping her mind empty. It's not kind to imagine rape.

Anna had a bathrobe wrapped around her when she answered the door, pink chenille with the belt pulled hard and knotted. Her shoulders were held tight. Her hair was wet. Her eyes had trouble meeting Alyson's.

She led Alyson in to the living room, and they sat down formally.

There was a bottle of wine and two glasses on the table. Alyson was surprised to see that it was all so neat. She had expected signs of a struggle.

Anna's eyes traveled around the room with Alyson's, checking to make sure everything was in its place. When she finally started to talk, it was in a strangely apologetic tone. The police had left shortly before Alyson arrived. Anna hadn't called them, neighbors had when they'd heard her screams.

"Screams?" Alyson repeated. It was hard to imagine Anna screaming. She was, in so many ways, so determined to control everything. Even her body was compact and efficient. All her moves were decisive and quick. Anna poured out a glass of wine for Alyson and sat down again, wrapping the robe carefully around her body, pressing her own wine glass to her cheek.

"I was just coming home. It wasn't even that late. I didn't think anything about it. When I'm really late I watch the streets more carefully. But it wasn't that late. I was robbed last year and I always look behind when I come in the building. I don't know where he was, out on the street, I didn't see anyone there. But just as I turned to close the door, there was someone behind me, and I slammed the door shut, quickly, I wasn't even thinking. I caught his hand in the door. I stood there for a second, I could see his fingers and he was yelling, 'Wait! You've got my hand! Open the door!' It's funny, Al, I felt horrified. I felt so *mean*. I looked through the glass and I saw a kid. He couldn't have been twenty. He looked all right, and I felt so awful about his hand that I opened the door. He was shaking his hand, flipping it up and down in the air, and he was asking me why I'd done that, he was just trying to find the super. He said he was looking for an apartment. And I thought, here I am, this horrible, suspicious person, and I'd hurt an innocent kid."

"You're not a horrible person," Alyson murmured,

Anna ignored her. "All of a sudden, there was a knife. I don't think I even saw him take it out. He held it in his left hand, he had his right hand under his arm now, it was still hurting. He said, 'You really fucked up my hand,' and I was so shocked, I just kept looking at that

Karen Heuler

knife. I thought, maybe he's right-handed and he won't be able to use it, because he had to hold it in his left hand, but he kept pointing it at me. That knife hypnotized me. My muscles froze. I just was there, waiting. I think my head shut down too. I couldn't think anything anymore, just, 'He has a knife,' and how the knife looked very long and gray and sharp and it seemed to want to come closer."

"Closer?" Alyson asked. She held on to her wine, forgetting to drink it. She pictured herself there, in Anna's place, it all seemed so vivid. She was pulled in by the strict detail of the story. Even her body was clenched.

Anna nodded. "That sounds strange, but it was the knife that seemed to be alive. I can't even remember exactly what this kid was telling me, but he was talking constantly—nervous, edgy jabber, he never let up. His knife motioned me down the hall, and I turned and went, trying to think, but it was so hard to think. I don't know why I couldn't think, why I couldn't figure out anything. Time went fast, my mind went slow. There was too little time. I couldn't figure out if anyone was home; if they would come if I yelled—and by the time I'd thought of anything it was already too late." She shook her head. "When it occurred to me to run up the stairs and take my chances, I'd already gone past the stairs to the door leading out the back. By the time I thought maybe I could swing the door into his face I was already outside. It was very dark. I couldn't see anything. And everything was so quiet. There's not much in the back, some garbage cans and some steps that lead down to the boiler room. The knife motioned me down the steps, and I felt my heart thumping. There weren't going to be any ideas now. He knew where he was going. I thought, you know, it wouldn't have worked, since he knows the building, I mean it wouldn't have mattered if I'd tried anything because he knew what he was doing and I didn't."

She stopped for a moment, and Alyson said, "How could you know?" It was a meaningless question; it was just a way to connect with Anna.

"The door was locked to the boiler," Anna continued. "I'm so glad it was, I think I'd be dead if he had gotten that door open. We were under the stairway now and he stood there, talking again. He shifted his knife back and forth from his left hand to his right and he told me again that I'd really fucked up his hand. And I started saying I was really sorry, and I was, because he was so angry. He started hitting me then, just back and forth across my face so that I had to stop apologizing and wait for the smack to end so I could finish what I was saying. I never felt it when he hit me. I just recognized there was some kind of rhythm punctuating what I was saying, but it didn't hurt at all.

"Then he stopped hitting me and told me to take off my clothes. I started pleading with him no, but he took the knife and he held it at my throat for a minute, just the point of it, and then he moved it down and held it so it pointed between my legs." Alyson closed her eyes and winced. "When it moved again I started taking off my clothes."

Anna paused there. She remembered the wine in her hand and took a drink.

"The stupid police. Do you know when I was telling them one of them asked, wasn't it cold? Can you imagine? Trying to lighten the mood. But it wasn't cold. It wasn't any temperature at all, unless it was knife temperature."

Alyson refilled their glasses. Her hands were wet with tension, and she rubbed them on her legs.

Anna took a breath. "I took off my clothes and he had me back against the wall. There was a piece of cement that stuck out, and it pushed into my back. I kept moving to try to get away from it, and each time I moved he hit me. When he was inside me he had his left hand next to my head, the palm against the wall, so the knife was almost in front of my eyes. He kept thrusting as if it would never end and I started thinking maybe I should do something so it would be over. Can you imagine it? I was trying to think what I could do to make him come." She shook herself and gulped more wine. "I think I must have been crazy. I don't know how I could think that. It makes my stomach turn." Alyson's hand reached out for Anna's.

"The police asked me if he did anything kinky. Yes, I think the

Karen Heuler

word they used was 'kinky.' I was so well behaved with the police, I kept answering them like a child. I just said no, I didn't think so, and then later I thought, isn't rape kinky? Are they looking for something, I don't know, juicier? They asked me a few times whether I was sure I didn't know him. They made me feel guilty. It was insane. Why do I feel guilty? Why couldn't I do something? Why couldn't I think straight?"

"You got through it alive," Alyson interrupted. "How can you blame yourself?"

"I should have learned self-defense or something. I always thought I could take care of myself."

"You can take care of yourself. This guy had a knife, it wasn't equal, you didn't stand a chance."

"Why didn't I fight?" Anna's voice was low.

"Against a knife? How could you fight against a knife?"

"I didn't even scream, until after. He was finished, finally, and he backed away from me. He told me to kneel down and I did. I thought, Oh God, he's going to cut my throat. He just looked at me. I know I kept shaking my head, pleading, it was as if I'd forgotten there was anyone else in the world, just him and me. And then suddenly someone came through the back door, someone was going to dump some garbage, and I started screaming, without thinking. My mind just went, it was totally blank, my mouth opened and there was nothing in it but a scream. And he took off, he rushed up the stairs and through the door, just like that. All done. I kept screaming, I heard windows being crashed open and people yelling. Someone called the police, I know, because I didn't and they came here. I put my coat on, and I pulled on my pants. I grabbed whatever else was laying on the ground. The guy with the garbage was just standing in the doorway, watching me. When I passed him, he said, 'What happened?' Just that.

"I came up here and I called you. And then the police came and they left. They wanted to know what he looked like. I'm not sure. He was young, and white, and he carried a knife. I can tell them exactly what the knife looked like."

"You should go to the hospital," Alyson said. She wanted to find some clean and professional way of helping Anna, some way of tidying up.

Anna shook her head. "I wanted to tell someone and I told you. I don't want anyone to touch me, to look at me, even. I told the police I wouldn't go. That's it."

"That's not it," Alyson said as gently as possible. "They can do things to help you."

"They'd scrape me," Anna whispered, her head hanging lower. "They'd scrape me, and they'd take notes, and what if I'm pregnant?"

Alyson was shocked. She couldn't understand this, she really couldn't. "You don't want his child, do you?"

"You don't understand. I went to the clinic four days ago. I was ovulating then, I know I was. I'm very regular. I might be pregnant from that." Tears ran down her face; she let them fall onto her hands.

Alyson's voice dropped to a whisper. She moved closer to Anna and pulled out one wet hand to hold it

"You'd never be sure," she said carefully, "where you got that child. Who the father is. Can you live with that? Can you live with that child?"

"I'd never know anyway," Anna replied and Alyson could feel the ragged jerking of Anna's fingers within her own. Anna gave a small laugh. "I think of that clinic as a bargain basement. Who knows what kind of sperm that was? Do you think it belonged to a genius? Is that what geniuses do in their spare time—fill little cups with their sperm to make a few bucks?"

Alyson smiled carefully. "Still that's different. Chances are good—whoever it is, it's not a rapist."

Anna's face bunched up. "It's not worth thinking about. I can't afford to think about it. Financially. Emotionally. It does no good."

Alyson rubbed her arm and kept quiet. It was Anna's decision, after all. Anna was crawling into herself, her legs tucked up to her chest, her arms around them. Alyson could see she needed to feel safe; no doubt she also needed to work it out, slowly, in her own mind.

Alyson spent the night there, watching TV with Anna and sleeping on the sofa. There was no dog to walk; no one to call to say she wouldn't be home. She considered Anna's position. She could understand the need to withdraw, to deny, to recoup, but there were consequences that needed to be faced, and as far as Alyson could see, the sooner the better. Better to sacrifice whatever it cost for that trip to the clinic, much better. How could you love a child, wondering if it would grow up to have the face of a man who held you up against a wall? Wouldn't you watch its eyes too closely, slap its hands too often? Alyson realized she thought of the child as a boy. Of course it would be a boy. Was it possible, too, that Anna could keep silent all the years ahead—never, in a fit of anger, in a careless moment, let that child know who its father might be?

She wouldn't be capable of standing that. But, then, it hadn't happened to her; she didn't have to live with any of the consequences.

She went home the next afternoon. Anna told her to; she didn't want to be watched, she said, like a tea kettle; she was okay.

Alyson checked the street carefully before she went in her building. She looked down the hallways and over her shoulders. Her keys were bunched in her fist, point outward.

She opened her apartment door quickly, slamming it behind her and taking a deep breath. She heard footsteps coming towards her from the room and spun around, unlocking the door.

"Alyson?"

"Peter!" She leaned back against the door, her heart pounding. A first wave of relief flooded through her. This was Peter; he was back! She sprang away from the door and took an eager step forward. "Where's Dingo?"

"He's home," Peter said quickly, and Alyson froze in place. Peter wasn't back, then. She eyed him warily, her muscles tight, conditioned to expect a hug when she saw him. She had to fight to keep her arms from lifting. He had said "home" and he hadn't meant here.

"What do you want?"

His fingers moved nervously, tucking his shirt into his jeans. He had a strained, uncertain smile on his face. He took a breath. "I tried calling. I've been calling since last night. You weren't home."

"That's right." Let him think what he would. "What do you want?"

"I'm looking for my birth certificate. Or my passport. I need some ID or I wouldn't bother you. I went through the papers in one of the boxes you. . . ," he hesitated, "you packed for me. I couldn't find it."

"It will turn up eventually."

His eyes glanced left and right, those beautiful eyes. He reached in his pocket for cigarettes, took one out and lit it, expelling air in a long, nervous stream.

"I need it pretty soon," he said, tapping the cigarette over and over again.

They were still in the little hallway that ran into the living room. Alyson eyed his cigarette, waiting for it to spill. She felt very alert: There was something going on. She moved into the kitchen to the left and ran some water. He followed, watching as she filled and drank a glass.

"Why do you need it soon?" she asked finally, putting the glass in the sink next to a knife that had lain there unwashed for the last few days. What had she used it for? She couldn't remember.

Peter shifted from foot to foot, flicking ash into the sink. A charcoal gray speck fell next to the knife. "I need it to get a license."

"What kind of license?" Both their eyes focused on objects around the kitchen. Peter looked from the shelf above the sink to the kitchen counter to the refrigerator. Alyson looked at the dishes in the drain, the glass and the knife in the sink. Their voices were superficially polite.

Peter closed his eyes briefly and then opened them. Alyson wasn't looking directly at him, but she was aware of it. Her heart seemed to be beating in a number of different directions; she could feel it lurch to the right and then to the left as he said, "We're thinking about going away for a while." His voice had a quaver to it. "And maybe getting married." How nicely his shirt was ironed, Alyson thought. Did Maggie do that? Eight years of living together, and did it really only take someone who would iron your shirts and say as she pressed the button for a spurt of steam, "Dear? Have you thought about marriage?" And after eight years of declaring his personal freedom to one woman did he suddenly look up at another woman one day and say, "Not a bad idea, honey. Where's my birth certificate?" Or did he get down on one knee, jubilantly, laughing at himself, and ask for her hand? A particularly good hand, maybe, a glad hand that grasped his penis with a special movement, exactly the way he'd always wanted?

Her fingers twitched their way to the sink. She picked up the glass and rinsed it out, shaking off the beads of water. She picked up the knife and held it under the faucet. Peter watched it too.

"I'm sorry," he said. "But you'd find out sooner or later, wouldn't you? I'm sorry."

She still held the knife. Her head was spinning. "Whose idea was it? To get married?"

"It was mine. She agreed."

"How nice. And you always told me you never wanted to get married."

"I thought it was true."

"And it just came over you, all of a sudden, this revelation?" Her hand closed over the heft of the knife.

"I'd been thinking about it for a while. It feels right." His cigarette was out; he looked for a place to put it. Alyson was still at the sink and she turned to face him, the knife still in her hand.

"For a while, huh? You mean when you were still living with me?" He didn't answer. "You mean you came home thinking of her, comparing, contrasting? For how long? How long were you judging what I said, what I did, against *her*, against that bitch? The two of you betraying me, lying and cheating, and you discovered that I wasn't good enough?"

"Maybe you were too good," he said nervously. Were his eyes watering; was he trying to pretend he felt something? "Maybe that was the problem. I don't know, I honestly don't know. I didn't ask for it to turn out this way. I don't like it any more than you do. But what can I do? I can't help the way I feel. How can I pretend that it didn't happen, that I didn't fall in love with Maggie?"

Alyson winced. Her hand was beginning to have a life of its own, cutting the air in very small circles. "I don't have your birth certificate, or your passport. If I find them, I'll burn them. And I want my keys back. I don't want you breaking in here again. Take the keys and put them on the counter. Now."

She had the knife pointing at him without even noticing. He looked at it, he looked at her, and then he began to go through his pockets until he found the keychain. He slipped off two keys and placed them on the counter. He sighed. "It doesn't have to be this way, you know. We could be friends. You've been so unreasonable lately. I think you need to talk to someone."

"Get out," she said, glaring. "Get out while there's still time. I *did* reasonable, Peter, and it didn't work. I don't want reasonable anymore. I don't want you anymore! Get out!"

She slammed the door behind him, gouging a chip of paint off in the process by forgetting she still held the knife in her hand. She looked at it with contempt. Another damn phallic symbol.

She turned and went straight for the left-hand bureau drawer, where she kept the important papers. She opened the window and hurled the drawer out. It made a dull, unsatisfactory thud. She walked calmly over to the lamp he had lit, unplugged it, and then threw the lamp out into the air. She felt relieved when she heard it shatter.

A window across the way was flung up, but she was finished; there was nothing else she needed to destroy.

Karen Heuler

Chapter 5

That was it. She turned away from the window (someone was yelling, "Are you all right over there?") and clenched her fists. She'd thrown two things out the window—was that really enough? Why couldn't she now, this minute, go racing after him, make a scene, threaten, endanger, claw at Maggie's door, break it down with her shoulder a battering ram, rip phones from the wall, spit on her clothes, rip their bed to shreds, throw the two of them out the window, grab a gun and take potshots off the nearest building? It was all she could do to keep from running downstairs and cleaning up the mess she'd created.

She knew what it was, of course. She'd been happy enough, being the woman, letting the men do the physical stuff (okay, okay, they had superior upper-arm strength, no reason to pretend it wasn't true) while she felt smart and happy and *equal*, idiot that she was. Because she was a woman, because she loved intolerably, permanently, in a female way; because she took what she could get and stored it for the future, dreaming for the future and waiting, waiting—she had lost everything because of this. She was exactly the kind of woman she had never intended to be.

If she'd been a man, none of this would be true. Men were certain about what they were doing—well, most men; maybe not Mickey. But in general terms, it was true: *she* never did anything risky, uncautious, aggressive (well, maybe she'd just stepped up to passive aggressive?); she looked for clues as to what the right thing would be before she did it; she had a fear of doing the wrong thing, as if the wrong thing could always be recognized.

She clenched and unclenched her fists, jabbing one against the wall, weak-willed, kitten-soft, a woman's punch.

She had decided she would not cry. That, at least, was in her power. But to stay, here, with these particular walls and that mocking chip of paint from the knife she had waved around—no.

She meant to slam the door but shut it quietly out of habit.

She walked around the block once, but it was cold. The wind crawled at her back like a wave, running down her neck, drenching her ankles. She kept her hat pulled low. She hadn't even taken it off when she'd seen Peter. And he hadn't mentioned her hair. She caught herself wishing he had. Did I want him to feel sorry? she thought angrily. Cut my hair off? Destroy something of mine?

She stopped in a bar on Second Avenue, hunching into a stool at the end. She looked warily along the row.

"Vodka," she said, changing her order at the last minute. She imagined drinking herself into a frenzy, her face lined from booze. If only she didn't get such headaches! She made a bad drunk.

The bar began to fill with Sunday-night traffic. The women sat, the men leaned against the bar or stood, feet planted firmly, glass in hand, gesticulating. Alyson looked at all of them with cold contempt; their loud voices, their tired jokes, the eyes that checked to see who else was listening. She ordered her second drink quickly.

She had just taken a sip when the man next to her said, "So what do you do, little lady?" He had boots, a sheepskin jacket, a Western hat. He put spurs into his voice.

"I don't believe it," Alyson cried, slamming her drink down and slopping a trail of vodka. "Did you just say 'little lady'?"

He blinked at her slowly, cautiously. "No offense," he said. "Just being friendly. I'm new in town." He grinned at her, flipping the corner of his coat back and putting his thumb in his belt.

"You didn't say 'little lady,'" she repeated. "I don't believe it."

His eyes got a far-off look and he turned his shoulder to her, staring in the other direction.

She clutched her drink. She should have waited longer, letting him skewer himself with his own stupidity. Peter would never have said such shit, not without a leer and a quick laugh. She wanted a fight; she had missed her chance.

"Slim pickings tonight," Madame Hope said. Alyson looked over her shoulder to the gypsy's face. She wore hot pink lipstick, a smudge of mascara, a knitted purple cap with the brim pulled over her forehead. Alyson felt an odd relief at seeing her. She was becoming a familiar face. She accepted the fortuneteller's presence without surprise.

"A bunch of fools," Alyson agreed.

"Hard to find the right sort on Sunday nights. Men coming out of marriages; men dropping off their kids, men dropping their lovers, all of them unsatisfied."

"Weekend daddies, slingshot lovers," Alyson agreed.

Madame Hope laughed. "A bad night. Cracked eggs." They both looked at the line of people at the bar, the women trying to look bright, the men assessing them. Poor fools, Alyson thought, looking at the women. What luck was there here? Alert female eyes, complacent male ones. Trash.

"Cracked eggs?" she asked.

"They look normal, but if you get real close, you notice chicken shit." She laughed.

Alyson nodded. "I just don't feel like going home," she admitted.

Madame Hope gleamed. "Come with me. Come to my place. We'll have some tea."

The vodka was making her head foggy anyway, Alyson decided. The first clear lift had disappeared. She nodded and left.

The wind sent a shiver down her spine. "Brisk," Madame Hope muttered. "The breath of lost souls."

They turned the corner down Sixth Street. "I like it here," the gypsy continued. "An interesting area."

"It's gentrifying."

"That's what I mean. Some people get squeezed, some ride the wave. They all want to know the future. Good for business."

A man was leaning against a car in the dark. He glanced at them furtively, his hands in front. The sight angered Alyson. "That car's not a pisspot," she said, loud enough to be heard. "The world's not a pisspot." The man made a few quick movements and rapidly walked away.

"Still, you have to envy them," the gypsy chuckled. "Damn convenient. If a woman has to pee in New York, she has to go home. Or buy a drink or get something to eat."

The gypsy's storefront was wedged in between two Indian restaurants. It was below ground level, and the three steps down to the door had a fusty damp smell like dirty laundry.

The fortuneteller opened the door quickly, waving Alyson forward. "This is it. This is home. My burrow, my cave. Come in."

The small outside room was furnished exactly as Alyson remembered—the little round table, the plastic chairs pressed close to the large plate glass window, the doorway with beads hanging down. Madame Hope grabbed the beads and pulled them aside. "Come through here to my living room. Watch your step there. I haven't had a chance to do much with this place yet. But you'll forgive me." She flicked on a light switch.

The walls were painted cement blocks, covered on one side with an Indian print, frayed and faded. There was a beat-up sofa, a coffee table, and an armchair, all looking like they'd been rescued from the street.

The dog lay in the armchair, his head resting on his two huge paws, his eyes trained on Alyson. Madame Hope and the dog ignored each other, as if there were hard words between them. Alyson stood still as Madame Hope went to a kitchenette small as a closet, and started rattling things around.

"I put the water on to boil," she said, coming back and drying her hands. She hadn't turned the light on in the kitchenette, and the gas burner glowed gently, dancing at the corner of sight.

"Just indulge me a minute," Madame Hope said, turning on the

TV beside the armchair. "The news." She sat next to Alyson on the couch and both women turned to the set. Alyson's view was slightly blocked by the dog's rump; his tail flicked occasionally, like a cat's, obscuring the view.

"I like to see what's happening," the gypsy said. The TV cut to an interview with a city official. "I can hardly keep up with the bribery these days. Scandals, suicide, murder. Nothing but gossip, really."

"But we need to know these things."

"Of course we do. I'm all for it. Wait!" she cried, jumping up and turning up the sound. "This one's familiar." Alyson caught the voice-over on a picture of firefighters aiming streams of water at a burning building. ". . . fire in a tenement building at. . ." Alyson heard as Madame Hope thrilled. "I knew it! I knew it! That's where I used to live. A much nicer place than this one." She turned down the sound and clutched Alyson's arm excitedly. "Just moved out last month! Can you beat it? Serves that bastard right, he was a miserable landlord." She snorted with contempt and, Alyson noted, undisguised glee.

"Good thing you moved, then. I mean—otherwise you'd be in that fire?"

The gypsy shrugged. "Would I? I always kept a sharp lookout, had to, that place was a real hellhole. Rats and all. Here there's centipedes, I admit, but they're not as bad as rats, rats are too noisy, don't you think? Miserable landlord. And what a scam. Five floors, all packed with welfare recipients, he nailed up some plywood in each room and kept dividing it so he could cram some more people in. At a thousand a month, I heard. Never any heat and it stank of roaches. It deserved to burn. If he wasn't a millionaire already, he would have been next month, he was raking it in." She smacked Alyson's arm with satisfaction. "Not that I didn't envy him, with all that money and perfectly legal, too, but that building should have burned down long ago. Squalor, endless yelling. Who can live like that? And he hardly gave me any notice, just told me to leave. Ha! The water must be boiling by now." She jumped up again, turning the set off as she passed. The dog's tail jerked once, irritably, and he blinked.

Alyson could hear the clink of cups and teaspoons in the still-dark kitchenette. To be honest, this room wasn't very bright either. There was a dim bulb in the ceiling fixture and an even dimmer bulb in a heavy wrought-iron floor lamp. The shadows from each crisscrossed in wide, curving bands. Studying the pattern, Alyson saw a centipede moving from one strip of half-light into dark ground. She lifted her feet and checked the floor nearby.

"In fact," Madame Hope continued, carrying in a tray of tea things, "these slumlords are the cream of the crop. They know the system inside out. They *are* the system." Her voice chattered in hostess tones and Alyson quickly revised her opinion of the gypsy. The cups and saucers didn't match, but they were not mugs. And there was a cloudy silver sugar bowl and creamer. "Genteel," Alyson thought. "She has aspirations of some kind."

"Someday I'll be rich, too," the gypsy crowed. "I'll be a slumlord too."

Alyson sipped her tea. It was sweet and had a strange taste to it. She sipped it again, trying to place it. Cinnamon, cardamom, allspice? She shook her head. "Why settle for that? Petty tyranny, cheap despotism." Her head was beginning to hum. Had she had two vodkas or three?

The gypsy gloated. "No cheap stuff for you, eh? If you're going to take the plunge, go for the big stuff? Why nickel and dime your soul to hell, hey?"

"Who said 'soul'? Who said 'hell'?" Alyson objected. "Besides, who knows if what they're doing is a sin any more than it's a crime? Walking the line. Shelter, but at a cost. Isn't that better than no shelter at all?"

"So he's performing a service, is he? Burning them up like bugs on a log, and all in the name of charity?"

"Probably the burning wasn't intentional." Alyson put a hand to her forehead, rubbing it. The room was warm; she had thought it was damp. She shrugged her coat off her shoulders. "And who's to say it wasn't a kinder, faster death for some of them?" She was vaguely surprised at her own words. They were not like her.

"You're taking the objective view. I like that view myself. Gets rid of the nasty emotional details. More tea?"

Alyson held out her cup. "And, let's face it, no one likes to look at people who refuse to get on; no one likes to meet them on the street or on your own stairs. If you look at success, you think success. You look at failure, and what?" Had she really been harboring thoughts such as these? She was interested to hear herself speak. Maybe she could be different; maybe she already *was* different.

"You see yourself?"

Alyson glared and the gypsy laughed. "You're right, you know. You can be anything you want. Of course there are sacrifices, of course there are incidental losses, but you have to stack them and weigh them, don't you? Timing's very important. Once in your life you'll see you can take what you want. If you're polite, you lose. But you have to learn to bargain."

"Bargain?" Alyson asked. She could feel the first trickle of sweat roll down the back of her neck.

"Well, we can't all be saints, can we? And lucky for us, too. A saint's life is no fun—did you ever imagine one of them slapping your back and shouting hurrah? Not a chummy group. Don't ever get trapped in an elevator with one of them; they're dead serious all the time."

"You're being ridiculous."

"I'm making a point. Goodness is shallow. Not just now but forever. Angels smile but they can't tell jokes. Now sinners," she clapped her hands, "tell jokes. Sinners understand punchlines."

"It's so hot in here," Alyson said, fanning her face with her hand. "I seem to have lost the point."

"Is it hot?" the gypsy jumped up. "I didn't even notice. It's the furnace, you know. Come on, come on, I have to check it." She pulled Alyson up by the hand. "This way." Alyson followed her through the kitchenette to a cinderblock room with two doors in it. The gypsy stopped and began to search her pocket for keys. "Which is it?" Madam Hope asked, gesturing to the doors, "the lady or the tiger?" She grinned.

Alyson considered the doors as if it were a serious choice, but she couldn't make up her mind. If it were true, she thought, if I really had to choose, I'd end up staying here forever. She bit her lip. *I've never chosen anything; I've never risked anything. Half-risks, hesitations, that's where I've gone wrong.* She pointed. "That one," she said, thinking, *But I do know what I want. It's obvious what I want.*

"Bingo," Madame Hope said, turning the key in the door.

I just want the things I was promised as a child, Alyson thought, watching as the gypsy busied herself at the door. *Love, marriage, a family. And a little more. Respect and hope. Or maybe not even hope. Maybe strength. Maybe ruthlessness. Things I haven't even considered yet. Power. Power would be nice.*

"Into the valley of death," Madame Hope said, opening the door and waving Alyson to follow. "Into the depths of hell."

The door opened onto a short stairway, but one so steep that Alyson had to clutch the wall as she went down. The heat and the roar were staggering, so hot she shielded her eyes. The gypsy jumped around lightly, flipping a switch for light, peering at dials and gauges, pursing her lips.

The furnace must have been six feet high and twice as long. Alyson had never seen anything so large, so hot, so ominous. It had doors that the gypsy opened and then slammed shut quickly, shaking her head, turning to look at Alyson and holding up her hands. She yelled something—Alyson thought she said, simply, "Too hot" but it was hard to tell under all that noise. Alyson worried that her skin was growing crisp, she felt so overwhelmed by all of it, the roar augmenting the heat. But Madame Hope was turning dials, nodding, grinning, as if she were a virtuoso with a cherished instrument. Alyson thought she was whistling. Finally the gypsy waved her over, shouting, "Come take a look," and she opened a whole row of hatches all at eye level. Alyson approached them cautiously; she could feel a breeze passing her, being sucked into the hatches, feeding the fires. The closer she got, the closer she wanted to get. The flames were wonderful to see, leaping from their spigots, shooting up blue and orange and white, making a roaring music, so tempting Alyson had to fight an impulse to stick her hand in, to see exactly *how* hot it was, it seemed so fantastic.

Karen Heuler

"They say hell's like this," Madame Hope shouted, turning a dial, adjusting the fire. "Hoopla, hoopla! It isn't at all." Her eyes gleamed and she slanted them in Alyson's direction.

"How is it, then?" Alyson asked automatically. The scene itself was so otherworldly that she felt no surprise at the gypsy's words.

"Just like this world," the fortuneteller laughed. "Noisy and groaning. Come on, we're fixed." She led the way up the stairs, her rump riding high in Alyson's face.

She slammed the cellar door shut and rubbed her hands. "Busy, busy. I love machines."

Alyson's mind was also busy. The gypsy knew all about hell, or so she said. Was she merely being funny; was this the whole punchline thing she'd been talking about and had Alyson missed the joke? Hell didn't exist, did it? Because that meant the devil did as well? This gypsy was merely being provocative; the fire and the questions were just her way of showing off. But showing off about what?

"Is your life everything you wanted?" the gypsy asked when they sat, once again, over their tea. She had a smudge of soot under her right eye, like a shadow.

The dog had walked down from his chair—there was no other way to describe it; he was too big to jump—and had come over to stand by Alyson's knee. He leaned against her, gradually increasing his weight. Alyson had no idea what it meant. She leaned her weight back against him.

"Do you know my life?" Alyson asked.

The gypsy grinned. This disconcerted Alyson. I wonder if I understand what's happening, she thought, but then she hastily corrected herself and added, But nothing's happening. Out loud, she said, "This life I have is worth nothing to me." The dog pressed against her even more. Her hand reached out to pet him, to distract him, but she got a sudden smell of something from his fur, and she hastily withdrew.

"I knew a man," Madame Hope said, "who wanted a second chance. He wanted to *taste* life."

"And did he?" Alyson whispered. The gypsy's eyes were burning into her, her body leaning toward Alyson, her voice smoky and rich.

"He did." She licked her lips. "I knew a man who wanted to keep his beauty, who wanted never to fade."

"And did he?"

"He did." The gypsy picked up Alyson's left hand—the future hand, she'd said, hadn't she—and stroked it once, twice, thrice. "Cross your heart, girl. Make a wish."

Alyson blinked slowly. "And what happened to these men?" she asked.

"One went to heaven, one went to hell. The odds are always there. It's a sporting risk."

The dog leaned so heavily against Alyson that she had to use her knee to push him back.

The room seemed soft and encouraging; and yet within the room was this woman and this odd dog, and the strangest conversation Alyson had ever had. It sounded like the gypsy thought she could grant her wish; it sounded like eternity was at stake. And even in her mind, Alyson shied away from naming names, but she knew about bargains and souls. She knew. At the same time: how stupid to fall for a joke! She had to feel her way carefully. "And are you the one to grant these wishes?" Alyson asked.

The gypsy flung herself back in her chair. "Of course, of course. You're stalling for time, that's all. It's plain as day." She grinned.

Alsyon felt the inevitability of her own question. "The devil?" she whispered. "You?"

Madame Hope frowned. She looked offended.

"It's just," Alyson said quickly, "I would have expected a man."

The gypsy snorted. "Stereotypes!" She waved her hand dismissively. "I know how it goes. 'In the beginning were two men, and one of them was God.' So much for feminism! Well, think about it, think about it. If there is a heaven, who would grab it? Men! And we know what that means—the women go to hell!" She looked theatrically annoyed; Alyson could detect a crafty gleam to her voice, an eye on the audience. "In eternity, too, there are men and women, and in eternity, too, only one has the upper hand."

"And it's not you."

"It's not me. But that's your advantage. God doesn't bargain."

"Bargain," Alyson repeated tentatively.

"What baffles me is that I don't do more business. The vogue with devils comes and goes, you know, though you'd imagine it should be more consistent. This century has turned out very practical—of course it would, you have the bomb now. Still, you'd think people would have a sense of history, a grasp of alternatives." She tapped her fingers on the rim of her cup, still eyeing Alyson. Her voice switched gear, it had become soft and cajoling. "What is your secret wish, your private little play, your starring role? What do you want out of life that you don't have?"

Alyson's head was clear now; and the gypy's practical voice made even this leap—this chance—this strange possibility seem businesslike. To have what she wanted! She thought of Peter, and her heart leapt with grief, but she saw him again, standing before her, saying he would marry Maggie, saw him floating away in the cab with Maggie, while her own small dreams collapsed. She forced herself to reason it out, forced herself to look logically at all the things she'd been thinking since it happened. Losing Peter, losing Dingo, getting older and less valuable every day; what did she have to look forward to? What was her future like? She could see it only too well: she would never stop being a woman, and she would never stop being treated like a woman, and she didn't think she was going to get much happiness out of it; at her age, her chances were slim. But there was a desire, a longing, a need for more. If this was all she got, she knew it wasn't enough. She wanted more, and better.

"I want," she whispered finally, "to be a man." She lifted her head up and gazed, wet-eyed, at Madame Hope.

"Oh my *dear*," Madame Hope whispered, "what fun!"

Chapter 6

By the time Alyson dragged herself to bed her head was clicking like a beetle and her skin felt on fire. She thought that now, at least, she had dared to do something exceptional, that her life was her own at last. But then her heart would begin to thud and she'd wonder, after all, what had she done, what kind of insanity was this? She didn't even believe in God; didn't that automatically exclude the devil? Was that woman laughing at her? Was there a drug in Madame Hope's tea, did she go about making fools of lost women? Wasn't Alyson always humiliating herself? And in the middle of a groan she would think with alarm, it *was* the devil, she *did* sell her soul, and she would run and check the mirror for signs of a change. The cycle repeated itself—ecstasy, shame, despair.

It came as no surprise, then, that she awoke the next morning with chattering teeth and pain in every bone. Flu, no doubt, and the real thing, too, not just a cold or a sniffle that some people *said* was the flu. Her head felt boxed in. She called the office, barked in her illness, and went back to bed.

There was no doubt she had a fever—maybe all of her conversation with the gypsy had been no more than a fever? She heard voices around her, as if she were in some marvelous party. People told hilarious jokes, jokes that made her laugh out loud, they were so clever. But a second later she couldn't recall what had been so funny, and she strained her ears listening for the next witticism. The party lasted all day; she had no sense of loneliness or self-pity. The thirst, of course, was annoying, but she stumbled into the kitchen periodically and made pots of tea, which she took back to her bed. The tea always had that undertaste she had noticed at Madame Hope's. "How strange to think I could have lost my soul over a cup of tea," she mused, and a wave of laughter from the ghost party reassured her of her silliness; or perhaps the ghost party, too, had all lost their souls and that was why it was so amusing.

Day and night passed by outside like cars on the street and Alyson woke and slept, sipping her tea, listening to her guests. She never actually saw them, but she imagined they were all thin and beautifully dressed. They lounged across the furniture or stood in waving groups clutching martini glasses, beaming at her, showering little spurts of conversation her way. She grew used to disconnected phrases that seemed to have extraordinary significance. "She's not herself today," passed through the company like an excited breeze, and everyone smiled, including Alyson. Not herself! How silly! Who else could she be if not herself! "Ultimate slice-of-life kind of thing," observed a flutey masculine voice, and heads wagged knowingly. Wasn't everything "slice of life"? Wasn't everything ultimate? Alyson shook with mirth, rattling her teacup or clutching her pillow.

Covered with sweat and shivering, she took a hot shower, the water stinging her skin. The party followed her into the bathroom and she was caught in one of those dreams where you are naked, and everyone else is dressed. "I've misunderstood something," Alyson thought bleakly, and covered her breasts with her hands.

Suddenly the water was turned off and Alyson was stumbling into thick dry towels while the hands of her guests gently pushed her back into bed. They shoved and clucked at her with sympathy. "Sometimes you just don't notice," a voice said in a slightly defensive tone. She felt the towels being pulled away and then felt herself being gently patted dry. The apartment was warm; for once, the heat was on when she needed it, the clank and hiss of the radiators was secure and comforting.

The ghosts began to massage her body, rubbing and prodding

the ache from her bones. Their fingers were gentle, but weren't they indiscreet? "Such beautiful small breasts," someone whispered as fingers kneaded them, prod, prod. "I don't have small breasts," Alyson thought defensively, but it felt good, whatever the circumstances, to be touched again, soothingly. How wonderful to feel them massaging her neck, gently, gently, and her throat, which felt like it had a lump in it, moving the lump, somehow, to a more comfortable spot.

Although sometimes they pinched, these fingers, especially when they ran up her legs, her thighs, and scratched at her pubic hair, pulling and pushing. How odd to be touched there and not feel aroused. It was sensual, yes, the rubbing, pushing at folds of skin, but the murmurs and encouragement had no sexual thrill to them. Alyson felt unashamed yet unaroused, equally content to have them stir at her ribcage, her breasts, or her clitoris, stroke her forehead or her vagina, tug the skin over her cheekbones, tap gently at her hip. Her skin glowed with well-being; she relaxed, thinking of glorious naked bodies, male and female, considering their parts as voices whispered, "A little more, move that over, push, push! It's coming along now, you over there, pull that tighter and don't forget the hair!" Alyson's hand wandered up to her hair, still damp, still short. Should she grow it out again, long and shining?

She woke to the sound of the phone ringing. She thought, vaguely, that someone else would answer it, but it rang again and again, insistently, Alyson turned over and grabbed the phone. Her voice came out harsh and sore.

"Bob? Is that you? It's Anna."

Alyson ran her hand over her face, rubbing her eyes, trying to clear her head. Her thumb scraped something prickly on her chin, and she scratched absent-mindedly, trying to peel it off.

"Anna? What day is it?" she asked cautiously.

"It's Thursday," Anna answered. "God, you sound awful. Have you seen a doctor?"

"I'm better. I'm almost better. My throat is sore." Alyson tried to clear her throat again, but her voice refused to move back up.

"Do you need anything? I can come by after work."

Alyson stopped scratching at her face. Her breath froze and she touched her jaw with the tips of her fingers. She gripped the phone tightly. "I've got to get off the phone, Anna," she said, no longer trying to control her voice. "I'll be back soon. I've got to go."

"Oh. But call if you need anything," Anna said and hung up.

"If I need anything," Alyson repeated to herself, and took her hand away from the stubble on her chin. She took hold of the sheets, paused, her knuckles white, and whipped them aside.

"Damn," Alyson muttered, and her eyes misted over. She lifted her hand and felt for her breasts. A man's hand rose and ran over a man's chest, lightly hairy, nipples puckering flat against his ribs. She opened her legs and a man's legs moved, revealing a soft, floppy penis drooped in a bed of hair. She felt for her vagina and met the loose sack of a man's scrotum, and behind that sealed skin to her ass. A woman's tears ran down a man's face, slowed down by the beard on her chin. The radiator hissed and spit and spit again and then clanked off with a venomous bang, and the cold edged out from the windows, running sly fingers along the skin of the man in bed, who lay there, staring down, as his skin prickled and his heart bounced madly, wondering if he'd lost his mind—or just his soul.

*O*ver the course of a lifetime spent with yourself, you must check the mirror a few million times. Do I look all right? you ponder. Is my hair just so? Do I have a smudge or a pimple or parsley in my teeth? Is that a fool looking back, have I worn that face again, and if I hold my head this way, don't I look better?

And what's more, if you never saw yourself at all, you might act differently; there's an irresistible impulse to act the way your face reveals you to be—big-jawed, low-browed, shifty-eyed, thin-lipped, angelic. Your nose will determine how you move your hands. You can't avoid it; you remember the image in that mirror, you do what it suggests. You develop your style and your style develops you. You were skinny once but now you're fat, and sure, you think of yourself as skinny still, but you've seen the mirror and you stick to your chair, and your fate is sealed. And you—

you rehearsed a thoughtful look until you thought it was your own, but one day you caught sight of yourself at a party—mouth hanging open, perhaps a speck of drool at the corner of your lip—and that sight pulls you back a hundred times from saying anything thoughtful; you clench your teeth to keep your drool to yourself and soon you'll discover you're not only stupid but bad-tempered as well.

But imagine for a moment what it would be like if you looked in the mirror and saw another face staring back, looking exactly as shocked as you felt. If you need glasses, perhaps you can understand the desperate attempt to focus, to blink, to squint, to get everything in line again. The eyes . . . the eyes are the right color, there's no denying it, but your jaw is different, stronger than usual. Although, if you don't look quite so hard, maybe it's not really all that different, your old jaw exaggerated, your cheekbones, higher or lower, but if you could shift them—maybe by turning your head or looking from the side—well, then, you can see how it really is the same old formation, slightly redistributed. If nothing else, those are obviously your teeth. In fact, taken separately, all the pieces are familiar, but it's uncanny, it's mocking how they've been redone.

Added to that, of course, was the fact that Alyson had a whole new body; in parts at least, vaguely familiar, but no longer, in any sense, *personal*. Her hips were narrower, her chest was flat, she had an Adam's apple and a penis, and, presumably, increased upper-arm strength. Her hands were broader, her shoulders wider, her voice deeper.

It's probably time to concede that it wasn't *her* voice anymore, it was *his*. There was certainly sufficient external support for this. Internally, he still thought of himself as a woman. Having to pee, for example, he made the mistake of sitting rather than standing, a habit that had served him well for thirty-five years. Obviously, a lot of habits were on the way out.

But lifting his hand and seeing another hand moving; looking at his face and seeing another face looking: these things confounded him. His identity was gone; he had no confidence in his body—the steady, daily, physical automation was gone. There was an abyss between what he had been and what he would one day be. The loss of intimacy with himself was more shocking than the loss of his soul. It had to be—he had never lived in his soul the way he had in his body.

Staggering around with this body, as if it were a shoe that didn't fit, he opened closets and drawers. All the clothes were new, unlabeled, unstained, untouched. He searched for anything familiar like an immigrant searching for native foods. He found nothing. It was painful to be so new.

He pulled out jeans and a shirt, socks, underwear, shoes. Everything fit him perfectly and, finally dressed, he felt oddly light, as if disencumbered.

Restless, still disoriented, he decided to go out. His hand was on the doorknob when he saw the polish on his nails. He jerked his hand back as if burnt.

His heart beat rapidly; he felt he had almost exposed himself. He didn't stop to think why he was so determined not to be "found out." He had almost given himself away; at any moment he could be careless again, and the old Alyson would come seeping out behind the new, forcing him to fail.

There was one thing he knew immediately: he wouldn't fail. Whatever was happening to him, however complicated it got, he wanted to win. The game was on; he would figure it out.

He dashed for the medicine cabinet, yanking it open. But there was no polish remover. There was shaving cream and razors and styptic pencils. Why should there be polish remover? He slammed the cabinet shut. Even more important, however, was why there was polish on his nails. Could the devil manage everything, and not manage that?

Or was it on purpose? The idea filled him with panic, and he was forced to dismiss it. What would Madame Hope get out of it? He chewed at his nails, biting off the tips, trying to peel off the polish. There were still streaks of red, it was impossible to get rid of all of it that way.

He found gloves in the bureau, and put on his jacket—buttoned left side over right, a *man's* jacket. The light was already fading on the street—midafternoon in December. He pulled his scarf up over his ears, tingling in the cold. The weather had turned while he was sick.

He hurried to the nearest drugstore. He was trying very hard to avoid thinking too much; he was trying very hard to act and decide and leave the thinking for later.

He strolled through the aisles, trying to be a man in a woman's world. Shampoo, toothpaste, deodorant. Hairspray, hairdye, haircurlers. Smiling women, women with bare shoulders, touching their hair. Curlers, combs, bobby pins. Lipstick, mascara, blusher. Women's eyes, women's mouths. He picked up a bottle of polish remover.

He felt awkward, going to the counter with just that item. He followed the aisles, drifting around. He stopped in front of the Tampax display, paused, then walked on. Near it was a display of condoms. After some hesitation, he picked up a package.

His eyes had ignored the tinsel and the fake evergreens, but when he went outside a wet snow was falling. Bing Crosby sang "White Christmas," a scratched recording piped out from next door. It was the week before Christmas, after all.

He walked slowly back, clutching his small paper bag, his shoulder feeling empty without a purse slung over it. Christmas again. Visions of Christmases past floated through his head like a holiday movie: buying gifts for Peter, opening gifts from Peter. Christmas trees and ornaments, wrapped packages, lies, lies. Even now it seemed impossible that it could all be lies. He stopped short, closing his eyes. He had to forget Peter. Peter was useless even as a memory.

He opened his eyes again; he was across the street from his own building. It was garbage pickup day, and all the garbage cans had been brought to the curb, filled with big black bags surrounding them on the sidewalks. In front of his building, someone was rummaging through the trash. At first he thought it was for bottles and cans, scavengers living off the five-cent refund. But then he recognized the weird guy from the first floor.

It was the Vulture, at it again. Everyone knew he went through the garbage, but a neighborly embarrassment had prevented all the tenants from watching what he retrieved. But now Alyson could see that the vulture was picking out pieces of paper—envelopes, letters, lists, notes,

Karen Heuler

anything handwritten.

It struck Alyson as an incredible violation, and one he'd ignored for too long. All those years, and the Vulture had been collecting her notes, her lists, scraps of paper with Peter's writing on it! Birthday cards, letters she'd never sent, pieces of paper with phone numbers and addresses! It was bad enough, thinking of him snaking his fingers through discarded Tampax boxes, identifying who they belonged to! Knowing her bouts with vaginitis, her mania for pasta—he was obviously methodical; he would know. And when she had a cold, the discarded tissues! The Vulture's fingers must be filled with germs, small wriggling microbes, he picked, picked, picked. The thought was sickening, he could feel an onrush of weakness again, a buzzing in the ears, and he stumbled across the street and up the stairs, causing the Vulture to replace a lid hastily and straighten up, his hands tucking paper into his pockets, his lips moving in some sort of incantation. The weirdo stepped back against the side of the short front stairway, into the shadows. Only half of his face showed.

Alyson fumbled for his keys and, he couldn't help it, he looked over to the Vulture, who was staring up at him. His head kept bobbing, as if he suddenly understood something. Was it Alyson's imagination, or was there a flash of comprehension in his face?

The phrase "dirty secret" leapt to Alyson's mind as he raced up the hallway and stairs to his apartment. He grabbed tissues and polish remover and took off the last streaks of red from his fingernails. He was about to throw the tissues in the garbage when he realized the Vulture would find them, so he flushed them down the toilet.

He caught sight of his face in the mirror, with its day-old stubble. What kind of person belongs to this face? he wondered. Who is he?

The phone rang. Anna again? He reached for it. "Hello? Hello?" he asked, hearing the sound of music in the background. "Who is it?"

"Bob? What are you doing there?" It was Peter's voice, and he felt a jolt. Of course it was Peter, he'd known it as soon as he heard the noise. Peter used to call when he was playing somewhere, taking a break, getting a drink, sometimes with his saxophone still looped around his neck, and there was always the bar buzz in the background, and the sound of music. He registered that Peter had called him "Bob"; and Anna had also called him "Bob."

"I live here." He cleared his throat.

"Where's Alyson?"

His mind worked rapid-fire. He felt cautious and oddly insulted (Peter should *know* who he was, even as a man). He closed his eyes to conentrate.

"Alyson's gone," Bob said slowly. He sat down on the edge of the couch, hunched forward.

"Gone?" Peter sounded impatient. "You mean you're living there now?"

"Yes. Yes I am. What do you want?" He could hear the sound of a match being struck, and an impatient, indrawn breath.

"I wanted to talk to Alyson. Where is she now?"

"What about?"

He imagined Peter's hand jerking in irritation or embarrassment, the way it did when he felt pressured. "Come on, Bob, I just want to see how she is."

"Are you still living with Maggie?" Alyson tried to keep his voice neutral. The mutual friend perhaps. Or an old friend of Alyson's? What was his role?

"Don't take sides," Peter urged. Alyson could tell he'd had a few drinks. "I know it looks bad. But that's just the way it *looks*. I guess you've heard her version. That's not fair to me."

Mutual friends, Alyson decided. "She doesn't want to talk to you. I can't give you her number."

"Are you subletting or something? You didn't even tell me."

Maybe *his* friend, Alyson thought. "I'm subletting indefinitely. I'm sorry. She doesn't want to hear from you if you're living with Maggie."

Peter snorted. "High drama." He inhaled. "Look, this feels awkward. Why don't we get together for a drink? I've been a little busy lately." There was another little snort, slightly self-mocking, hoping to make the best of it, a good guy caught behaving badly. "So. So, let's get together, maybe shoot some pool?"

"Yes," Alyson said slowly. "I'll call you."

"If you don't, at least I know your number," Peter said. "Just like it was my own." He had a rueful little laugh.

Alyson hung up, thinking. He had a new history—obviously. But what was this past like? And this business about being called "Bob"— was the gypsy laughing at him? And did Alyson still exist somehow? No; Alyson was gone as long as he was Bob; she was just part of the history around him.

He felt a wave of loneliness at this new relationshp to Peter. The one person who knew everything—every nuance, every crack in the armor, every failure, every hope—no longer recognized him. He went to the closet, dragging out the photo albums.

Alyson was still there, at least. She laughed and smiled and held her hand in Peter's. She wore jeans and dresses and swimsuits. She looked out from behind a waterfall, raised her foot coming down the stairs. He felt a sharp nostalgia for her: her eyes, her hair, her breasts pushing up against her shirt. He rubbed his own chest, missing the soft companionship of breasts.

He looked up and saw Madame Hope sitting on his bed, smoking a cigarette and regarding him with amused eyes.

"Everything all right?" she asked. Her hair, which she used to wear swept back from her face, was now loose and untidy. She wore a polyester pants suit instead of a dress, and she poked the hand with the cigarette as if she were poking someone's chest.

Alyson was repulsed. "Did I ever really like her?" he thought. He was disgusted with himself, forced to admit that she had seemed, at one point, clever and resourceful. Impervious, preternatural, wise. Now she wore black oxfords; she crossed her legs so that the ugly shoes caught Alyson's eye.

"Or are we feeling the least bit sorry for ourselves today?" she continued mockingly. A short laugh and a cruel twist to her lips made her seem like a different person. But it passed, briefly, as if he'd had blurred vision, and she straightened up, smoothed her hair back to its regular style, and smiled politely. "You're feeling a little out of sorts right now?" Her voice had the old familiar undertone of concern to it.

"Why are they calling me Bob?" he asked curtly.

"They have to call you something."

"Everyone called me Al."

"Well, we can't have that," she said companionably. "Old associations. Too familiar."

"But—Bob?" He sighed. "It's so usual. So neutral. Generic, even."

"Hence the irony." The gypsy grinned.

He ducked his head and shook it. "I don't know. This is all happening so fast, and I keep having to figure things out. I can't get my bearings. I mean, I don't know what's going to happen next." He felt close to tears and blinked hard.

"Well, of course it's a new life; why would you know what's going to happen next?" Madame Hope answered benignly. She got up and walked over to the closet and inspected his shirts. "A few surprises and you'll be at the top of your game. It's good to have to think on your feet. And you have to admit I have good taste in clothes." She didn't wait for a comment. "You wanted to wake up a man, but you forgot to ask whether you'd be comfortable, is that it?" She walked back to the bed and sat down casually. "Oh, lordy," she said in a mincing tone, "where are my sweet, sweet breasts?"

Bob leaned back against the wall, his eyes narrowed. "Were you spying on me?" he snapped. He felt the blood rush to his face.

Madame Hope jerked upright, her eyes gleaming. "Dear me," she said apologetically. "I've had a busy week. Shouldn't take it out on you." She grinned coyly. "And the holidays are so difficult, aren't they? I know I always get depressed—spending them alone, no goodies under the tree, carols nagging at you day and night. And then I get annoyed." She patted Bob on the shoulder. "Don't worry, you'll get into the swing of things. Anything new is confusing at first. But look at how well you've done so far—you didn't fall to pieces when *he* called, did you? It's beginning to work."

Bob nodded, determined to be calm. "I suppose it takes a while. I was confused at first, when he called me Bob."

The gypsy shrugged. "It's just a name, you know. Never occurred to me you'd want something fancy."

He ignored that remark. "Peter thinks I'm his drinking buddy."

"Peter thinks of you as a close friend he's neglected by becoming involved with Maggie," the gypsy corrected smoothly.

Bob digested this. "And how will other people see me?"

Madame Hope shrugged vaguely. "They'll all have different ideas. A kind of guessing game, that's what makes it interesting."

"Interesting?" Bob said uneasily. "You mean, interesting for you?" A look of disbelief crossed his face. "You mean you'll be watching me?"

"Oh, come on, now," the gypsy laughed. "You didn't really imagine I'd be sitting back and waiting for a postcard when your soul comes due? I've got my reputation to think of; I've got an investment." She leaned forward, her brows pulling down over her eyes. "You and I, Alyson, we've become partners." She smacked her lips hungrily. "We've got a soul in common."

Chapter 7

$\mathscr{B}$ob went back to work, his beard itching, his clothes now buttoned on the wrong side, eyes darting, trying to analyze everything at a glance. He felt like he still had a fever; his skin was flushed and damp, his mouth dry. He kept checking the mirror, studying his face. Yes, that was it, he seemed to *have* more face. The bones were heavier, his ears larger, his neck more sinewy, his chin thicker. At first, whenever he'd looked at himself, he'd seen fear at the edge of his gray eyes, in the thin lines that ran between his mouth and his cheeks. He removed the fear by staring slightly beyond focus. After a day or two he stopped shaving, and the uncertainty around his lips seemed to slip away.

He had clipped all his fingernails short and, as he turned the doorknob to *Adventure's* offices, he felt sure that every physical detail had been adjusted; now it was character alone on which he would win or lose.

Anna's smile at his entrance was unmistakable. It made him feel welcome, but he stopped his own smile as soon as he noticed it. Friendship, warmth and ease were dangers. His first rule was to hold his tongue and get his bearings.

"How are you feeling? You look so pale!" Anna said.

He shrugged. "The flu is no vacation. I still don't feel altogether myself." He walked to his office, and Anna followed.

"I'm glad to see you're growing your beard again," she said.

"It was too much trouble to shave," he answered, rubbing his chin. He unbuttoned his coat carefully, hanging it behind the door. "Anything happen while I was gone?"

"Well." She hesitated, moving mail on Bob's desk into an orderly pile. "Pierre and Eliot have gotten thick. You know Eliot's sharing Pierre's office!" She glanced up quickly for his reaction; he very carefully didn't have one. "They go to lunch together; they close the door and discuss things together. Of course, Eliot is Pierre's friend; it may not all be business, but if even half of it is . . ." She trailed off. "Maybe inviting Pierre out to lunch would be a good move."

Bob nodded.

"He keeps asking me about subscriptions, every day," she complained. "There's been some talk of making TV commercials about the magazine. And I know he's trying to raise more money."

"God. I've only been gone a week," Bob said crossly. He sat at his desk and stared gloomily at the mail.

"And just see how it all falls apart. Eliot isn't good at handling queries," she said carefully. "He wants to check with Pierre on everything. And you know he can't type, so he writes it out in longhand, crosses it out, and then hands it to Ellen to type. She does it after she finishes Pierre's letters, and she doesn't rush herself." Anna grinned. "Pierre is deliberately ignoring it. He's been waiting for you to come back."

"Well, I'm back."

Anna remained where she was, her arms now crossed, looking at Bob. "Other than being sick," she asked finally, "is anything new?"

Bob picked up an envelope and slowly ripped it open. "No, nothing new," he said evenly.

"You haven't heard from Peter?"

He forced himself not to break the rhythm, unfolding the letter, placing it on the desk.

"He called once," Bob said, keeping his voice as neutral as possible while his pulse skipped suddenly out of beat. He realized the implications of Anna's question all at once. Could he be mistaken? He hoped, he begged that it was a mistake. But Anna had always known about Peter—all those confidences Alyson had shared, the perpetual "we" of the references.

Couldn't Madame Hope have shaped it a different way? Did she have to twist it against him? Was this the "interesting" part for her?

"Are you two getting back together?" Anna continued.

Bob balled the envelope in his fist and forced himself to smile. "No."

"I'm sorry."

"It's all right."

Anna shook her head. "It's a rotten business. Love," she said angrily. "Unspeakable."

Bob kept the smile creased on his face. "The chapter's closed."

"That's so easy to say," she protested vaguely and sighed. "I know how it can be, so if you want company sometimes, tell me." She turned to go. "You could have called me when you were sick," she added reproachfully. "We're friends. I can make tea. I can hand out aspirin."

"I know. I appreciate it."

"Male stuff," she said. "You should know better. Mickey's away. I'll tell Pierre you're here."

Bob sat perfectly still, his hand holding the envelope in his fist. "Gay," he thought, and he could feel his face grow white then red, cold then hot, back and forth. Gay. To Anna only? To everyone in the office? Did Pierre think he was gay? What impact would it have? Could he deny it, overcome it? Or was it too late?

Gay. Had he traded his soul for this? He felt a balloon growing in his chest, hatred of Madame Hope, hatred of Pierre, of Eliot, even of Anna. To be labeled as gay! To go from being a woman to being a fag. Queer. Queen. He could hear the words, the whispers, catch the condescending looks, the contemptuous smiles. Not so different after all, not much progress here.

He finally threw the envelope away, his back as straight as a coat rack, bile flowing through his veins. The fortuneteller bitch had issued a challenge, then; objectively, he could see how much fun this would be for her. His hand strayed to his tie, knotted correctly after three tries.

It was a good thing Peter had worn ties and that Alyson had liked to watch him dress.

The intercom buzzed. "Glad to have you back," Pierre hummed. "Feeling all right? Let's meet in about an hour, to go over the next issue. Try to get through the mail."

He bent his head over the mail—his gay head, he told himself, frowning, his emasculated, effeminate head.

There was a question at the back of his mind that worried him. "Am I attracted to men or women?" It was a confusing question. He had been sexually happy as a woman; if that part hadn't changed, then indeed he'd still be attracted to men, and hence gay. But if he was now attracted to women, and he was still, psychologicaly, a woman—gay again? "Keep an eye out," he told himself, his jaw clenched. He scratched his beard.

He went rapidly through the mail, sorting it into discards and possibles. When in doubt, he asked himself how Pierre would see it, and he heard Pierre's voice, saw Pierre's dismissal. If *he* hesitated, Pierre would definitely reject it. He felt his mind grow sharper. Pierre's mind was black and white, there was no hovering on the edge.

He was surprised to see that Anna was also at the meeting; she was rarely invited.

Pierre smiled at him; Eliot smiled, too, but reluctantly, as if at a subordinate not entirely encouraged.

"Good to have you back," Pierre repeated. Eliot leaned forward. He had an open briefcase in front of him, brown with clasps of gold.

"Did you have a chance to get through the mail?" Pierre began.

"There are a few possibles," Bob began quietly. "Hang gliding, spelunking, a man building a plane in his garage. Not invigorating, but good in a pinch. The main interest is in a gold-mining expedition in South America. It's a pay-your-way proposition. There's a stake fee, and then you're free to tap anywhere on the mountain. The slant wouldn't be on the gold—that story's been in a few periodicals already, so it's not an exclusive. But over a dozen men have died so far in rock slides and tunnel collapses. Nothing is provided, the miners go there empty-handed. So the struggle is primitive. That's where the story is. There are some photos," he said casually, "amazing things. Ants on the side of a hill, only they're men."

"Has anyone found gold?" Pierre asked.

"Oh yes. About ten percent. That's what keeps it going." Bob passed him the photos.

"Fantastic," he murmured. "Elemental. Man against the forces of nature."

Eliot leaned over Pierre's shoulder. "A cover story," he said.

"We need something snappy," Pierre agreed. "Whoever took these photos is no good, we'll have to get someone else. Lots of pictures, a couple of good spreads. Men working themselves to the bone, risking their lives, and for what?"

"For gold," Eliot obliged

"For a dream," Pierre corrected him. "Fame and fortune, every man's dream. Better than a lottery." He grinned. "The risks make it a better story. There has to be some risk, you know. We'll have time to do it, I suppose?" He turned to Bob. "When's the next cover date?"

Bob looked quickly at his schedule. "We could squeeze it till the end of next week. No later."

"We'll do it, then."

They discussed the rest of the issue—a hypothermia piece, a volcano photographer, speed-skiing—most of it unchanged since before Bob's illness. The queries Bob brought from the mail went as he anticipated; Pierre agreed with him on three, disagreed on two. Eliot made comments but only gave an opinion after Pierre had given one. After rejecting one idea, Eliot glanced at Bob and said, "Yes, well it's a little *soft*, you know." The skin on Bob's neck prickled; what did he mean by saying *soft* in exactly that way?

He fretted over it while Pierre asked Anna for subscription breakdowns. She glanced pointedly at Bob before reading her numbers. Just over 50,000. Not bad for a new magazine, Bob thought, but he caught Pierre's frown, the way his fingers tapped his thigh, once, twice. Bob knew that the ad rates were tied to the circulation figures; the higher the number of paid subscriptions, the more *Adventure* charged for an ad. Magazines lived by their ad rates. Were they in trouble? "We've got to get the subscriptions up," Pierre said after Anna was finished. "Give it some thought. I'm open to suggestions." He nodded at Bob. "Keep your eye on the mail. If we have to put more money into promotion, I want to tie it into something good."

"Will do," Bob responded, gathering his papers and heading out the door with Anna. He caught the low, mocking sound of Eliot's laugh as he closed the door behind him, and he knew, he knew for a certainty that whatever the remark, it had been aimed at him. He didn't hear Pierre's laugh, only the businesslike mutter of a reply. But Eliot's voice—slippery, sly, belittling him—hung around his ears like gnats.

These gnats buzzed as he saw Pierre go out to lunch with Eliot, they bit tiny gnat teeth into his skin as he went through the mail and the schedules, trying to find an idea for Pierre, not knowing what kind of idea it should be. They circled him and irritated him, snickering through their gnat-like teeth, so that his mouth set hard with annoyance, with impatience, battered by small wings of despair. They were little bits of fury, these gnats, and they ate at him for a while until he felt exhausted with frustration. Sitting there, going through the mail—it was familiar; it would get him nowhere.

Pierre and Eliot disappeared for the day. He was aware of it, he brooded over it. His shoulders ached, he looked through all the magazines he could find. What was everyone else doing? What could he think of that would give him the edge he needed? He had to do something or fall down the chute, lower and lower, a drone, a letter-opener. And he wasn't going to do that; no matter how stupid the situation was—why, after all, hadn't he insisted that the gypsy make him *important*, for instance? Why had he asked for so little?

He drank coffee, hoping coffee nerves would give him a rush of energy and confidence. When his bladder began to throb he got up and then stopped, as if casually, in the outer room. He glanced slowly around, but the one man who worked in the room looked at him incuriously. Bob walked toward the hall, trying to see through the doorways into

Circulation and Advertising. By the time he reached the men's room his palms were sweaty. He prayed silently that he'd be alone.

He forgot, of course, about the offices on the rest of the floor. He took his place at a urinal, unzipped, fumbled, and aimed, but his muscles refused to release. His eyes kept darting to the left and right as the other men unzipped, stepped forward and peed. The little puffs of flesh poking out between those other fingers fascinated him. How did one get used to it? He closed his eyes to concentrate, to be able to pee in front of other eyes. He had to open them again immediately because his aim was off, and the man to his right took a half-step away and grunted. One flick, two flicks, a little sideways fillip, each man to his own routine, and Bob followed suit, red-faced, wondering if they suspected him. All the details he had to get right! All the silly, silly details!

*B*ob nicked himself under the chin again and grimaced. He had decided to shave off his scraggly beard; he couldn't keep his hands from roaming up to his beard and checking it. It was like a girl who kept playing with her hair, he thought. And speaking of hair, his own was coming off in his fingers. It came off in the shower, too, and he told himself there had always been hair in the drain before. But he found a few strands on his pillow, and on the collar of his new jackets, even his shirts. Just one or two at a time, enough to make him frown and worry. He left his hair alone now, treating it gingerly. He never rubbed it dry, he patted it; he never brushed it, he combed it. He looked at ads for hair restorers thoughtfully, but convinced himself it was normal wear and tear, he was just too sensitive. But it was another insult. He wanted a full head of hair.

He still had moments of absolute terror—though nothing he'd done so far was dramatically wrong. Still, he was afraid he would get caught out by his own stupidity. He knew he'd been hasty, and he knew he should have bargained for more. He had never given any thought to the details, and that's where the gypsy was having her fun. He was a man but he hadn't thought out what kind of man to be; he had to be twice as alert to be even a mediocre man. But this was what he'd bargained for, and it wouldn't get better by fussing over it. He had to fit in, he had to succeed, he had to triumph. He dressed right, he grew a beard and shaved it off. His eyes watched everything: the way other men walked, sat, stood, held their drinks at the bar, the way they held their eyes. They stood straighter, legs apart, leaning, if anything, a little away from each other, sat with their knees wide, hunched slightly forward. They didn't hold on to their drinks but lifted them, gulped them, and sat them down again on the bar. They didn't lower their eyes or stare down at their hands. They even handled money differently, casually, as if they had plenty. Older men, waiting for an elevator, might stick a hand in a pocket and jingle change.

He listened, too, not only to what was said, but to the tone of voice. Men's voices were more inflected than he'd assumed, with faster rhythms, less shading. They took out words and snapped them like dollars.

He went to neighborhood bars at night, refusing to take a book or anything to read. It was odd how often there was a division of the ranks—men crowded to the right, some of them standing around their dates, women seated and talking to each other as their men waved arms and stepped in, stepped out, talking to one another. Women alone sat on the left hand side, and at first Bob sat next to them, feeling safer. But they were aware of him, sometimes staring at him, waiting for him to say something, sometimes moving their bags to the other side of the stool and leaning one arm around their drinks. Bob found it hard to talk, especially since, like them, he had always waited for the man to make the first comment. It was not easy.

He watched, he listened. He was interested in how men bought drinks for women they didn't know. The bartender would come over to a woman, place another drink in front of her and say discreetly, "The guy down at the end bought you a drink." The woman would look that way and a stranger would nod. Sometimes the bartender would ask, first, if she wanted it. Usually not. There were two kinds of men who did this. The first would nod and keep his counsel, never making a move. The woman would look his way occasionally, uneasily. He tended to be older than she was, not at all the kind of man she'd encourage, and the drink made her uncomfortable. She didn't know whether to reciprocate or not, and she drank quickly and left, stopping hastily to thank him before she went out the door.

The second kind of man usually sat closer, to begin with, and moved over after she thanked him, saying, for example, that he was celebrating a good day at work or a piece of good luck. This led to a conversation, and once again the woman was uncertain whether to reciprocate or not. She felt she should, but that meant she would have to talk to him for at least two drinks (his glass was full). If she was waiting for her boyfriend, the situation was perfect: men, after all, place more value on women that other men find desirable. But if she was alone, she was claimed, and stuck with him, and if he was an idiot she would have to leave quickly, and her night was over.

Of course there were other women, too, who smiled and asked for a light, a cigarette, or the time. Bob could never keep their attention, even when, eventually, he tried to. They moved on, abandoning their drinks on the way to the ladies' room, sitting somewhere else when they returned, trying their luck with another man. These women seemed to typify the complaints the regulars had about women's inherent treachery. The regulars in the sidestreet bars where Bob felt more comfortable were generally in their fifties, with lined faces, thick hands, loud voices and aggressive bantering. "Yeah, sure, get yourself another drink, why don't you? Never mind about me, I'll get my own," was their style of conversation. Their words and their gestures demanded constant attention. They had a sort of wide-eyed disbelief in their girlfriends' lack of appreciation. These girlfriends nagged, too, and demanded things, just like a wife would, and these men all had current wives, also a source of irritation. They were surrounded by traps, forced to sit down to an endless dinner when they only wanted a snack.

Everyone held a grudge. It came as a surprise to Bob to hear so many men confiding so much to each other. Of course they boasted and of course they strutted; why did the peacock have feathers if not for that? But these bitter, undisguised complaints surprised him. Sure,

Karen Heuler

women complained. But women usually tried to be careful not to go over the edge—after all, if your man treated you like shit, what did it say about you?

Men had emotions all right, but all their emotions went through a process of translation. They were the financial victims of women, those sharks with teeth set for their wallets. In fact, in summing up the differences between men and women, one drinker had said, with emphasis, "Men pay." Bob felt he had skipped back to some former generation, before the advent of Women's Lib and Equal Pay. The women he knew by and large paid their own ways, and if at times they seemed somewhat niggardly, somewhat reluctant to part with their coins, it was understandable. Even now women earned less than men; a coin too casually discarded was not easily replaced.

But men were always trying to get value for their money. It was quite true, as far as these men were concerned, that paying for a woman's dinner gave them certain expectations. They didn't mind paying for sex; they would have preferred all their negotiations to be that straightforward. What they resented was coyness, was breaking the unspoken rules. They would spend an entire night arguing with a woman, insisting they were not after "one thing and one thing only," but the argument was a kind of business negotiation, a saving of face necessary, it seemed, for the woman, and adding spice to the chase. An eager woman was no contest at all. But a woman who didn't repay in kind was not just a bad sport, she was a thief, because she used his money and gave him nothing. Conversations didn't count; talk was cheap. These were the men who gave expensive gifts, who boasted of their gifts, who found it easier to price things than to value them, who used money as a substitute for being able to love.

So the coins jingled and the bills were peeled and Bob listened, nodding and sometimes objecting, hearing every accusation women had ever made against men confirmed. There was something comforting about it, because none of it could ever affect him again. He had changed sides, gone from labor to management, and if he had sacrificed idealism in the process—well, who needed idealism once you gained power?

He had, for the moment at least, a clear viewpoint, as if he had settled on no candidate and could listen to both sides without prejudice. He heard not only what was said but how it was said. He concluded, from years of listening and from the kinds of explanations he too had offered, that women liked sex with men, they liked their own feelings when they were involved with a man, but beyond that, didn't really like men, who either behaved badly and left, or turned into bores. The men felt the same. There was no friendship between the sexes; the most you could hope for was love.

And even that was more properly broken down into romance and passion. A woman built a whole story out of infatuation, where a man built a magnificent scene. Men fell "in love" faster, were more passionate, wanted passion to take them over and control them so they never doubted anything again, whereas women, despite their varying degrees of impulsiveness, expected to be steadied. Women wanted understanding, the myth of the man who knew her better than she knew herself. Men wanted to be driven mad.

But Bob didn't learn this in one night. As a matter of fact, he learned various things and forgot various things as he evolved. One week he thought he knew what men wanted, the other week what women wanted, and as much as his insights might vary in usefulness or accuracy, week by week he also learned more about what he wanted.

And he wasn't just keeping mental lists, he was urgently trying to assimilate. Success depended on it. No more waiting for life to happen to him; he was determined to get results.

Results from what? That seemed obvious. First of all, he must be unquestionably a man, a successful man. He had a nervous, nagging fear of being "discovered" a woman: laughed at, dismissed.

Restless, on edge because of Eliot and his remarks, Bob stopped off for a beer at a bar on First Avenue. He sat to the right, with the men. Down to his left was a young woman reading a newspaper. She was plain, he noted quickly, dispassionately. She folded the pages carefully to avoid taking up too much space.

Bob leaned slightly forward each time he took a sip of beer. He

Karen Heuler

hoarded his drink, he had no intention of having too many. His irritation sought an outlet. Finally, he waved the bartender over, and bought a drink for the woman at the other end. He didn't want her to be told who ordered it.

Bob watched carefully, seeming to stare at his own beer, as the woman got her drink.

She looked cautiously around, trying to figure out who had sent it. Her eyes roved down the row, pausing on each face. One man looked at her accidentally, and she smiled tentatively. He gave her a blank stare, and she blinked and rubbed her eye. Bob could feel her embarrassment.

She went back to her paper, but her eyes kept pulling away to see if anyone was watching.

Her movements got smaller, although at one point she shrugged her shoulders and swept her arms out wide to turn a page. Then she cowered back in on herself, pursing her lips.

All of this pleased Bob. He had intruded on her world, he had affected her. Even anonymously it felt good. It was power without risk: petty, trivial power, but sweet. He raised his head and looked around the bar. Another woman had come in; better-looking, apparently waiting for someone. He could buy drinks for other women, if he felt like it. He could introduce himself, or just watch. He took a last sip of beer and left extra change on the bar.

The plain woman with the newspaper sighed as he walked past. She was determined to stick it out, waiting to see if another drink would appear or if the sender would make a move.

There was a slight swing to Bob's walk as he went through the door.

Chapter 8

A man bends down smoothly to a woman seated at a table, extending his hand. Her head falls back slightly as she lifts her own hand to his, rises, and follows him to the dance floor. Her arms are naked, her neck long, her legs in sheer stockings, tickled by a skirt that moves as she does, her hand on her hip, her hips swaying. A band, all eyes and mouths, sweat beaded on their foreheads, plays music that makes you want to cry out with desire. There's just enough light to make you seem young forever, and room on the floor to spin, to keep your ankles free and your elbows clear and the arch of your back in full view as you dip, dip, your breath not even holding, your eyes locked, your heart plunged straight down to your groin.

Bob watched, imagining himself as the woman. It was beautiful, the man's hand inviting you to dance, leading you and following, the strict sway of hips, the pressure of hands on hips. At the very least, though, he should be picturing himself as the man. It made him irritable—or maybe it was just the people who were dancing that made him irritable.

"You dance well together," he said grudgingly, hanging tight to his drink as Maggie and Peter came back from the floor.

Maggie's teeth showed. "Making love in public," she grinned. "That's what dancing is. Extended foreplay." She sat down, leaning against Peter.

Bob imagined the dampness of Peter's shirt as Maggie rubbed her hand along his back. Peter always sweat so much when he danced.

They leaned against each other, the two lovebirds, they swooped and dipped in inches, testing what it was like to be a millimeter apart, a microsecond closer. And though they stared at each other, Bob could see a blue iris, a brown iris, flicker towards him. What they were thinking was obvious: How was Bob reacting? Did he see they were in love? Did he see how good they were, how good for each other? He could feel their insistence.

Even in the dim light of the club, Maggie's hair shone like buffed pennies. It was cut straight below her ears, but the heavy waves fanned out like wings. She wore bronze earrings, a dozen strings to each, almost six inches long, so that the tips lay on her shoulders, and they rippled as her head moved. Her skin had an amber tone to it; her brown eyes seemed to have flecks of rust; her coloring—hair, skin, eyes—seemed an illustration for coordinated tones. She wore a dark green sleeveless dress, belted low on her hips. Maggie was long-waisted, her worst feature, she always wore things that took the eye to her hips.

Maggie's hand bushed against Peter's arm. She had a tendency to touch men lightly, gently, when she was laughing, and Alyson had long ago noticed that most men responded by stepping closer.

Peter had invited him to listen to a band he'd discovered. Bob had expected a cramped sea of tables and loud rock and no Maggie. He'd forgotten that Peter had been heading away from rock and towards Ellington. Although that wasn't his fault, forgetting it; Peter practiced elsewhere; all Alyson had ever heard him play was "Take the A Train," and how could you tell it wasn't for fun? He dismissed the question of whether it was something he should have known; more than likely Peter had been withholding all sorts of new inclinations from Alyson; there was only so much a human being could guess without being given a reason to guess.

Peter could play guitar, too, but he loved his sax. The choice of an instrument had sexual overtones, anyway. Drummers and violinists must make love differently. When Peter blew on his sax, he bent his back and threw his groin out. Just watching him pick up a horn used to make Alyson sweat. It would have been different with a piccolo.

"Well, so how's work going?" Bob asked, to break their concentration on each other.

Maggie answered first. "Great for me. I got a raise, a good one. I brought in a new account." Bob was slightly startled. The agency Maggie worked for placed public service announcements. Somehow, he had always imagined that the pay was low, that the employees were dedicated. But Maggie mentioned a $5,000 a year raise. Bob accepted it with a grudging admiration.

Maggie turned to Peter encouragingly. It was his turn. He leaned forward. "Good. Good. I'm putting together a new band. Eclectic stuff. We'll be playing in a place in Chelsea next month. And I'm doing some backup for a record. That's good. It was a lucky thing." He gave a mock sigh and blinked his eyes and grinned. "Life's good. Life's real. I feel I've finally got it."

"Things are going your way, huh?" Bob's smile was politely frozen.

Peter hung his arms out and shrugged happily. "Do you know how you can keep going at the wrong thing, compromising, waiting it out? You know you want something, and you know you don't have it, so you keep treading water, holding out until you get there? And you never get there. You just keep floating." Bob nodded. "I stopped that. I'm getting somewhere now, I can feel it. This band is great. One of them's a keyboarder I knew ten years ago. He was in on a few records, thought he was hitting it. But he didn't like what he was doing. Another sax player too, tenor, the sound now is brass, it's a big sound. New Orleans, kind of loose. We're looking for a singer, and Maggie says she knows someone. I've never felt so sure of anything as I am of this. A big sound," he repeated.

"I've heard them," Maggie said proudly. "Big is not the word. Great is the word." She laughed.

Peter patted her hand. "Prejudiced, of course."

"You're on a roll," she said happily. "You can't lose."

They smiled at each other and squeezed each other until Bob's teeth hurt.

"I hope success won't spoil you."

"Spoil me?" Peter scoffed. "I hope it destroys me." His eyes half-closed with pleasure.

"Peter dreams of corruption," Maggie said. "Out loud. He laughs in his sleep. His snores are different when he's in front of an audience." Her eyes were squinting, too, out of merriment.

Bob had a picture of her, lying alongside Peter, leaning on one arm, watching him as he slept. Alyson had done the same, watching the ripple of Peter's eyeballs under the lids, the slack mouth with its slightly too-thin lips, edging, forming phrases.

"Most people just talk in their sleep," Bob said, as if by way of a comment.

"He does that too."

"I do." They laughed at each other merrily.

"As a matter of fact," Peter said, taking a gulp of his bourbon-and-soda, looking quickly around the room before coming back to face Bob, "that was one of the things that was so bizarre about Alyson. I caught her trying to *help* my dreams." He glanced apologetically at Maggie. She shook her head slowly in sympathy. "I must have been talking a lot one night. She woke up easily. I was just starting out with a new band, and it wasn't going well. I was really worried, because at the time I wasn't making much money and it didn't look like this was going to work out."

"I remember," Bob said stiffly.

"Do you? I thought I kept quiet about it. Anyway I woke up with Alyson leaning over me, saying, 'You play very well, Peter. We all like the way you play.' It was weird. I tell you, it gave me the shivers. With Alyson I couldn't even dream alone."

"That's like her," Maggie agreed. "Very controlling."

"I don't see her that way," Bob said peevishly. What shits the two of them were!

"I didn't either, for a long time," Peter said quickly. "And I wouldn't tell you, but I know you've heard her side. It's only fair to hear a little of mine."

"Nothing is ever simple," Maggie agreed. "Of course she's hurt. We're all upset. On the surface it all seems so nasty."

"Only on the surface?" Bob found it impossible to keep his mouth from settling into a bitter line. He felt tricked into this; he wouldn't have come if he'd known Maggie would be there. But Peter had called, and Bob, listening to Peter's voice on the phone, had asked himself, Do I still hurt? So much had changed; surely his own feelings had, too? If criminals go back to the scene of their crime; do victims go back too? Do they both ask themselves, is the crime really over? How can anything so violent be truly past?

They had no right to be happy, no right to parade it around like a moral victory. But what could he accuse them of? He was now an outsider in every sense—no longer part of their triangle. Wasn't that a good thing?

"I loved her," Peter was saying, "for a long time. But there was . . . I don't know how to explain it—I always felt uneasy—as if she expected something, as if she were watching me. You love someone, you know you love her, and yet there's always the feeling that you're supposed to be doing more." His eyes were wide open, his eyebrows raised, a man trying to explain a mystery.

So this is what hatred feels like, Bob thought, hating Peter's smug innocence. "It's vague," he said shortly. "I don't know what you mean. Alyson never judged you, she never expected anything mystical. She just loved you. And trusted you."

Peter looked at him impatiently for a moment "Well. it's hard to explain. Maybe it's my fault. It's amazing it lasted as long as it did. Seven years."

"Eight."

Peter frowned. "That's the kind of thing *she* would do—point out how insensitive I am for not knowing how many years." He turned away from Bob for a second, slightly ruffled, and patted Maggie's hand. "Sorry. This has to be hard for you."

Maggie shook her head, waving her thick hair like a fluid wedge, her earrings—dull though they were—managing to catch some flicker of light. The stoic, the understanding lover. No dream-sucking expectations there.

Peter moved back in his chair, glanced at Maggie, put his hands on the table. "Her hair," he said, dropping his voice dramatically, and Maggie snorted, her mouth twisted to the left. Yes, she seemed to think, the hair will prove it. The hair's the last straw.

"What about her hair?"

"You know she cut it off, you've seen her. Did you know she sent it to me?" His voice had risen on the last few words, outraged.

"She saved it, that's all. And you ended up with it when you got your stuff."

Peter shook his head. "She told you that? I'm surprised you bought it. She cut off her hair and rolled it like her own, packaged it and wrapped it. My stomach turned when I saw it. It's crazy, but for a split second I thought it was her head." He laughed once. "Why do you think she did it?" His eyes had a sharp radiance, almost narcotic.

"Grief," Bob said quietly.

"Guilt."

Bob's head snapped up. "What would she have to feel guilty about?"

"Not her. Me. She wanted to make sure I felt the right amount of guilt. So she shocked me."

"I think you've got it wrong." Bob rapped the bottom of his empty glass on the table. He was growing irritated with the way Peter insisted on misinterpreting everything. "She was showing you her pain. Better her hair than her throat."

"Is that what she said?" Peter asked in alarm. "That she's going to kill herself?"

"Over you?"

Bob's sarcasm shocked Peter, making him rock speculatively back in his chair, as if trying to decide something. "You're not involved with her, are you?" Peter asked finally.

"No. I'm not. I'm just a neutral observer."

"You don't sound neutral. Why are you so mad?"

"What you did was hideous."

"Falling in love was hideous? Should I have stayed with Alyson out of—out of duty, out of despair? I did that, you know, I did that for over a year before I finally found the courage. . . ." His hand crawled over and clasped Maggie's hand, like a spider settling into its web.

"You told her you loved her. Besides which, you never 'found' the courage, you *were* found—you and Maggie." His breath was coming in short pants, he had to be careful or he would let something slip.

Maggie was watching Bob with her cold marble eyes, a kind of amber with a band of yellow in them, like the aggies children rolled on the street. He could feel her suppressed anger, could see the twitch of her lips as she fought back words, wanting to let Peter answer for himself.

"Well, as for *that*," Peter scoffed, "I could have lied, it was easy to lie to her, she was always willing to believe what she wanted to believe." He warmed up to his argument. "I could have lied and she'd have found some way to accept it. Not only that, she'd have found significance in her jealousy, everything was significant, even her turning victim the way she did, sending her hair and then disappearing like a martyr. She couldn't behave reasonably, oh no, this is a cosmic event, the moral order is shattered because I stopped loving her! No wonder it took me so long, I was afraid of war and pestilence, she gets so goddamned *wound up!*" His free hand waved as he spoke, ending with a small slap on the table in front of them, causing them all to feel slightly embarrassed and, consequently, even more annoyed.

"Well," Bob said, standing up and reaching for his coat, "time for me to get going." He thrust an arm in a sleeve.

"No, wait," Peter pleaded, his voice suddenly losing heat. He half-rose from his seat. "I'm sorry, I really am. Of course I'm defensive, I feel really bad for her."

"You feel entirely too much," Maggie said stiffly.

"We don't have to talk about her. It was a mistake—but I wanted to explain. I'm not sure exactly why you're so set on defending her—aren't *we* friends, too, don't you have a responsibility to me, too, to listen to my side, to hear what I have to say?" He sat back, ruffling his hair with one hand. His voice was apologetic. "It hasn't been easy on me, either, you know."

"It hasn't been all *that* hard," Maggie pointed out quickly.

"You haven't said anything kind or even fair about the woman you lived with for eight years. You take her dog—"

"Dingo's my dog!"

"You cheat on her with her best friend—"

"We were hardly 'best friends,' " Maggie said acidly.

"And then you leave her behind like outgrown shoes." He could feel, even as he said it, that the shoes image was a bad one. It certainly didn't flatter Alyson; there was no reason to keep old shoes. "Well," he said vaguely, trailing off. He realized, too, that leaving in a huff might absolutely close all doors with Peter, and he didn't want that to happen. He had an unpleasant need to know more, to see the end of the reel, as it were. He hesitated, shifting quickly from foot to foot, one moment leaving and the next moment staying. "I don't know what to say," he ended lamely.

Peter's eyes lit up and he nodded. "We go back a long way. I hate to lose so much—Alyson, and then you. We don't have to mention her, you know, we can just get together and be ourselves and talk about other things."

Bob looked away for a moment. He wanted to keep an eye on Peter and Maggie. He should probably let go of them, but he couldn't. He wanted something; he just didn't know what, yet.

"Oh well, old girlfriends never die," Maggie said with a little pout and then smiled. That smile was one of her finest achievements; she had practiced it often and hard. It was slow and partial, with just the tips of her teeth showing. It was remarkable how white and neat and businesslike the tips of her teeth were. "That's what they mean about 'baggage,' isn't it? The past stays with you and weighs you down, even when you don't want it to." She looked suddenly pleased with herself, as if she'd explained away the entire conversation.

Bob's eyes lingered on her thoughtfully. He knew that tone, that dismissive, false naiveté. He knew the two of them much better than they knew him. That conclusion, for a moment, elevated him. He had some power over them, even if it was only just the power of more knowledge. It was a good feeling.

He relaxed and smiled. "Baggage," he repeated. The two of them suddenly seemed transparent and obvious.

This sudden revelation swept over him almost tenderly. The saddest thing isn't facing what you no longer have, he thought; it's facing what you no longer want. He nodded at them both, saying, "Some other time. I'll be in touch," and left, still buoyant with his new-found feeling of distance.

It frayed a little when he hit the outside air, so cold it forced him to stop in the doorway while he put up his collar and wondered where to go. His empty apartment had no appeal, and there was no one else to see, no one else who expected him. He thought, bending into the wind, I may as well have another drink, and he remembered a bar he had passed on 14th Street that looked interesting. He took off, his neck pulled into his coat, his ears already freezing. He rewrapped his muffler to cover them.

He passed a man walking a dog that looked like Dingo. Or maybe it was the jaunty swing to the dog's walk, the happy anticipation of all those sidewalk smells showing in his eyes, that reminded him of Dingo. Immediately he thought, it's not fair that Peter took the dog.

And it wasn't just that Peter had the dog—Maggie had the dog, and she probably didn't even like the dog—she was not an animal person. There she was sitting pretty, with Alyson's dog and Alyson's boyfriend—and she didn't like dogs! The two of them bobbing together like little birds puffing up their feathers, chirping over what they had, clucking over Alyson's faults. With a start Bob realized that they must have discussed him (discussed her, Alyson, he quickly amended), defended themselves by pointing out her failures. How much had Peter disclosed? Was there no privacy left after a lover's departure? And in bed, after they'd made love, did they whisper together, trailing fingers on a shoulder, a thigh, summoning the image of Alyson and shooing her away like a diseased pigeon? "Poor Alyson, so awkward."

And obsessive. And controlling. They'd both rushed to agree on that. The more he recalled the conversation, the angrier he got at them—after all, they were the ones who had forced her to sell her soul, weren't they? Everything was going so well for them, happiness sanctifying their actions. And if they were happy together, then they proved what they did was right.

All of this led to only one conclusion: Bob had not yet gotten what he wanted, what he deserved. It wasn't enough just to be a man—not if Peter and Maggie were satisfied. It galled him to think of how much he had suffered, and how immune they were to it. Was this satisfaction?

He reached 14th Street and turned the corner with his feet slamming hard into the patches of dirty ice. He could see the bar through the plate glass window, tinsel Christmas decorations hanging limply from the ceiling. The look was brief; he went inside. The floor was bare wood, uneven and creaking. The barstools had worn-red oilcloth covers, torn in spots. Two people, sitting next to each other at the bar, raised their eyes indifferently and watched Bob sit down. Back in the corner stood two videogame machines, both with signs that said "Broken." A smell like wet overcoats competed with the smell of beer and a strong disinfectant odor which Bob traced to an unmarked door next to the machines.

He ordered quickly, and he ran his thumb absent-mindedly over the rim of the glass when it was placed in front of him

"It's clean," the bartender said briefly. There was no real animosity in his voice.

"Just a habit," Bob lied. He was happy with the seediness of the bar, the dank, failed air it offered, its sullen lack of pretense. He was grateful to reach such borderline territory. Not because it was dangerous—danger requires energy and The Green Stone Bar had none—but because it reeked of other people's decay. At this bar he was confident that he had more money in his pocket than anyone who regularly came in, and he liked the idea.

The bar had a sullen air about it. That old, drink-embalmed couple at the end of the bar, Bob thought—people like them, certainly, lived an honest life; one could kill the other out of jealousy or despair and never have any doubts about it.

Bob studied his drink, thinking of Maggie and Peter, imagining what it would be like if he had raised that knife against Peter, if he had gotten even with him. He had been too polite, he had let Peter go too easily. Maybe he *should* have killed him! But Peter, bleeding, dying? No, he couldn't have done it. Even filled with rage he couldn't imagine forgetting that it was unalterable and wrong. It occurred to him, with a nasty little frisson, that selling his soul was, by most definitions, wrong, too. But it was *interesting*, he thought; and he was harming no one else. It was a kind of suicide, wasn't it—and wasn't that better than homocide, on the karmic scale of bad moves? Lost in these musings, he looked absent-mindedly along the bar and then out through the window to the street. He was struck by a figure, face up against the glass, gazing in at him; once it had caught Bob's eyes, a hand was lifted and beckoned urgently. Bob squinted, frowning; he suspected that it was Madame Hope, but the figure seemed to be wearing a man's overcoat and a tweed cap. The hand outside the window gestured impatiently. Bob took his change from the counter and pulled on his coat leisurely; if it was Madame Hope he wanted to show her how little importance he placed on her urgency.

It had begun to snow, wet flakes spilling like a cheap paperweight scene; Bob stopped in front of the figure, whose shoulders were hunched against the cold.

"You took your time," Madame Hope complained. Bob regarded her suspiciously. There was a dark smear on her upper lip, a woman's mustache. The hair was cropped in a butch cut, and the devil seemed to have gotten both shorter and stouter, coming up only to Bob's eyebrows. He felt insulted by this inept transformation. Was this some kind of mockery on the gypsy's part?

"Why do you look like that?" he asked rudely. "Not quite a man, not quite a woman?"

The devil wagged her head impatiently. "It happens, it happens.

I told you before, we share a soul now." She started to walk quickly, slapping her arms across her chest for warmth.

"I took you to mean that metaphorically."

"Metaphors, metaphors," the devil muttered. "A metaphor makes you pick up on a resemblance you might have missed before, doesn't it?"

"I wouldn't have missed this."

"Maybe not." The devil cocked her head at Bob, wheedling. "Don't let it bother you. I'm still myself; you're still yourself. It's just a change in style."

"I don't like it," Bob said shortly. "It's obscene, somehow. Don't you have any control over things like that?"

This offended Madame Hope, who straightened her back and slowed down. "You're a good one to talk about control. What were you thinking about just now? Reveling in squalor, weren't you? I don't like places like that; it's the kind of atmosphere that can pitch one straight into salvation; no one there thinks they can get anything out of this life."

"You're afraid I'd find salvation?" Bob scoffed. "I'm not interested in salvation; I never was."

"Weren't you?" the fortuneteller asked, pulling herself up short and pushing her face close to his. "People say they're not, of course, people say it all the time, but they keep looking for a loophole, a small way out, a tiny, technical detail that gives them everything. Whatever you have, you'll want more; that's my experience. And you can have more, that's what I want to tell you right now, before you get fuzzy and start hanging out in churches—"

"What are you getting at?" he interrupted, pulling his arm roughly away from Madame Hope.

"You're not following the formula," the gypsy snapped.

"What formula?"

"Where are the revels?" the gypsy moaned, "where's the mad, passionate frenzy? Don't you have any poetry in you? It's a poor showing, I can tell you. I was warned about it. 'Don't do it,' they said,

The Made-up Man   89

'that particular soul has no courage, it will fizzle out.' And I stood up for you! I won't say I regret it, I won't go so far as to say that, but—have you asked yourself what you're doing? Have you really given any thought to your potential right now? You gloat over hating them, and you forget you're a man! Don't you see there's a beautiful potential here, oh a very pretty piece of vengeance, the kind that makes me clap my hands? Don't you see it?" She pulled him up short, tapping his chest in her excitement.

Bob watched her carefully. "Potential?" he repeated. "What are you talking about?"

"I could give you time to think about it; I'm sure you'd see it eventually. It's so obvious. Maybe you *have* thought of it already, and you just don't say it out of modesty. But don't be modest, it's so *small*." She waited impatiently for Bob's reply, but getting none, she burst out, "Revenge!" She sang it out, hopping from one foot to the other. "It's pure and simple, it's got a life of its own!"

"I'm years ahead of you," he snapped. "Of course I want revenge." He resented her presence, her prodding.

"Then take it," she wheedled.

"I will."

She laughed harshly in his face. "You don't know how. You're not taking this seriously, are you? You don't see what you've done, *or* what you can do. You're going bald, you need a shave, but other than that, what are you doing any different? 'I'll wait till I get my bearings,' you think. Wait for what? What are you doing?" she almost shouted, her face wrinkled in annoyance. "You've got a duty to act in good faith!"

"What the hell are you talking about?" he asked, genuinely confused.

"You sold your soul. Your *soul*. Don't you want to get anything out of it? Even now, you're just pretending that you know it. You seem to think it's like borrowing money, that there's no danger if you behave yourself. You hate them and you think what a miracle you are for your 'suffering,' your 'sacrifice.' You don't believe you have to do anything, you think you can earn points just by existing."

Karen Heuler

Bob swung his head around, slowly, to face her as she continued. He had to admit that her words rang true; he didn't feel he was doing enough. He did feel he was being too cautious. Was there too much of Alyson left in him?

"Doesn't it eat your guts out that Peter, right now, is with Maggie, talking about you or forgetting all about you? Tell me," the gypsy said, once again placing her hand on Bob's arm and pulling him closer, "when you're alone at night, is your heart filled with forgiveness or with hate? It's hate, isn't it? Why else did you come to me? Did you think it was a gesture only, a symbol of desperation—because you, more than anyone else, would be driven to desperation? Do you want Peter happy, no matter what? Do you want Maggie happy? You don't; you know you don't. You want them to pay for what they've done. If it takes your soul, you mean to do it. It's not a game. You've lost your soul, and you won't get anything from *them* for it. Hell is misery, unending misery, so you'd better make the most of your time."

Bob was alert. "You said there was no pain in hell."

"I lied," she said, her lip curled. "Did you expect me to be honest? Or maybe I didn't lie. But it isn't peaceful; it's never peaceful; you'll wish you had lips to scream with."

Bob drew back. He began to shiver, and stuck his hands deep in his pockets.

"It's best to make the most of your time," the gypsy said, suddenly businesslike again. "There's nothing you can regret anymore; nothing you do will change eternity and everything you do can change this life. Why waste it?" She slapped Bob on the shoulder. "I've never known anyone who needed to be pushed as much as you." She turned to go and then looked back again. Bob saw her features, coarsened by the cold and the wind, sneering at him. "Think ahead," she whispered. "You're damned; you're a lost soul. And *they* made you do it, if that makes it any easier for you. Make sure you get what you want while you can." She turned the corner as Bob watched, shivering.

The cold seemed to creep into every nerve in his body, as if all natural warmth had been sucked out. Damned, he thought, and for the first time it seemed real. Even now he couldn't spend time thinking about what it *meant*, to be damned. With a snort he added, And not good enough for the devil! But he knew that he *was* good enough for the devil, that no matter how he played out his side of the bargain, the conclusion would be the same. So what was he doing with this opportunity?

Madame Hope was right: he'd been driven to this. He blamed Peter for that, he blamed Maggie. Peter and Maggie were the ones who should be damned, without them he would never have been forced into this bargain, never, never would he have agreed to it. He was paying for their betrayal! And they were getting away, free, free as birds!

Triangles. Triangles. He and Maggie and Peter.

He and Maggie. And Peter. Another triangle.

He smiled and felt warmth returning to his fingers, to his cheeks, to the small, closed pocket of his heart.

Chapter 9

Up to now, Bob had been far too tentative, but he finally realized he was damned and there could be no harsher consequences, no matter what he did. Therefore he was free. It was a tremendous relief. He didn't have to worry about hell yet, hell only came after death, and at thirty-five death still seemed a long way off. But if he was going to hell, he should really figure out a way to make it worthwhile.

He was going to get decisive, and he was going to get even.

The first thing he did when he got home was to retrieve all of Alyson's photos from the closet shelf. He flipped through them quickly as if they were cards. Was there anything to save? Nothing. Anything to regret? Nothing. The stack fell together at his feet. Faces smiling, faces serious, eyes squinting, eyes closed, summer and winter, year after year. He noted how, as the year went along, there were fewer pictures of the two of them together; when, exactly, had it become unnecessary to be documented as a couple?

The only photos he kept, quickly putting them back on the shelf, were two pictures of Dingo running down a hill. Everything else he shoved into a crumpled paper bag and took with him when he went out. He was getting in the habit of taking his garbage two or three blocks away before putting it in a can, a different one each time. The idea of the Vulture or anyone else touching anything of his was too repulsive.

In minutes the bag and the photos were gone and Bob felt tall and straight, determined and unsentimental. He felt clean; he was in control. He was sure that he had no love left, certainly not for Peter, and the absence of that love gave him strength and an almost technical interest in revenge. He could go ahead now, his mind was bursting with clear and concrete images of what he would do next.

As quickly as he had one idea, another one followed. Perhaps only the first one is hard, perhaps like a chink in a dam everything rushes through with incredible force once the outlet is found. He did not doubt that he could get Maggie. He knew what women wanted, after all; and he knew Maggie.

Revenge now seemed so logical that he began to see its potential everywhere. After all, he hated Eliot, too, his restrained sneers, the inflections in his voice, the way he altered statements to suggest that Bob was unnecessary as well as homosexual. When he gave Bob a story, he held it by the corner of the paper with his pinkie curled. When Bob gave him anything, Eliot left it pointedly on the desk or held it again in the corner, flapping it lazily in the air as if to shake off germs. Pierre sometimes picked it up himself, with an amused glance. Sometimes he absent-mindedly licked his finger to turn a page, and Eliot winced.

Bob deliberately began touching things in the office. He handed out papers at meetings. When there were sandwiches ordered he made sure he was the one who distributed them. He always unwrapped them first, and when he found Eliot's order he would lift the bread to make absolutely sure. This, too, amused Pierre, who would fight to keep the smile off his face as Eliot glared, protesting, "I'll get my own. Don't touch someone else's food."

"Someone touched it already, you know," Bob said reasonably. "It doesn't get made by machine."

He ran into Anna a few mornings later, after he'd started his new plan of attack. She was standing on the street, leaning against the railing or the subway. He almost didn't notice—she was across the street, coming from the downtown side, while Bob was on the uptown side. But some ripple of movement or obstruction made him look over and he saw her. At first he thought she was waiting for someone, but her head was down, she had her hand on the grillwork, and her coat was open despite the cold.

"You're sick," he said, hurrying over.

She waved her free hand. "It'll go away in a minute."

"Dry toast. Weak tea. Come with me." He took her by the hand, careful not to be too firm. "We can be late for work for once. I'll call. There's a luncheonette just a little bit down the street." She followed him along weakly.

When he'd settled her into a booth, taking her coat and folding it neatly by her side, he asked, "Morning sickness? Why didn't you tell me?"

She leaned back slightly. Already she seemed less pale. "Subways are a bitch." She licked her lips and then carefully ran a finger over her upper lip. "I found out I was pregnant while you were out sick. Somehow it didn't seem like a good time to call you up and chat." She looked down at her hands. "Can I tell you something? I don't seem to have anyone else to tell." Her voice was very low; he had to lean forward to hear her. "I'm scared." Her face tinged pink, the first healthy color he'd seen so far. "What am I doing?"

"Having second thoughts, that's all. Perfectly natural."

"Isn't it bizarre, what I'm doing?"

Their hot water came, and she slowly opened the tea bag, dangling it in and out of the cup like bait. When the waitress sauntered away, Anna looked at Bob bleakly. "You know how much money I make? Less than $30,000 a year. I wanted to do this and I did it. I cheered myself for making a decision, instead of just thinking about it. Applause, applause. Fadeout and a standing ovation." She dropped the tea bag on the saucer and added milk and sugar, stirring nervously. "Only no fadeout. I'm trapped in a machine now. We don't cut to the next scene, with a beautiful two-year-old, a good-paying job and an organized life. Instead it's morning sickness, fighting the subways—do you know I get groped at least twice a week? You wouldn't know, you're a man. And every time someone gropes me," her eyes narrowed bitterly, "I want to kill. I want to kill. I try to find out who it is, you know, but none of them are looking at me, we're packed in like sardines, it's not possible to turn around and find out who it is. It's not possible to even turn around. Sometimes I grab his hand, but I still can't find out who *belongs* to the hand, you know? If I can move even slightly and try to see who it is—everyone's eyes are staring at the ads, at the top of other heads. No one *owns* that hand. I could cut it off and when the doors opened and everyone got out, no one would miss that hand. I'll never find out who it belongs to. And I want to. I want to find out who owns that hand so I can scream and point at him and cut his cock off and put it on a stick." Her shoulders fell. "But no one owns the hand." She took a sip of her tea. The waitress slapped down toast, and Anna broke off a corner.

"Is that all of it?" Bob asked gently.

She shook her head. "Have you ever been pregnant alone? You're sick, and no one knows it. You'll get fatter, and no one will make it easier. You'll go into labor alone, with no one to call a cab or an ambulance. No one to rub your back. There won't be anyone in the delivery room, no one peering through the glass at the baby, you'll go in alone and come out alone, with something infinitely fragile in your arms, depending on you alone. Nights and days, looking at the bank account while a baby cries and no one lets you sleep, just this once, through the feedings and the diapers. And the decisions! Where to go, what to do, when to do it. And how much it costs. And what will be best, always what will be best.

"And, you know," she said finally, wearily, her eyes dull. "Those hands aren't accidental. Nothing is accidental. Sometimes I think I'll find out who belongs to that hand, and it will be my child's father."

"God, Anna."

"You were right, you know. I've never forgotten what you said. I think about it all the time. Who was the father? You warned me, but when do warnings ever matter? I got what I wanted. That's all, that's it. I'm scared." She took the last of her tea, gulping it noisily, taking another piece of toast, eating it greedily.

"You stay here," Bob said abruptly. "I've got to make a call." He came back quickly. "You've got the day off," he said, pleased with himself. "I've got the day off too. I told them I'd found you passing out at the station, and that I was taking you to the doctor and then home." He stopped himself abruptly and asked, "You don't need to go to the doctor, do you? I was hoping I was lying."

She smiled. "You were lying. I even have something I can take for the nausea. I just didn't, I resented taking it. It annoyed me." She began to unfold her coat. "What'll we do? I wasn't planning on taking the day off."

"We're going to do pleasing things," he said. He liked her, after all. She deserved a break, and he could provide it. He knew she would be grateful—not just for a friend, but for a *man* friend. "We're going shopping for baby clothes. We're going to a movie. We're going to have an elegant, civilized dinner. Or are you too delicate for all that?"

She laughed in surprise. "Strong as an ox. But I can't afford it. Some of it, yes; I can treat myself to a few things." She seemed to perk up. Her eyes had some sparkle.

"Good," he smiled. "You'll need maternity clothes, too. That will be your treat. The rest is mine."

"Of course not," she said quickly.

"This is a bribe. I want to be the godfather."

She hesitated. "I hadn't thought that far ahead," she admitted. "Godparents."

"And besides, you'll be helping me out. It will add interest to my life."

"You miss Peter," she said, and her eyes grew warm with sympathy.

They were back on the street. Only very late employees were dashing down the avenue now, looking tense, checking their watches.

"Who's Peter?" he said heartily. "Just someone I knew. Just a bad experiment. My life is changing and believe me, for the better. Look at it, just think about it. Yesterday I was alone in the world; today I'm almost a father."

Anna laughed. "You sound awfully sure of yourself." Bob raised his arm and hailed a cab. "Where are we going?"

"I think the baby boutiques are on the East Side."

"There are a couple on Second, in the Sixties," she agreed.

"Sixty-fourth and Second," he told the driver.

"It's really a beautiful day," Anna said contentedly. "I didn't even notice." Bob took her hand and squeezed it and she pressed back, happy.

This could be perfect, Bob realized. I like Anna, I've always liked Anna; we're friends. This child isn't mine, but the next one could be. She's alone, and what chance does a pregnant woman have to meet someone new? He smiled. This is one possibility for me. And who knows? Maybe I could even love her. It wouldn't be such a bad thing. He was glad that he had money with him as well as credit cards. He wanted to treat her right. Oh yes, he knew Anna thought he was gay, but didn't all women half-love their gay friends? Wouldn't Anna end up believing Bob could change simply because that change might make life good for her? A family. It was laughable how easy it was. This was how men did it—shopped around for the best deals in life. He took hold of Anna's elbow as they entered the store.

He couldn't keep from fingering the booties, the buntings, the soft receiving blankets. He picked up and unfolded tee-shirts with snap closings, spreading them out, pleased with their size. At first he planned on buying just one item, one token gift, but at the sight of these little things, these small things, these packages for tiny arms and kicking legs, he wanted to buy them all, take them all.

He settled on a layette, a few gowns, white socks the size of invitations. The package weighed nothing, yet he shifted it, squeezing, prodding, as if it were a small kitten he wanted to make sure was still alive. He hated giving it up finally, to Anna.

It wasn't until the next morning at work, as he went over the article on gold mining, that he finally got the idea that would tie all the rest of it together. This, he thought, this is the trick that can get the magazine going. It's the edge I need over Eliot.

He stared at the photos of men crawling on the mountain, men numerous as ants. It was so obvious! A challenge, a competition of some sort, sponsored by *Adventure*—done right, it would get the buzz that Pierre wanted and it would give him a substantial edge over Eliot. (That alone was worth it.) And then his mind jumped even faster and he thought he could tie it in to Maggie, that this would be the link he needed in order to get to her.

He called her immediately. She was cautious over the phone. Of course, she would be after that last time, but he coaxed her into lunch with the promise of a great business coup. Her curiosity won out. He rushed through the morning.

He was charged, he could feel it. Just thinking about Maggie, about what he had in mind, all the delicious pieces of the puzzle, invigorated him. "My God," he thought, "it's so sexy!" He stopped for a moment to savor it. Of course by now he had woken once or twice with an erection, the aftermath, as he supposed, of some lost dream. But it had quickly passed; quickly because he had stopped each time to try to form a fantasy to work with. He stopped himself from thinking of men and he tried to think of women and then his mind went blank and his prick went soft. How long would he be in this in-between state? How would he get out of it? At such moments he thought of Madame Hope with loathing, for it seemed to him that there was no alternative but to go to her with his problem. And by now he despised her, because she was the one being in the world he could never be free of. He suspected that she even knew of his dilemma, knew and was waiting for him to mention it so she could leer and snicker, poke and prod. The trouble with being owned was that it left so little room for negotiation.

So he humored his responses, indulged them that morning. Was it the first real sense of power that went to his groin? The first identification of a sexual target? Both? It was like being hungry and looking forward to a feast. I will taste this, I will rip that apart with my teeth, my chin will be slick from the juices, I will gorge, gorge, gorge.

He took the subway down to Maggie's office, on Park Avenue South. When she met him at the receptionist's, he said, "Ready? Pick someplace nice. I don't know this neighborhood."

She had a cowl that she carefully draped around her hair. "What's the mystery?" she asked. "You were very brief on the phone."

"Don't worry, it's business."

"A sudden interest in public service? Or are you looking for some sort of connection you think I have?"

"We're going to be nice and civilized first," he said. "We're going to talk to each other like friends. How do you like living with a dog?"

"I'll assume you mean Dingo. Isn't that friendly of me? He sheds."

"You have my sympathy. This way? I hope they take cards. This is all an impulse."

"Oh well, the first impulse is always the hardest. But yes, they do take cards."

"You don't like the dog?"

"It's better than a kid, I suppose. I kind of like it when he wags his tail. It's nice to be appreciated. And I don't have to walk him very much. Just once in a while, as a favor. I don't like cleaning up after him, and anyway, he's Peter's dog."

"In here?"

Maggie nodded. The entire front of the restaurant was a solid wall of glass, intersected by thin strips of metal, suggesting a greenhouse. There were ferns in Victorian stands on the inside. There was a coatcheck.

They sat down and ordered wine.

"Are there any other questions I'm supposed to answer?" she asked with a professional smile.

"This isn't an interrogation."

"No? Oh come on, Bob, let's have it out in the open. Why did I do it? How could I do it? Right? You've got some strange sort of status here, you're like Alyson's lawyer or father or something. Well, I'll tell you about me. I look at what people want and I get it done for them. I match things up. I have a knack."

The waiter came with the wine, stepping aside as Bob tasted it. Bob nodded with a slight frown; he knew nothing about wine.

Maggie picked up her glass. "I got involved with Peter because I found him attractive and because he was available. Does that surprise you?"

"He wasn't available. He was living with someone."

"Yes, I know." She took a sip. "My dear friend Alsyon. Look, let me explain a few things to you. There's no way a woman can keep a man when he's finished with her. And I *do* know when a man is available—when *he* thinks he's available. It's not so hard to tell. They start talking to their lover's or wife's friends, and they throw in sad little *if*'s all the time." She picked up a menu and put it down again. "You know, 'Sometimes I wonder what it would be like if,' or 'I would do that right now, this minute, if....' They trail off their sentences, they look at their hands and shake their heads. They start asking how their wife acts when she's not with him, what she says. They want to hear what she was like before he came along. Imagining her without him seems very attractive. 'So she managed on her own before, huh?' You see, I've been somebody's sounding board often enough to know. Oh, the ones who start with 'My wife doesn't understand me'—they're the ones looking to go to bed with you, and they don't count. Somehow they think that phrase relieves them of responsibility, because, of course, they all understand their wives. But the others—the ones who really want someone to *help* them—they're trickier. They're heartrendingly sad because they're so sincere. 'You know her,' they say, 'tell me what to do.' Well, you can tell them the same thing a million times, or try a million different answers, but they won't hear it unless it's the one they've already decided on, only they're afraid of it. The easiest way out for them is to fall in love with someone else, because the wife can't argue you out of that, and besides it's easier to run away from home when you've got another home to go to. I've seen it over and over—I've even been there once or twice—the woman who supposedly broke up a happy home is herself dumped a year later. Sometimes not even a year. They were instruments only, a half-way house, the exit off the highway. That's all." She put her hand flat on top of the menu, jiggling her fingers on it. He found—and it surprised him—he found her almost strong, almost brave. Almost admirable.

Of course, she wasn't admirable. She had ruined Alyson's life. "If you know all this, why did you do it? You're telling me that you've got a limited lifespan, too."

She shook her head. "Not this time. Not with Peter. For one thing, the talking stage lasted a year."

"A year," Bob echoed bleakly. How could he have missed that?

"That's never happened before. Men don't like to think too long. It's like we nurtured each other, Peter and I. We took a long time discovering what we were doing. No headlong rush. All my life it's been a frenzy—in or out of love—so I can tell this is good, it's right. We were family long before we went to bed together, we just kept discovering more and more."

"Everyone believes it's magic, don't they?"

"You can say what you want," Maggie answered smoothly, shrugging her shoulders and flipping her hair. "But I've got him now and I can't help feeling that that's what matters." She bent her head down to study the menu. Bob did likewise, but Maggie's head rose again in a minute. "There's just one question I want to ask."

"Go ahead."

"Just what makes you so incredibly righteous about all this? Just what makes you Alyson's defender?"

Bob took a long time to answer. He weighed his words carefully. "Peter seemed to think I might be interested in Alyson." He paused deliberately.

"Well?"

He smiled at her, almost absent-mindedly. "I like Alyson, but she wasn't the one I was interested in. And that's all I can say. Believe me." He held up a hand. "It's time to order now."

Before he moved his eyes to the menu he caught the sudden look of speculation in Maggie's eyes. He hoped he hadn't overplayed his game, or underplayed it for that matter. Maggie liked to flirt, she had always boasted of it. He meant to take advantage of that.

After the waiter took their order, Bob unfolded his napkin and said, "Now, business. I have a proposition for you." He watched her settle back in her chair. She cocked her head and her mouth shut in a serious mood.

"At the moment, this is just between us. I need your opinion on a purely speculative idea. Something occurred to me that might be good for both of us if we handle it right." He eased himself back. "I work for an adventure magazine; you try to place public service ads. What if we got together on that—organized competitions for some of your clients? They'd pay for the sponsorship: ads, banners, promotions, and additional fees for having their names on our advertising. We'd run an editorial article about the particulars of the competition or prize. We'd get paid for the ads and they'd get publicity throughout the campaign." He became more businesslike, reaching in his pocket for a pen. "I'm not sure of all the details, of course—but it's a thought. The advantage on your client's side would not be just ads in the magazine but media coverage. After all, we'd want to get as much notice as possible. Our advantage, of course, would be the income. And, since we'd be organizing the whole thing we'd get coverage and publicity as well. What do you think?" He put down his pen abruptly, settling back in his chair and looking at her attentively.

Maggie's left hand was crooked around her wine glass. Her right hand tapped one finger thoughtfully against her chin.

"Full cost for the ad?" she asked. "Even though you'll be co-sponsor?"

"Definitely. It would have to be full price." Bob spread out his hands. "Our circulation's small right now, so it's not expensive. But there'd be a hell of a payback, much more than just an ordinary ad would get. You know as well as I do that a race or a mountain climb—or whatever, that wouldn't be my decision—generates a certain amount of interest."

"Yes, it does," she agreed, "but our clients stay away from hyped-up publicity. They want a respectable profile."

"They'd get it," Bob assured her. "They'd know what the challenge is before the final agreement. Honestly, I don't see how either one of us could lose, if it was done the right way."

"It does sound good," she said thoughtfully. "Let me get some reactions on it, though." She toyed with her food, a smile spreading slowly across her face. "This could be quite a good move for both of us.

I mean, professionally," she added. Her eyes glanced at him brightly.

"To a good idea," she said, raising her glass.

"To us," Bob corrected her smoothly. "This is our baby."

Their glasses tipped giddily towards each other and clinked.

Chapter 10

*E*liot's mouth managed to keep a consistently disdainful pinch to it while he assembled his neat, repetitious bites of food. He'd ordered veal in some sort of sherry-and-cream sauce. His hands fussed over it, gathering a piece of tortured calf and a wedge of rice, blending sauce over it with his knife, and then holding it an inch above his plate to see if it would drip before quickly assisting it to his mouth. And all the time he seemed to be belittling it, not only the meal itself, but his surroundings. Pierre, on the other hand, sometimes forgot his food when he was talking or listening intently and then came back to it with smooth recognition. He ate beef. Mickey had a stew which he approached carelessly, holding meat or carrots on his fork too long while he thought out a question or an answer, and then quickly reaching for a napkin when the food splashed back down on his plate.

Bob regretted his choice of an omelet. Light lunches were an ingrained habit. He was glad he'd passed over his first inclination for a salad. That would have deepened the line of contempt on Eliot's upper lip.

His attempt to exclude Eliot had failed. Pierre was going away for a few days, and when Bob had approached him about discussing business, he had included the others automatically.

It had taken two days to hear back from Maggie. Adpub had, at first, been uncertain about the idea, but they had suggested she talk with a few of the contacts she knew best. There was definitely some interest, she told Bob; people were referring the matter on and discussing possibilities. Adpub was willing to consider the idea officially.

That was half of the cast, he had known as he hung up the phone. He had to talk to Pierre, and this lunch was what Pierre had settled on.

Bob was nervous. He spent too much time thinking about what he would say rather than saying it. He was fighting a tendency to burst out abruptly, interrupting the steady flow of talk about ad rates and publishers of other magazines. Bob didn't care about any infighting, about who folded or sold out or changed format. He listened hostilely as Eliot inserted his snobby, inflated comments about his editor, his publisher, his reviews. Bob personally had seen Eliot's book remaindered in the Strand bookstore; he was waiting for the right moment to mention it casually.

When coffee came he felt with a thumping heart that it was now or never. "There was a reason I suggested lunch," he began, forcing himself to stop the frowning attention he had been paying to his plate.

Pierre grinned. Over the past year Bob had catalogued Pierre's grins: encouraging, indulgent, dismissive, ingratiating. Now it was expectant and fatherly. Pierre evidently liked lunches; they allowed him to feel relaxed and gave him public visibility.

Bob laid down his fork and gripped his drink for support. He started to describe his plan about the nonprofits and the sponsored competitions. He found himself, at first, making light of his ideas by inserting phrases such as "I felt," "maybe," "it might possibly," but he began to discard them as he warmed up, as he mentioned his contact, Maggie, at Adpub, at Adpub's expressed interest, at the potential for increased circulation as well as the ad revenues. He stopped abruptly. No one had interrupted him. Pierre had nodded once or twice, and Mickey had done little more than watch Pierre's reactions. Eliot had continued to digest his food, sometimes pausing to study other people at other tables. Once Bob was finished, however, Pierre sat back and asked him, "What do you think?" His voice was neutral.

Eliot shrugged indifferently. "I can't see how we're equipped for it. And it's one of those projects that ends up costing more than it's worth."

Bob tightened his mouth, then arranged his face neutrally. At this point, Alyson would have been close to tears in frustration, but he stepped back from his emotions and waited.

"I like it," Mickey said easily. "It all ties in, doesn't it?"

"Of course it would take money to run any sort of competition," Pierre added. "The price of an ad wouldn't cover that."

"Entry fees?" Mickey hazarded.

"There'd have to be entry fees. It would be good if we could include subscriptions as part of the entry fees. Ad rates go up as our circulation goes up–of course, you know that. We'd have to work out the details for the financial aspects. But it might be worth it." He nodded at Bob. "A good idea."

Bob sat back, congratulating himself and replaying Pierre's approval in his head, when Pierre interrupted him, saying, "If you act fast enough, we can put something about it in this issue. How soon can you put something together?"

Bob cleared his throat. "Adpub's having a meeting today with the sales staff. Maggie thinks she'll have a sponsor in a day or two. Then it's just a question of choosing an event and organizing it."

"Good," Pierre said approvingly. "You have almost a week to get the details together. Can you do it?"

Bob said yes automatically. He felt a lift of triumph. He would get it done, somehow.

"And who'll take charge of it all?" Eliot asked casually. He lifted his napkin to his face, using only the corner. "An amateur could botch it, don't you think?"

"You don't like the idea," Pierre said. "But you don't have a better one. Every expense here is deductible. I'm not saying we have money to burn; we don't. But it catches the spirit of the magazine. Men like a challenge. We can review it every step of the way. If it doesn't work— well, we're not married to it. It's worth the chance. Well worth it." He turned to Bob. "I assume you want to manage it?"

Bob nodded.

"Sometimes amateurs take the biggest risks and get the biggest payoffs," Pierre said smoothly. He grinned. "And sometimes they lose and get fired." Eliot appeared happier. "But risks are part of the game."

The bill came and Bob reached for it.

"Put in for it," Pierre said. "And whatever you do with those Adpub people—what did you say her name was, Maggie?—if it's business, put it in."

"Oh, it's business all right," Bob said.

Bob called Maggie later that day. "Well," he said, "it's settled on this end. Pierre has guaranteed the first event. We're going to announce it this issue. By the next issue we'll be ready to go. How's your end?"

"Very pleased. We may have the first account already."

"Oh—one thing. We have to be careful about advertisers. No cancer or alcoholism associations. We can't lose the cigarette or liquor ads."

"No, this one's good," she said with satisfaction. "Red Cross."

"Ha," Bob said thoughtfully. "Disaster coverage. Just in case."

"God, this is great," she said, her voice light and friendly. "I feel like thunder."

"You should," he laughed. "We're in control." He heard a new edge in his own voice, certain and authoritative.

"Are we?" she said, suddenly breathless. "Or do we turn it over to the honchos?"

"We *are* the honchos," he said with conviction. "Pierre is leaving it to me. And I insist on working with you."

"Do you?" she asked. "And do I have any say?"

"Why should you?" he argued lightly. "You may be thunder, but I'm the storm."

A month ago he would have sneered at anyone who talked like that. Now it was just funny and free and right.

*B*ob began a systematic search for a good event. He combed

Karen Heuler

through travel magazines for ideas, sports magazines, even the kind of newspapers that featured alien invasions. These last fascinated him, but Maggie dragged him away from the bizarre, and they settled for the simplest arrangement. The competition would be in March. It would still be snow season and perfect for a picturesque white-covered mountain and a mock-rescue. That should fit in with the Red Cross. He and Maggie started researching areas. Bob wanted something with various approaches, so that different levels could participate. "Ideally," he said, "a north side with a sheer face for the mountain-climbers; a south side for hikers—rugged but not too much so. I suppose the best would be to have a slope, too, somewhere, for the skiers. Picture it," he said, excitedly, "we have a Red Cross station on a plateau. We time the various approaches so everyone has an equal chance."

"If it's a rescue, though, that's only half the problem, isn't it?"

"Well, that's where the Red Cross comes in. Maybe they take the winner away by helicopter."

They got approval on the preliminaries. Maggie was invaluable, Maggie could track down anyone, any agency, any supplier of goods.

She immediately researched all the ski areas around them. They both agreed that for a successful project they needed to appropriate an already viable operation and for their own convenience, one close at hand. They settled on upstate New York's Shawangunk Mountains. There were a number of resorts in the area, and since the event was scheduled past the peak season there would be plenty of available rooms.

The "victim" was to be positioned in the hills above New Paltz. Rock climbers had direct access from the road—they were there all the time, it seemed, parking their cars in a caravan along the highway. There was a cross-country ski trail, lots of rugged country, part of the Appalachian trail—it looked good for any kind of approach.

And what was to be rescued? The winner not only had to find the "victim" but transport it back to the finish line. Planning all of this was great—seeing his own ideas become real and watching as more and more people got pulled in, answering to him; but something about it was unfinished. He was the man behind a great idea—but was a great idea enough?

He wanted a challenge; he wanted conflict; he wanted drama.

"Tell me something," Maggie said carefully one night as they went over the details for the challenge. "I can't make you out. Every once in a while you seem very friendly, and then you get very cold. What's the deal?"

Bob looked down at his hands. He felt a quick burst of adrenaline; he had to find exactly the right touch. "That's a strange question," he said, looking at her and then deliberately looking away.

Her smile was crooked and she tipped her head slightly. She leaned across the table in the diner and touched his hand lightly. "I don't want to make you uncomfortable. I'm only asking because I like things clear."

"Well, I do, too. But some things can't ever be clear, can they? All the time I've known you, you've never been free." He did a quick glance again, trying to look secretive. He had already run through this line in his mind.

"Not free?" she questioned. Her face was pink and her voice rustled across the table to him. "Are you flirting with me?" She sat alertly on the edge of her seat.

"You've crossed my mind, that's all." He grinned, suddenly finding the rhythm of the conversation.

She laughed. "Nice and ambiguous." She pressed the edge of a teaspoon against her lower lip. "Don't you ever go after anything that interests you?" she asked thoughtfully. "I do. Whatever is life for?"

"Whatever," he repeated.

"It makes it nice to get up in the morning. You wake up and think, 'Anything can happen today.' It's a nice thought."

"It sounds nice," he admitted. "But you're living with someone. The possibilities must be a little more limited."

"Oh, they are. They are. A little." she smiled. "That sounds terrible, doesn't it? But it isn't, not really. After all if you wake up every day with the unlimited, and then, every day, you choose the same person, that's something, isn't it?"

"I guess it's love."

"Oh, yes, love." She swirled her coffee slightly. "And what do you think love is?"

The question surprised him, it came so suddenly. "It's choosing the one person for whom you can find no substitute. Who fills your life. Who never ceases to engage you. Even when you can't stand it. The one person you can give up the rest of the world for."

She laughed. "You see, that's the paradox. Love isn't giving up the world, it's being completely alive to it. And to be alive you have to keep your eyes open. You have to be honest, too; if love can't stand the test, then it isn't love, is it?" She brought out the question as if she'd handled it often.

"Which test are we talking about, Maggie?"

Her mouth curled. "I'm not making a pass at you, if that's what you're asking."

"Why not? Am I so unattractive?"

"No. It's not that. It's—how can I put this?—I think you have something up your sleeve, something you're hiding. I don't know what it is. But you always seem to be *not* telling me something. It's like you knew something about me that even I don't know."

He snorted. "That comes straight out of a romance novel."

"It does, doesn't it?" she said, smoothing her silverware out on the table. "It would have a certain appeal, if I were that kind of heroine. But I'm not a heroine, am I, in your book? You're playing with me now, right? You're on Alyson's side, aren't you?" She looked steadily into his eyes. Her own were bright and moist.

"I'm not on anyone's side. Except my own, of course. Anyway, I think you should drop the idea of sides. It's not that simple, not that black and white. You know that from the way Peter feels about it."

Her fingers froze over the alignment of the fork. Bob could see that it rested at an angle next to the spoon, the knife, the salt shaker. There was a slight twitch, almost at the wrist, before the fingers began, again, to sort the implements in rows. He saw this all peripherally; he dropped his remark so casually that his own senses seemed poised.

"The way Peter feels about it?" Maggie echoed him. "Oh, I know he still feels a little guilty. You mean, how guilty?"

Bob shrugged. "He could ask me how Alyson was out of guilt, but why keep asking me where she lives?"

Everything on the table was now in place. Maggie looked at it all vaguely and frowned. "It was a long relationship. I suppose he *would* want to talk to her," she said neutrally.

"Yes," Bob said, "eight years. Hard to get that out of your system overnight. It must be rough on you."

"On me?"

"He must talk about her a lot."

"No. Not much."

"Well, maybe he would feel easier talking to me. But then, I'm not very sympathetic about it."

The conversation seemed to die listlessly. Bob could hear fragments of talk from the other tables; a buzz of inflections met and merged into a pleasant, jumbled sound.

He approved of the way Maggie's lower lip tugged downward, pulling her mouth into a tight, unhappy line as they went over the ads and the latest arrangements for the contest.

When he got home, Bob bent down and picked up what looked like a white square of paper in front of his door. He turned it over and saw a picture of Alyson.

There was a sound down the hallway, on the stairs, he was sure of it. He moved swiftly, on the balls of his feet, to the stairwell, and listened intently, careful to make no noise. Even so he couldn't be sure that the sounds he heard—small and furtive—weren't merely his own sounds. When he stopped, peering up to the next floor, squinting in concentration, he heard nothing definite, nothing suspicious: the faint sounds of voices through doorways, a phone ringing, water running, a horn sounding dull but angry in the street.

Karen Heuler

He heard the front door slam downstairs, and voices cheerfully discussing dinner, so he gave it up and went back to his apartment. Perhaps he'd dropped the photo when he'd thrown all of them out and hadn't noticed it lying there. But that was weeks ago. Was it possible he wouldn't notice?

He turned on the lights and studied the picture. He saw the fine line of a ballpoint pen, drawing in a mustache on Alyson's face. At first he thought it was some child's joke, but then everything became clear. He had thrown it out, along with the others. And no matter how far he'd gone, the Vulture had found the bag of photos (maybe even following Bob?), retrieved it, and lightly traced a man's own mustache on Alyson's lip.

Bob leaned back against the wall, his heart racing. The Vulture knew. Bob had no doubt of it.

He thought rapidly. The Vulture had no contact with any living being; he hid in the shadows when anyone came near, his enlarged Adam's apple bobbing up and down anxiously, his bony head sunk forward. Why would he leave the picture where Bob could find it? Where anyone could find it, in fact? What if some neighbor had found it and thought, It looks familiar, I know this face? How well would his new identity hold? No one else in the building had shown any surprise or suspicion at seeing Bob come or go. No one asked after Alyson—and why should they, Bob thought, when they were no more than nodding acquaintances, New York neighbors who only knocked on the door to complain?

He tore up the picture and burned the tiny pieces on the top of his stove, wondering if the Vulture had any others, and what he planned to do with them.

Chapter 11

The snow fell around him, caught up in gusts, spilling everywhere. Bob reached into his pocket and pulled out a sheet of paper. He lifted a garbage can lid and dropped the note inside. All it contained was a random word or phrase; he'd written a few dozen on separate sheets of paper right before going out, and now he was leaving them in cans all along Seventh Street and along First Avenue. He was on his way to Madame Hope; he was laying a trail for the Vulture, just to let him know he knew. Would that skinny, woolen-wrapped idiot check every can in the East Village?

Bob had gotten another note that day. It asked, simply, "Alyson?"

What difference did it make? Of all the people in the world, did the Vulture matter? Did the idiot ever talk to anyone? And yet Bob wanted to crush him, stamp him out, wipe him out. He was not going to be challenged by that crazy, creepy piece of crap.

It was typical of Madame Hope—the little twist she gave to things.

He was on his way to the gypsy, who had been noticeably absent lately. What was she up to? It was odd how irritated Bob became when he saw her, and how insulted when he didn't.

He hesitated when he heard the throb of base notes from her storefront. Hesitated? He was offended. The fortuneteller obviously had a life independent from his, an indifference designed to put him in his place. Annoyance accumulated around him faster than snowfall.

Karen Heuler

She wore a velvet tuxedo suit with a ruffled white blouse. Bob eyed her. The cut of her jacket and the line of her trousers hid her figure; she was squat, plush, barely coming up to his chin. Had he grown? Maybe he had grown. He stiffened in disapproval

The gypsy laughed in his face. "Perfect timing! I thought of giving you a call, but I hoped you were busy."

"I'm not busy."

The fortuneteller smirked. "Then come in. By all means, come in. A belated winter celebration. A select group, I assure you. You'll stand out in a big way; we need another man." She clucked. "Beggars can't be choosers, but there are some luscious items here." She gestured him in. "I don't like the cold. Keep it outside."

"I wanted to talk to you," he said in a low voice.

"Bad timing," she brushed him off. "What, am I supposed to be open twenty-four hours a day like a vegetable stand?" She dropped her voice. "Do you need someone to feel your lemons? Are they turning brown on the shelf?" Her voice rose. "Maybe you should give them a little squeeze, dearie?" She cackled and winked.

"There are a number of things," he said stiffly. "A number of problems."

"There will always be problems," she said, waving him off. They were still standing in the outer room, where the gypsy had read Alyson's fortune. Did she still do that, Bob wondered, then caught himself. Did he think he was her only client?

"I have a lot to do," she said, as if answering his thoughts. "Reading the future. You'd be surprised, but the future really just means tomorrow, this week, for most people. Are you worried about tomorrow?"

"Of course I am," he snapped. "What happens tomorrow affects everything, doesn't it? Listen," he hissed. "I think someone knows about me."

She sat down reluctantly. "So what?"

"So he can ruin everything."

"How?"

Bob sat down opposite her. "I can't be questioned," he said slowly.

"If I'm questioned, I'm deflected. No one can be allowed to interrupt me. No one."

"You're too important," the gypsy supplied agreeably. She leaned back, crossing one leg over the other.

"Don't play games with me," he said quickly. "I can't be found out, it would ruin everything."

"Which 'everything' are you referring to?" she asked with interest.

He settled into his chair, glaring at her. "I'm a man now. I have all the things men have. No one doubts me now, no one questions whether I can do it or whether I can go there because women don't do it or don't go there. No one will ask to speak to the man of the house, no one will tell me to go get my husband to help me with that, no mechanic will rip me off because a woman knows shit about cars, no one will ever assume I'm a secretary or a prostitute or an old maid; no one can take advantage of me or dismiss me. When my hair turns gray I'll be distinguished, the lines in my face will show character, weight will add substance, and if I have to get nasty I'll be decisive, not bitchy." He stood up and began to pace the room—hard to do in a space this small, with the shabby chairs and the weak little table where she spread her cards. The cheapness didn't matter; he shrugged it off. What she had to understand was his urgency.

"I can go where I want without anyone making an unpleasant judgment," he continued. "I'll get a higher salary no matter what job I take. Maybe you added a little twist to the mixture by having some people think I'm gay, but Eliot can't use it against me forever. A lot of people in the world are gay; Eliot has to be careful because he can't always be sure what useful person might also be gay.

"But let them know I was a woman! I won't stand a chance!" He stopped and glared at her. "And listen to me now, I mean it, I won't give it up! I've barely started, you know, I want everything, as much as I can grab and then some; I won't have it destroyed because you see an easy joke. I'm going to get my share; I want *all* the goodies. No tricks, you understand! This isn't a game."

"Tsk, tsk," the gypsy said, shaking her head. "So suspicious. So

Karen Heuler

forceful. But let me in on it, will you? So far I'm in the dark."

"There's this person—the Vulture. I think he knows everything."

"He'd be the first."

"About me, I mean," he snapped. "About the change."

She shrugged. "Who would he tell? Who does he know?"

"Does it matter? Everything is a threat when you've got a secret."

The gypsy took out a cigarette. "So?"

"So I don't know what to do."

"What would you like to do?"

"I want him stopped."

"So he's stopped." She lit a match and flicked it off into the shadows. Bob waited.

"Well?" She inhaled.

Bob eyed her warily. "How will you stop him?"

She smiled. "What would you like?"

He pulled back. Suddenly the Vulture seemed less threatening. "I just want it it to quit, these notes and the wondering. The wondering—what does he know? What will he say? No more."

"Fine. What else?"

It irritated Bob, the way she took it so lightly, the way she minimized his concerns. But there was something else. He squirmed, ever so slightly, in his chair.

"There are so many women in New York," the gypsy said benevolently.

Bob dug for his own cigarettes.

"You know, it's interesting, the changes I've seen," she continued. "What is virginity worth these days? Who does it benefit? An academic question, now. It once formed the whole basis of society. Men, of course, were never supposed to be virgins. Did you say something? No? Sounds like the party's going fine." She cocked an ear. "I still know more women than men in New York, more women at loose ends. They complain that there are too few men, too few experiences left." She laughed. "They can forgive a lot. Women forgive a lot." She scratched her chin. "But then you know all about women, don't you? You have enough of a viewpoint to be a real winner."

"True," he admitted.

"Sex," the gypsy said. "It's not all hormones and happiness."

Bob waited.

"I can introduce you to some very helpful women here tonight."

"I don't need help."

"So everything is falling into place easily?"

"Mostly," he hedged.

She laughed at him. "I like that 'mostly.' It says a lot. But it's just first-night jitters, I bet. It's really not such a big deal, you've been studying for the part all your life."

"What do you mean?" He was surprised—was she saying something about Alyson's sexuality?

She waved it away. "You know exactly what the man has to do and exactly what's pleasing from the female point of view. You've got it made."

"All right," he agreed. "It's just that men can fail, you know; obviously fail."

"You won't," she said with assurance. "I'll guarantee it. Come," she said, gesturing. "You need a party."

"I need a party," he admitted.

She led him through the beaded curtains. Where was the dog? he wondered, and then he ceased to wonder.

The buzz—the busy-ness—the *sound* of it brought back the strange dreams he had while he was being changed. It didn't matter that the snow fell outside; in here the people were lithe, supple, with naked shoulders, long hair and fair skin. The heat was up, the coats were shed. He was reminded of the vast heat engine located under the floor—it seemed to throb throughout the room like music.

The gypsy handed him a drink and he drank it greedily.

"This is Helen," the gypsy said with a smirk. She pulled a slim woman forward, with brown wavy hair to her shoulders, a slip of a dress, and huge blue eyes.

"Hello, Helen," he said, trying to sound seductive.

Karen Heuler

Helen nodded, and the gypsy left.

Where had the gypsy gotten her music? There was a recording of "Do You Wanna Dance?" playing and Bob asked Helen—with a twist of his shoulders and a lift of his eyebrows—and she danced.

Helen—he could guess she weighed 120 pounds and dieted constantly—leaned into him occasionally, when the records changed. She moved her hips, slowly, slowly. Bob could imagine he was Helen, moving her hips. What had the gypsy given him to drink? He raised his glass between dances, as if trying to gauge its contents. But Helen came back to him, and he danced with her, smoothly, gently, how beautiful it was to swing one's hips, grinding into hers with one motion. He felt happy. Helen's hair dipped below her shoulder blades when her head fell back, and he closed his eyes, their bodies separate, yet meeting. His head orbited; her head orbited. They were together.

Did the gypsy have a jukebox? He wanted to throw his head back like Peter and roar. Was he becoming Peter? Who was he becoming?

He stepped into it. He was another person. The lift of Madame Hope's drinks, the lift of the music: who was he? His left arm crept out in an almost Spanish declaration as he danced with Helen. Poor soul, she never spoke, and he liked it. With each drink, he liked it more, her silent, yielding lips and her lapsing hair. He liked her hair the most, the way it swooped and fell. Like Alyson's hair.

He held her close, and began to hiccup. He asked for lime and sugar, feeling embarrassed. Helen, with her hair below her shoulders and the slim waist, laughed.

He loved the fact that Helen laughed. His own mouth opened, his head rolled back, and he laughed too, stopping right in his tracks. He turned to see who was noticing; he wanted to make sure he was seen.

Smoke slid around the room like a fog. Music still played—could it be Chopin? he wondered; such an extreme change and he hadn't noticed?—but everyone else seemed to have left. Or maybe not totally gone. It was possible, if he concentrated, to detect a murmur through the doorway, the inflected tones of pleasant weariness.

Helen stepped up to him and placed her arms around his neck; he circled his around her hips. The music had switched again to something he didn't recognize, Spanish or Italian, a voice was singing and he kept changing his mind about what language it was.

Portuguese? Helen's hips slipped back and forth gently. He sighed, his hands slipping along the cool fabric of her dress, rubbing tentatively at her ass. She pressed herself firmly up against him, so close her breasts flattened against his chest.

He knew that moment, it was so familiar, slipping in the borderline between sensual and sexual; she would be getting so delicately moist, pulsing between her thighs, just as he felt his own flesh tugging and growing rigid. He held her tightly.

Their feet were barely moving, dance or no dance, and they leaned themselves into the darkest corner. It was wonderful to feel a breast again, so resilient, so smooth, cool, firm; his hand pulled at her straps and slipped inside, remembering the feel of it with something close to gratitude.

She was leaning back against a sofa, her own hands unbuckling his belt, squeezing gently at his fly. His erection was so urgent and so seriously specific as she touched him—yes, he wanted more of that—but he noted, too, how every time he touched her it was a recognition, a sense of being able to recapture, from the outside, what it had always felt like. To touch her breast was to re-experience the pleasure of his own breasts being touched, to lift her dress and run his fingers over her clitoris, her cleft—to remember the quick intake of breath when it had been done so to him, how good it felt, this finger probing, pushing. Outside, remembering, and at the same time in a new body, at moments thinking he would burst, explode, and not metaphorically, but with expectation and a slight dread, as his penis swelled so full he feared for it. Her fist, riding cupped up and down him, made his eyes roll back and he had to clench his muscles to hold out longer.

She guided him into her, the two of them slipped down now to the cheap rug on the cement floor. His pants were down around his knees, her dress up around her waist, and he had barely started to move, pumping erratically, when her hands slapped wildly on his shoulders, she gasped, and he came so violently that he was shocked.

At first he could only lie there, making sure he would be able to breathe again. When he'd caught his breath he realized just how grateful he was; how pleased with himself and her. He lifted a hand to brush the hair off her face and whispered, "I love you." It was out automatically, before he'd even had time to think, and his hand froze as soon as he'd said it and lay still on the carpet. He could feel the cold creep up through the floor.

He went rigid at the sound of a harsh laugh. "Success so soon?" Madame Hope scoffed. "You've restored my faith."

Bob rolled over on his side, tugging his pants up. His eyes searched through the layers of smoke, all of which seemed to emanate from Madame Hope's cigarette.

Helen must have jumped up and left as Bob fumbled with his clothes, because when he stood up, tucking his shirt in, she was gone.

"Was it every bit as good as you hoped?" Madame Hope continued.

"How long have you been here?" He saw the dog come in, lower its head and sniff at the rug, black tail twitching.

"I've been here all the time," the gypsy said. "I live here. Don't tell me you're embarrassed? Don't tell me you're modest? You did a great job."

"Where did she go?"

"Helen? I don't know. I'm not even sure how she got here. Of course my doors are always open (and of course my floors are free); she just showed up in time for my party and I let her in."

He looked fretfully around the room. There were hardly any traces of a party; the ashtrays were full, but then Madame Hope smoked like a fiend. Two glasses only stood abandoned near a chair. Either the guests were very neat or someone had tidied up. His eyes caught sight of a centipede rippling near the doorway. The dog watched it intently and Bob shivered.

"She *was* here, then?" he asked.

"I deal in reality, after all," the fortuneteller assured him. "I work in flesh and blood. It wouldn't be any fun otherwise, would it?"

"Sometimes I don't like your idea of fun."

"My idea's the same as yours. But you like to keep things to yourself, you're so exclusive. You think you can't be criticized; that you're noble and proud. But don't let it worry you; I know you through and through. You'll never be closer to anyone than you are to me. Someday you'll look in the mirror and see my face staring back. Two lovers growing to look alike."

He had his coat on now; he had been watching her as he dressed, his arms had lifting every piece of clothing as if it were heavy. The gypsy's words struck him as true; he could feel her personality, her will, tightening in him like sore muscles.

He left her without another word, pulling aside the beaded curtain, walking soberly to the door. The cold air braced him, made him feel cleaner, although he felt indifferent to cleanliness. Instead he wondered if there had been a Helen, and if Madame Hope had watched. Or was it some sort of hallucination? What if there had been no Helen but Madame Hope had still watched, grinning at Bob's solitary performance? He was like a drunk trying to convince himself that he hadn't, indeed, behaved as badly as he feared, that if he remembered one more detail he might discover that no one had heard, that no one had seen, that someone else had been worse and his behavior would be forgotten. But try as he would, no more palatable explanation of the night's events presented itself. He was stuck, bested, and it was better to look upward and see the white cold stars still stable, untouched.

The stars reassured him that none of it mattered, anyway, that if there was a Helen she was silent and gone.

He would refuse to think about the gypsy at all.

Having decided that was a relief. It was impossible to pit himself against her, impossible to feel anything but distaste. He told himself that she was vulgar, obscene even, but her vulgarity did not debase him. He was his own master.

Still walking slowly, but with a more certain step, he began to notice the few inches of snow on the street, still white and relatively untrampled.

Karen Heuler

It sifted when a mild wind blew around the corner, rearranging the small white hills on steps and around the garbage cans.

A few of the lids had been blown off during the snowstorm, twisted to the side or turned upside down. Someone had put an armchair out on the street, and it stood covered in snow like a fluffy slipcover.

This was the best time to walk Manhattan, when the snow was still white and obliterated the garbage.

He must have noticed it before he reached the steps to his building, he must have been aware of it because he wasn't alarmed, he was curious. A bundle of clothes next to the garbage cans.

The Vulture sat with his back to the railing, his knees drawn up to his chest. His eyes were open and unblinking, as if he were thinking of something. The cap was pulled down to his forehead and the shadow from it darkened his face down to his eyebrows.

Bob took off one glove and touched the Vulture's face. It was cold.

He stooped down to pick out the pieces of paper the Vulture held in his right hand. He was afraid he wouldn't be able to pry them from the Vulture's grip but they came free easily, like hairs with a tweezer.

Chapter 12

"That wasn't my fault," he told himself. "No one could ever trace that back to me. What did I have to do with it? An accident. A coincidence! Everyone dies. It was just his time to die. Careless. Or crazy. Everyone knew he was crazy. He went through garbage and he froze to death. It didn't look like anyone had touched him. I certainly didn't touch him. I was somewhere else. I have an alibi, if it comes to that. If I need one. But how would anyone connect me with him, anyway? I did take the papers. I even looked through his pockets. But that was just garbage. Nothing points to me at all."

He felt guilty, all the same. He had said something to Madame Hope, but could that really have resulted in this?

He told himself it was coincidence. It was exactly the sort of thing she would capitalize on, inferring something from it. But it implied something, it implied causality. He had never said he wanted the Vulture dead, had he? Just wanted him to stop. Just wanted it ended. That could mean anything.

"And it won't matter to anyone, anyway," he reasoned. "He's been dead for years, the way he lived. He wasn't really a person at all, just some kind of walking psychosis."

He was struggling to accept it—however it had happened. He had coffee at a luncheonette on Second Avenue. The Vulture was sick, obviously sick, and wasn't doing anything to help himself. It was amazing he'd lived as long as he had; this might even have been a blessing of some sort. No, that was going too far.

He finally called Anna, telling her that someone he knew had died, and she told him to come over, don't worry, it wasn't too late.

He didn't feel good until he was in the cab, riding away from the area, farther and farther away, where no one could find him.

"Who died?" Anna asked gently as soon as he arrived.

He busied himself with his coat and his gloves, thinking rapidly, and then finally he sighed. He would have to tell her some semblance of the truth or he might—somewhere—get tripped up. "There was this weird guy in my building, he never spoke to anyone. In fact, he seemed frightened of people. Strange eyes. Once or twice I tried to talk to him, but he just sidled away. I came home today—I didn't even make it up to my apartment. There were ambulances and police cars outside the building and a covered body on the street. I asked and I found out it was him."

He raised his hands helplessly. "I didn't even know his name, it wasn't on the bell, and I can't remember ever asking anyone about him. It just seems so wrong somehow; he was young, obviously disturbed and completely isolated. I feel I should have done something."

"You feel responsible? But I'm sure he'd ignored you too."

"Of course. But I'm alive, I can be ignored."

She smiled gently. "I understand how you feel. Deep down, I'm sure you know there was nothing you could do."

Bob found, strangely, that he was getting sentimental about the Vulture. "If I'd been even five minutes earlier, I might have seen him, we might have stopped to say hello, he'd be alive."

"You don't even know how he died. Maybe he was sick."

"That's what I think," he said hopefully. "Or maybe he just needed help."

"I'm sure that you're thinking about your own death," she said tentatively, after a pause. "It's hard not to. Of course it's what you'd think. Everyone would. He was a neighbor, much too young to die. If he could go, just like that, without notice, then you could too."

"I wasn't thinking that at all," he said, horrified.

She was quick to soothe him. "I'm not saying you don't regret his death. But he wasn't part of your life." She took his hand and squeezed it. He squeezed back, nodding.

"You're such a good friend," he sighed. "You understand so much. I think you're the best friend I have." Magically, a tear welled up in his eye. She saw it and bent his head on her shoulder, patting him. "You've been a friend to me," she said, "through hard times. I have a lot to thank you for. I just wish I could say something to make you feel better."

"Oh, you have," he said. "Just being here means a lot to me. I don't want to leave." He hoped there was no stray note of calculation in his voice. "I feel relaxed with you," he admitted. "I feel at home." He settled his arm around her.

She continued to pat him. He hugged her hesitantly, wondering if he'd struck the right note. "I don't want to get maudlin."

She laughed. "Don't worry. You've seen me at my weakest, you know. I understand what you mean, and I'm sure it's obvious; we trust each other."

He sat up, smiling ruefully. "Thanks. I don't want to make a fool of myself. You don't have anything to drink, do you? I wasn't thinking or I would have brought something."

She got up. "I'm not drinking, and there's a bottle I opened for a friend and didn't finish. I don't know what it tastes like by now."

"Someone should do a book on how long things last," he said, following her to the kitchen "When do leftovers go bad? When does salad dressing go bad? When do bacteria take over? How long can you forget to put the mayonnaise away?"

"The only thing I ever know is when the milk spoils."

"And if it goes bad long enough, does it become sour cream?"

"Or cottage cheese?" She laughed. "I don't know how anything is made; I just know what brand I prefer. We're so removed from sources."

He nodded.

She poured the wine and handed it to him. "It doesn't smell like vinegar," she said hopefully.

"And if it did, could you use it in a salad?"

"If we had a nuclear war the survivors would have to discover everything all over again."

"If we had a war, the food manufacturers would be in charge. At least they understand how to make stuff."

"Food *manufacturers*," she sighed. "I'd rather get down to basics; I wish I had an old midwife who would tell me the myths. I want an old woman who'll say, 'Eat three beans every Tuesday and the baby will be strong.' I think I'd respect that. I think I'd believe that."

"You want magic. We all want magic. This wine is all right. See? Nothing goes bad, nothing goes wrong. We're just afraid it will, as if we had no control."

"Well, we don't, really, do we? Your neighbor proves it."

"It happened to someone else," he said abruptly. "We're safe. Nothing can hurt us." She raised an eyebrow.

"You know what I've been thinking? That we're good together, good for each other." He sat forward and spoke earnestly. "We can give each other comfort and understanding. Maybe that's not everything, but it's better than what we each have alone. And there's affection and respect, too. I've been doing a lot of thinking about this, so don't be afraid it's all coming off the top of my head. It's not so easy to raise a child alone. And there's no reason for it, either; we could live together, you and I. Then you wouldn't have to worry about being able to handle everything by yourself. Having a family appeals to me, it really does. Between the two of us, we could handle anything."

Anna's skin had a faint pink tinge to it, and her eyes looked bright. "Oh, Bob," she said sadly, "that's sweet, it really is. But it's not so easy. It sounds so practical, so logical. 'Why not be roommates? We get along so well.' But there's the baby...."

"All the more reason," he assured her. "The cornerstone of my argument."

She shook her head. "The problem is, I don't want to rely on anyone, I don't ever want to depend on anyone. Every man I've ever trusted has done a bunk. I'm sure I attract only the kind that will. But this, this is too important to take any risks. I've got to do each step on my own because if I ever rely on anyone else, it will all go to pieces. I have to stay strong day by day, it's like having money in the bank. I can't touch it, I can't share it, I can only try to keep it safe and out of anyone's hands. I'm sorry."

Bob sat back and sipped his wine, which didn't taste very good, really. The idea about the two had suddenly had so much appeal that a refusal hadn't seemed possible. "You haven't had time to think about it. Maybe I should have taken more time before suggesting it." He shrugged and looked determined. "But I'm not withdrawing my offer. I want you to know you can rely on me as far as you want to." He looked around, wondering how long he could stay; maybe the Vulture had been cleared away by then; maybe that part was over.

"I'd love a baby," he added softly. "It wouldn't even have to be a boy."

Anna laughed.

*D*id you see this?" Anna asked the next day at work. She pushed a folded newspaper at Bob and pointed to a small item, "One Dead in Snowstorm."

He read it quickly, snapping up phrases in the brief paragraph. Police stated that there was evidence someone had discovered the body, searched it, and left.

"It sounds like he was robbed," she said.

"I can't imagine why. He was a bum, really."

"Or maybe they just left him to die. There are crazy people who have money hidden away. Maybe someone thought he was rich. They said he froze to death."

"Oh, bums get rolled all the time," he said dismissively.

She was shocked. "That's cruel."

He recovered quickly from his mistake. "Sorry. He wasn't a bum. If he was, he wouldn't have made the papers."

Anna nodded once. "I get your point. Selective sympathy. Yes."

$\mathcal{E}$verything was going smoothly, everything was falling in place. The Vulture's death made the news for a day or two, but then he faded from view without regret. At first Bob was worried, but as his anonymity seemed secure he felt a certain satisfaction. He was safe; he didn't have to face consequences. Even Anna's discussions about moral issues—she liked morality—made him feel comfortable. She could discuss morality; he was above it.

Anna's eyes brightened when she saw him now. He could tell that she looked forward to his visits. Her smile gave her away; he could see her eagerness. She was bursting to talk to him, she wanted to tell him everything.

"It's funny," she said one night when she'd invited him for dinner. "I really don't think I like people that much. People are greedy. Or at least demanding. That's probably why I don't give money away very often. I think I should give money to anyone who asks for it, but I don't, not usually, but then suddenly I'll give someone twenty dollars. Of course I'm wrong; I just get taken in by a sad story that happened to hit me the right way. I should give everything away, I know it. But I don't."

He smiled at her, pleased with her. She was in a soft mood, and that allowed him to feel hard. "Give it all away and you'll be begging yourself. You and the little fish. Is it a fish now?"

"A guppy, a porpoise," she sighed, hugging her small belly. "Gills and all, a free-swimmer. Little fool." She shook her head wonderingly. "Better than I am, always better than I am."

He smiled at her, sinking deep into the sofa. How nice to make good and evil so simple. How pleasant to discuss things without consequence, just for companionship. Quite like love, without the illusions. Quite like love, without the risk.

Chapter 13

$\mathscr{B}$ ob kicked through the dirty-gray snow, considering life in general. He had awoken, startled, from a nightmare. In it he had been discovered naked, and his hands had gone to cover his genitals and his chest. He had hidden in corners and in bushes; he had woken with his heart pounding and his armpits sweating. Perhaps there had been more to it than he remembered. "I had a bad dream," he said out loud. "Everything is fine. It's just a dream." His teeth felt gritty; that must be why the words seemed to grind themselves out as he said them. "I'm tired," he thought; "I'm under stress." Too much too fast.

He pulled on jeans, he pulled on a sweater; he laced his sneakers tight. He found his gloves, his thick wool jacket and his muffler. He pulled his cap on tenderly over his hair. To think he had once cut so much hair off—heaps of it. Women were so wasteful.

It was Saturday morning; he was heading for midtown to talk to a travel agent who might agree to handle all the disparate reservations if this idea of his paid off. He folded his wallet in half; he put a comb in his back pocket.

His jacket was short; it only came to his hips. He'd read somewhere once that women withstood cold better because they had more layers of fat. He could believe it. If he went out without a cap the cold hooked into his scalp, pinching it, making the remaining hairs stand up and out, allowing eddies of frost in, he could feel it.

And his balls! No wonder men did that peculiar winter shuffle—step sideways, slap your thighs together, *tuck*! Bob found it unnerving, the sensation that his genitals were shrinking in the cold, growing raw, he could swear they were growing red, they puckered. What kind of insanity was it to pull such sensitive, squeamish organs outside the body and expose them to the elements? He was more conscious of his balls than a woman was of her breasts and as for his prick—it rustled, it shrank, it jumped like an unruly child; it moved ahead of his thoughts and behind his thoughts. He found himself making it jerk, once he actually found the muscle, at odd moments, when he was bored or thinking of something else. It was like the time he'd learned to raise an eyebrow—once he started doing it, he found it was a hard habit to break.

He would have to wear looser pants; he didn't always know what he was doing with his body when his thoughts were elsewhere. And no wonder the Elizabethans joked about noses and penises. You could visualize them freezing and falling off. He would never wear a jacket again; from now on it was long coats only.

He raised his arm and grabbed a cab. They made all the lights for the first mile or so but slowed down after midtown, and then just crawled the last two blocks. Bob paid his money and decided to walk the rest of the way.

He got out, went half a block, and saw and heard a crowd ahead of him, obviously some kind of demonstration; he decided to see what it was about.

As Bob moved into the crowd itself, he could hear series after series of small roars alternating left and right. He was still a half-block away from what he judged to be the center of activity. He pushed forward and found, suddenly, that the center of the street was clear, with a cordon of policemen and barriers keeping masses of people back to either side of the street. Two ranks of people faced each other, fists and heads bobbing, leaning out over the barriers to point accusing fingers, pushing against the deliberately impassive police, with intermittent placards bobbing and twisting illegibly in the wind.

"What's going on?" he asked the man in front of him.

"Abortion." The man turned away and raised a fist.

Bob could feel rage and righteousness rippling the air like a winter wind. He was standing almost in the center of the street; he wanted to take time to figure out the alliances (which side was which?) before deciding whether to push his way through on the left or right side of the street.

He could have sneered at how easy it was to tell. The right-hand sidewalk was almost exclusively female; the left-hand side had a cadre of men at what looked like the center of the demonstration, where he could see some kind of makeshift platform. Men deciding a woman's issue, he thought. It wasn't a biting thought; it was just interesting. The men who shouted "baby-killers" were the same men who were against gun control; they did not disapprove of death; they simply wanted to be the ones to decide it.

He had a moment as he looked around, a moment when he saw the women with their angry faces as shrewish and inappropriate; when the men seemed more reasonable. Just looking at it objectively, he thought, weren't the woman supposed to be on the side of babies and weren't the men supposed to feel trapped by babies? He wavered, considering if he really wanted to go over to the women's side, now that he'd made a deliberate choice to go over to the men's side; but there were of course women on the men's side and men on the women's side; it was just easier to stand and watch than to take a side.

That was really how he saw it, he finally thought: opposite sides of the street, arms raised. It was a good illustration of the divide between the sexes.

He shuffled forward slowly. He intended to cross the street before he reached the main barricades, but the closer he got to the center of the action (he could see there was a clinic across the street, where the women stood twenty deep), the harder it was to break through the lines of people around him. He allowed himself to look noncommittally at faces, the distortion of faces, really, altered with emotion. He paid no attention to the continuing outbursts of chants, and even less to the garbled speech from the man on the platform.

He stood, debating whether to push his way back and then go on to his appointment, when clouds started to blow across the sky, sudden black clouds, and a wind whipped up. More and more people were peering at the sky, and the strained, angry mouths were changing into distracted, evaluating mouths. The group was losing its focus.

The wind died down suddenly. It simply removed itself, so that people discovered they were tensed for it, expecting it. The clouds got so thick that it seemed like sunset. The speaker was including "God" or "judgment" in every sentence. It was not hard to believe in some kind of apocalypse, and both sides of the street began to shift, so that small lanes formed as the outer edge of the crowd drifted off in search of shelter and those as yet undecided began to hedge, moving backwards or slowly sideways, their heads still turned to the speaker or to the clinic.

It was through one of these lanes that a figure ran from the clinic, clutching a bundle hard to identify in the increasing darkness. Everyone's attention was on the weather, so the women in front of the clinic didn't hesitate to move out of the way as the figure called, "Please! Please! I'm sick!" They turned concerned faces away from the sky and opened their mouths, beginning to lift their hands in sympathy, but by then the figure had burst to the edge of the barricade and screamed out stridently, her arms raised with the bundle in them, "Help me! Help me! They were throwing it out! Save the poor thing! I think it's hurt!"

Her cries hit the crowd like an electric charge, at once snapping everyone to attention. All eyes were on the figure still moving forward in the darkness, all eyes were squinting, straining, forming images, their pulses beating faster.

A fork of lightning split the sky, giving everything a hard, sharp edge, and at exactly that moment the figure tripped and started to fall down, in the cleared space between the two opposing groups. The lightning seemed to last whole minutes, everyone could see very clearly as the bundle flew up into the air, hovered, and began its descent. A collective groan of hundreds of people swept down the street like the onrush of rain.

The bundle split apart before it even hit the ground, and a soft, round, bald object hit the ground with a loud thunk! A man immediately got sick as something wet and stringy splattered up into his face. A shriek, a scream, a roar, a twisting away, and then a surge forward as those who saw it least clearly raised their arms, bared their teeth, bellowed in rage with their tongues showing, and then the barricades were pushed aside, the police were surrounded and ignored like lampposts. Rocks, bottles, even pieces of wood from the sawhorses were raised and twirled and shouts of "Murder! Murder!" ripped the air.

The thunder smacked out angrily, making the hair stand on every neck, and there was no choice but to strike out, strike back, protect yourself. There was no chance to turn and run, the people themselves created a fierce web drawing everyone tighter and tighter together and forward, irresistibly forward.

Bob had time to wonder what happened to the blanket-wrapped bundle. Everyone was screaming or shouting, and all around him objects were colliding into flesh. Someone moaned very briefly, pitifully even, and then the next moment struck out with no hesitation, as if pain was self-indulgent.

But none of it mattered to Bob. He knew who had run from the clinic, and he didn't believe for one moment that the bundle in her arms had been alive.

It was all so theatrical, it was all so dramatic. People were smashing each other's faces because of mere trickery! He knew it was Madame Hope, and he knew the whole point of it was to make them all fight over a lie.

He would have bet any money that tomorrow's papers would show that blood was spilled because someone had dropped a melon on the ground.

He turned the corner as police sirens and ambulances pitched their way up the avenue. At his back was the sound of breaking glass and the simple voice of the crowd.

Chapter 14

"Come on, Maggie, don't fail me now," Bob urged.

"They want to back out," she said over the phone.

"Meet me for a drink." He looked at his watch "Six o'clock."

"I can't—I really can't—I'm supposed to meet Peter—"

"You can call him, can't you? Tell him you're stuck. This is *work*. What you're doing is important! He'll understand."

"All right," Maggie said with sudden decision. "But we're in trouble."

"Trouble," Bob thought to himself angrily. "It's probably something silly, something minor." He picked up an article he'd been working on. He frowned, looking at Eliot's copy. Eliot still didn't know proofreader's symbols. He was using arrows again. With a start of impatience, Bob got up and took it into Pierre's office. "I can't do this," he said without preliminaries. "I can't work this campaign out, play nursemaid to Adpub and decipher Eliot's arrows. It's not working, Pierre." He rapped the papers down on Pierre's desk, ignoring the fact that Eliot was in the room with them. "Something has to give here," he said firmly.

Pierre picked up Eliot's copy and said, "Okay. I'll handle it." Bob turned and left. If Eliot's fired, that's it, he thought. Not my fault at all. He doesn't pull his weight. What does he do but make snide comments and scribble on the articles? If his feelings get hurt, all the better. He didn't care about Eliot's feelings.

$\mathcal{M}$aggie rushed into the bar, breathless and late. Bob had been tapping his pen restlessly. He was in suspense. Maggie and drama; was this problem even real? He didn't like how she tried to pull these little power-trips on him. But he made sure to look up and smile when Maggie crept into the seat next to him, shrugging her coat off.

"You look wonderful," he said. "Not at all like the world has collapsed."

She smiled gamely. "Well, it's not quite as bad as all that."

"Get settled," he said. "Settle yourself. Relax. Wine?"

She nodded and he got the bartender. She shook her hair, smoothing it with her fingertips. One of her earrings, long hoops that glinted off her neck, caught in her hair and he leaned over and released it.

"Now. Let me have it. The worst."

"They said the copy was too sensational. And a few lines in the article. My boss was called in, too. It was high-level meeting time. Lots of suits. Power suits," she grinned apologetically, relaxing.

"Did you tell them we'd change the copy?"

"Bob, you said it was already at the printer."

"Don't be silly. We'll change it. What didn't they like?"

She searched through her bag, pulling out her copy of the page. The Red Cross had only taken a half-page ad; Pierre and Bob had used the rest of the page to draw up an entry form and particulars.

"This," she said, "DARING and ANYTHING CAN HAPPEN. And here, NO HOLDS BARRED, and then, THE ONLY RULE IS TO GET OUT ALIVE." Bob felt the blood rush to his face; most of the copy was his.

"We'll change it," he kept repeating, putting aside the printer's costs and what Pierre would say. It was impossible to back out, anyway.

"Give me the paper," he said, taking it from her. "You've circled everything? Good, it will give me time to go over it."

She looked relieved. "I can tell them it will be changed?"

"Of course," he said impatiently. "We want to keep them happy, don't we? Even if they're a week late. I'll call you tomorrow with the changes and you can get it over to them right away. We can't lose any more time. No mistakes."

"I was so worried. I thought I'd lose my job if this got nasty."

"Shouldn't worry," he said, willing himself to be soothing. "I don't see you as the worrying type, anyway."

"Maybe you don't see me clearly," she suggested. Her eyebrows pulled together; her voice was resonant.

"I can take care of it," he continued, misunderstanding her. "We can take care of it."

"I almost got an ulcer," she mused. "Can you get an ulcer all at once, like a heart attack?"

"No. Everything requires preparation." He sighed and put his hand on top of hers. "Besides, it wouldn't be the end of the road if you lost your job."

"I can't lose my job," she said, a little edge of coldness added to her voice. "I'm good at it; I've always been good at it. I'm known for it," she said simply. "It's part of what I am."

"Not ethical, moral, courageous, humane or insightful?"

"Why? Is that what you are?" she snapped, and he glared but kept himself from answering. Those were loser's virtues anyway, they were women's virtues—the feeling qualities, the worrier's qualms. They didn't matter to him.

The next day he went straight to Pierre; he brought his changes in, laid them out and told Pierre what had to be done.

Pierre's mouth tightened slightly; his eyes got a bright, sharp look. "Printer's costs," he said swiftly. "Are we on press yet?"

"I called last night and checked. We're scheduled for late this morning. We'll face late fees, but it was no good giving them corrections over the phone. We need approvals straight down the line—Adpub and the Red Cross. We'd look like fools if it didn't seem we were handling this smoothly."

Pierre nodded, curtly. "I agree." He handed the copy back and added, "This had better work."

"No reason for it not to," Bob answered.

"Nine to the side pocket," Peter said. He leaned over, the cue stroking his fingers. He pulled back and then shot. He wore a neatly ironed shirt; it was new—or at least Bob didn't remember it.

"Luck," Bob said, unmoving.

Peter grinned and raised his eyebrows. His face was rubbery and his eyes slightly bloodshot. He was in one of his antic moods. "Did I do that? Did I get that ball in, too?" He breathed on his nails and polished them against his sweater. "Five to the corner."

Bob watched as that ball, too, cracked pleasantly and swept home. Peter took a sip from his beer. "I don't know how I do it," he sighed.

"Cheating?" Bob suggested.

"It must be hard just standing and watching," Peter answered and whistled, peering with exaggerated ease at the table. "Now which one will it be?" he asked lazily. "No, wait! I'll do this one with my eyes closed to make it fair. Three to the corner."

Peter memorized the table, took aim, and closed his eyes. He hit a little too softly, and the ball missed.

"That's funny," Bob said, "I thought you'd be at your best with your eyes closed."

"And I always thought you were such a good sport about losing," Peter mocked him. He sipped his beer as Bob studied the table carefully and then leaned over. Just as he was about to strike, Peter let out a loud sneeze. His eyes shot wide open in a pantomime of embarrassment.

"Oh God," he said. "Sorry about that."

Bob grinned to himself. What would it be next? An accidental bump on the elbow, a clumsy knock against the table, a startled question or remark? Or would he just sidle up to Bob, closer and closer? This was the Peter he knew, Puck-like, playful. Now he was trying to unnerve Bob with advice, a volume of it, nonstop. "You could try the four in the side pocket, it's an easy shot. I'm sure you could do it. Not flashy or anything, of course, but at least you'd get something *in*, and that's what this is all about, isn't it? Don't go for the six; that's tricky one, you're bound to touch the eleven—unless you think you can do that all of a sudden? Do you? You couldn't last time. Last time you tried you

138   *Karen Heuler*

scratched, remember?"

He rattled this out, circling the table, with odd little jerks to his walk, making fun of anyone who thought about playing seriously. Yet he always won.

"Drink your beer and shut up," Bob said. Peter wanted him to be the straight man, and he was inclined to play it to the hilt. Let him think he was in charge.

"Do I make you nervous? Do you want me to go away? I could play with someone else if it's too much for you. But you've improved, you've definitely improved. All your balls are still on the table; none of them are on the floor. Want some chalk?" He held his hand out to Bob, then pulled it back and popped something into his mouth. Bob could hear the crunch. It was a potato chip.

"Good for stomach acid, chalk," he said, grinning.

"Six to the corner," Bob said quickly. It went in and he whooped.

Peter went to the next table, tapped a man on the shoulder, pointed, and said, "He got a ball in." He walked back innocently.

"Four to the side," Bob said, and blew the shot.

"Better luck next time," Peter said and cleaned up the table, prancing and making little baton twirls with his cue. Bob leaned against the wall and watched.

The place was loud with the crack of balls and the staccato undertone of voices calling out shots. Except for Peter, everyone was very businesslike. Peter was the only one having fun. Competition of any kind brought out the performer in him. It was not enough to be good, he had to be fun as well. This was the third game he'd won.

"Enough," Bob said. "Let me go home and shoot myself in private."

"You want to hit the rest of your balls in for practice?" Peter said, dropping his act and showing Bob where to hit, when to tap, how to start a spin, all of it things he'd shown Alyson before at one time or another. He could be a good teacher.

"Okay, okay," Bob said finally. "Someday you'll beg for mercy. Just wait."

Peter racked up the balls, putting them on the tray. They walked over to the counter where beer and potato chips were sold. Peter paid.

"Let me get you a drink, then," Bob said.

"No, gotta go," Peter said, looking at his watch.

"Just one drink?"

"Really. I can't. Why don't you stay and play some more?" Peter glanced along the wall, where single players usually lounged, waiting for a partner. A figure shambled up.

Bob saw the flicker of amusement in Peter's eye as the new player approached. Bob had a feeling he knew who it was.

He didn't turn around.

"You have to run home?" he said impatiently, still addressing Peter. "Not allowed to stay out late?"

"Got things to do," Peter said jauntily, slapping him gently on the shoulder. "But have I found a partner for you." He grinned and turned. "Call you soon," he said over his shoulder.

Bob didn't follow him. He turned to face Madame Hope and looked at her angrily. "You couldn't let me win *one* game against him?" His eyes took in her squat figure; the rolls of flesh protruding over her pants. A man's pants, he thought with disgust, belt and all.

"Listen," she said, smirking, "you have to tell me what you want. What am I, a mindreader?" She took a small black cigar out of her mouth and laughed.

"What's with the cigars? Do you know what you look like?"

Madame Hope took the cigar out and showed it to him.

"Sherman's cigarillo," she said. "Not a cigar. Can't do *my* lungs any harm." Her mouth gaped open in a wide grin and then she popped the Sherman's back in. "Want to play a game? I'll let you win."

"No, I don't want to," he said, getting into his coat and turning.

"Then maybe a drink?" she suggested, following him companionably out the door and turning toward the avenue.

"I'd rather drink alone."

"It's not too much to ask, is it?" the devil protested. "One drink? I'll pay. Or are you afraid people will think we're together?"

"Nonsense," he said roughly, hating to be caught out so easily. "All right, yes, that's it," he said abruptly, stopping suddenly on the street. "Why do you look like a, like a—" he couldn't fix on a word.

"Fag? Dyke? Butch? Queen? Will any of them do?" Madame Hope hissed. Her face had gotten red.

She feels insulted, Bob realized. He frowned at her. "Do you have to let yourself go like this? You just look cheap and second-rate," he said finally.

The devil champed down on her Sherman's, which had gone out. Her eyebrows seemed almost pointy as she spat out, "You have standards to keep up, huh? You're too refined for me now?" She spat. "I made you into a winner."

"Look at you!" he cried, exasperated. How was it possible that he owed this creature his soul? One of them must be insane. "Everything you do is cheap. I can't figure out what you really are—I mean, maybe I had some kind of fever that screwed around with my head. You make so many promises and I believe you and then you give me cut-rate results." He ran his hand through his hair, shaking away the few strands that came off. "How do I even know you are what you say you are? Look at you, it's laughable. Am I really supposed to believe that you're the devil? Just give me some proof, nothing twisted the way you usually do things, all smoke and mirrors. Prove it." He stopped dead in his tracks, jamming his hands into his pockets, sticking his chin out.

Madame Hope laughed. "That's funny. You're afraid I don't exist? Me?" The gypsy turned away and then spun back, grabbing Bob by the collar of his coat and pointing her finger in his face. "Listen, sonny, look in the mirror sometime! Where do you think you'd be without me? Beating your breast on the edge of a bridge, stroking your wrists and dreaming you had nerve? I gave you possibilities, I gave you life! If I didn't exist you wouldn't either. You're nothing without me! And I can make you nothing again!" Her fists pulled Bob down to her level. The stench of cigars sickened him. The gypsy's pupils opened wide and he saw a miniature of his face reflected in them, wobbling back and forth between Alyson and Bob.

He took her hands and pulled them off. "All right, all right, I apologize. I'm yours heart and soul. But I like to know what's going on, I like to know what's coming, and you're always letting things slide. You make a bargain like this, you expect to have attention. Sometimes you make me wonder whether I made the right choice."

"What's wrong with the choice you made?" the gypsy asked impatiently.

"What if I'd just held on? Maybe things would have changed Maybe there would have been a miracle; but you can't get a miracle from your side, can you? I mean, this isn't quite turning out the way I'd hoped." He tried to say it in an inoffensive way.

They tramped along in silence. Finally, the gypsy sighed. "That miracle business—it's all P.R. The only time you see one now is on TV. I admit to some faults, but God doesn't do the kind of personal service I do; God is all for deprivation. You could pray as hard as you like, and you'd still be a woman past her prime."

"I know," he said after a moment.

"I don't get the whole heavenly bit, the sanctimonious shit," she muttered. "What's really so great about it? Bottom line, everyone has to fight against the instincts God gave them. *That's* cheap, if you ask me. That's stacking the decks. Create people who love sin, and then punish them if they're true to their natures. Me, I like fun. I like humor. I admit it was at your expense sometimes. I love puns; my mind works that way. So I couldn't resist some of the jokes. But I admit it wasn't nice." She stopped and stuck out her hand. "I apologize." Her lips stretched wide, the cigar dipping down to her chin. "I don't like getting bored, so I keep changing things around. The devil is in the details, eh? God gets the big stuff—earthquakes, Inquisitions, floods. God likes awe; I like twists. Take that man over there." The devil pointed with her chin. "That's a very important man; a man who wakes up every morning with power on his tongue, like coffee. I can let him alone, you see, but there's no *development* in that. He'll be just the same tomorrow morning as he is today. But I had a thought about him. He's going to be mugged, you know, and knocked down a little. Not hurt seriously. But he'll *forget* himself. A little tap on the head and he'll forget the details he takes for granted—his name, where he should be going, who to order around. I don't expect anything very novel, except that he's too used to power to act differently. What will he do, do you think?" They continued to walk after him, the man in the camel overcoat and fresh-creased trousers, his feet moving swiftly and his arms swinging wide. His head was bare; Bob couldn't keep his eyes from the top of his skull. He wanted to warn him, but that would probably annoy Madame Hope, and he thought he'd gone far enough already.

"I could even move the bump just a little bit and produce a certain suggestion of paranoia. Sometimes I like to do that. But today, I'm interested in the simpler dynamics."

"You told me, once, that you couldn't do anything without being summoned."

"That was a lie, of course. I can do as I please. What's to stop me? God? God likes experiments as much as I do. Maybe even more. God likes *proof*. He's rather old-fashioned in that respect."

Chapter 15

"This is terrific," Bob said. He gestured to the sky and then made a sweep of his hand to include Maggie.

She noticed it and smiled. "Perfect day," she said. "Crisp and clear. Clean. Like everything's out there waiting for us to do something."

He raised his eyebrows. "I think you're right; I think it's time we did something."

She raised her eyebrows back at him. "You've got a different way of talking to me when Peter's not around." She tilted her head. "Almost flirtatious."

"Almost?" he said neutrally, and moved ahead of her again.

They climbed up the hill. The path was clearly marked, even in the snow, and there were wooden benches and rough gazebos dotted intermittently along the route. Some of these were perched on jutting rocks or ledges on the tops of cliffs. Down below was a frozen lake and a few ice-skaters. The crack of the ice splitting on the lake made a distinct sound even up on the hill, cold and clear.

Maggie's cheeks and nose were red. She had a cowl-like scarf over her head, draping the sides of her face. Alyson would have envied the way it made her look; Bob merely wanted to lift his hand and brush it back a little. He found it inviting.

The sky was low, almost on top of them; they were so used to the city that the sky surprised them with the way it was laid out everywhere.

They stopped on ledges to look up and to look down, continuously surprised.

Bob went first, turning half-way around to offer his hand when climbing over rocks. Gradually this became more habitual, and Maggie expected it, pausing and holding her hand out, though she was perfectly capable of climbing on her own.

When they reached the top of the path, a clear round plateau with an old watchtower on it, they stood side by side, leaning gently against each other.

"Where will it be?" she asked, scanning the range around them.

"Over there," he pointed to the west. "I went up there this morning, with one of the rangers. We found a few good spots. I didn't tell him which one it would be."

"You're enjoying this, aren't you? Knowing something other people don't know?"

"Well, you know it too, so how does it make *you* feel?" He liked where he was and he was enjoying Maggie. He kept fighting an impulse to touch her; it was strange to see himself want that. Strange but not bad. Alyson might have thought that lust and hatred were mutually exclusive, but obviously they weren't.

She shrugged. "Oh, well, I do like it, I have to admit." She grinned at him then looked back to the lake. "Peter said he was up here with Alyson once. Did you know that?"

"Yes; she told me about it once. It's hard to avoid coincidences," he told Maggie smoothly. "And new memories blot out the old." He smiled at her. "We're the ones with the new memories, anyhow. Not those two."

She sighed. "It is beautiful here."

He put an arm around her and squeezed briefly. "Enjoy it to the fullest. To the impossible fullest. It won't be here tomorrow."

She laughed at him, shaking her head and moving slightly away: not too far, he noticed; just half a step. "It better be here tomorrow; the contest is next month."

"Okay, then, business," he said, starting back down the path.

"Everything's worked out perfectly. Applications are coming in by the bagload. The hotels are booked; all the cabins in the area are reserved. We've already got a good sum for the prize money and our subscriptions are up by over a thousand already. The Red Cross is setting up a mobile station, the local chamber of commerce is providing police; the machinery is humming. They're already figuring out extra areas for parking lots. All we need is some music and we'll have a new Woodstock."

She laughed. "The real Woodstock is only twenty minutes away."

He stooped to tie a shoelace, letting her get a few paces ahead. He scooped snow into his hand and packed it. He caught her on the shoulder.

She whipped around, her eyes flashing, and then ran off for cover. She slipped and whooped, scrambling on all fours to get behind a bush and sweep some snow towards her. "You're on!" she yelled.

Bob ducked behind some trees and began making snowballs, packing them swiftly together and stuffing them in his pockets. He packed a bunch into the crook of his arms and began to stalk Maggie. "Watch out!" he called. "You're under attack!" He ducked from trees to rocks, approaching her.

"Cad!" she yelled "Villain! I'll defend my honor to the death!" Her snowball missed his head by an inch, smacking into a tree trunk and getting down his neck.

"Ha! Ha!" he sneered. "A lucky throw!" He aimed one at her and caught her foot as she jumped.

"I was on the softball team," she answered, and a snowball smacked his wrist.

Damn, he thought, she's got a good aim, and he stood up straight, clutching his stockpile in his arms and throwing off a salvo of shots. He hit her shoulder. "You're weakening!" he cried. "It's only a matter of time! Surrender!"

"You'll never take me alive!" came back with a wet smack to his forehead and he toppled dramatically backwards into some bushes.

There was silence for a moment as he stayed low, crawling unseen towards her.

"Bob?" A snowball shook the bushes he'd left. "What are you doing?" Her head appeared at the side of a pine. Bob jumped up, aimed, and snarled, "Your virtue is my own reward!"

She let loose with her own storehouse of snowballs, pummeling him as he staggered towards her, his arms outstretched to ward off blows. "Fall down, bastard, you're hit!" she cried indignantly as he lunged forward, reaching her and throwing her to the ground under him. She laughed, squealing and hitting him lightly with her fists, so he was forced to fight her down. When she looked up at him, her breath warming his cheeks, his head bent low and he kissed her.

Her hands settled themselves on his back and he kissed her harder, cramming her head into the snow and twigs on the ground, feeling her jaw loosen and then open.

His plan was to play the reluctant admirer, the man with integrity and doubts, and he hoped to stall for time until he found a way to pull off his seduction. But she fit so neatly into him—their arms settling in the right nooks of their bodies, her legs around his—that he found it hard to stop. His mouth wanted to crush hers. His left leg slid between hers. It came to him automatically, the moves and sounds of make-believe passion, and he realized with surprise that it was no longer make-believe. He wanted her. He pinned her wrists down with his hands. He heard her quick breaths, and suddenly he wanted her to think he was better than Peter, and he suddenly got what Peter saw in her. Her eyes opened and stared at him, searching.

He moved off her slightly, looking back at her. "I don't know," she whispered, "is my honor still intact?"

He kissed her again, his tongue just lightly tasting hers, and then he kissed her on her eyes and the part of her neck just below her ears. She sighed and shifted under him.

Then he rolled off her, got up and offered her a hand, pulling her up. He dusted the snow off, lingering, as though accidentally, on her chest and her ass.

They turned and walked slowly down the path. They were almost at the hotel, a wide, sprawling collection of floors and hallways, when Maggie said, "What was that all about?"

He smiled tightly. "Believe me, I'm as surprised as you. I apologize; I promise to keep myself under control."

"I wasn't complaining; I was asking." They left the path and began to walk up the long driveway. Their steps slowed imperceptibly until they came to a complete standstill.

"I'm glad," he said. "I'm glad you're not sorry anyway." He hesitated. "You must know that this isn't easy, considering the circumstances." He laughed shortly. "I feel so close to you; but there's a question of loyalty—"

"Yes, there is," she said soberly, and he was afraid that it was a warning, but she continued. "Although I don't know who you're being loyal to—Alyson? Peter? There's a whole mix of loyalties here, a terrible mix. Maybe I should have realized that before I got myself into this." She frowned, and sighed, and pushed the hair back from her face, and lowered her head.

"You sound unhappy." Bob heard the disappointment in his voice; it sounded real, at least to him. He wanted her to come to him, though; that was true; and it didn't matter if he felt something for her. It was a pleasant sensation; he didn't have to question all his responses. For the moment, in this time and place, it was good enough.

"Well," she said reluctantly. "It's like you said once, Peter is fun—a lot of fun—and a great, great guy. But there's something on his mind. He keeps his mind—well, away from me. I can't *feel* what he's thinking about, you know? He's holding back, reserving something. He must be still thinking of her." Bob waited. "He just doesn't talk the right talk, somehow. There's nothing reassuring about him; he dances around you. You can tell, in his heart, that he's flickering." She looked up at Bob, smiling apologetically. "It's bad manners, I know. I mean, talking about someone else with the man you've just kissed?" She looked at him and smiled. "I'm looking for reassurance here. I'm feeling shaky."

"I'm the one who made the moves," he said, taking hold of her hand. "So I'm the one who's on the hot seat. Yes, I'm loyal to both

Peter and Alyson, and this isn't what I was looking for at all. I don't like complications," he said, trying to sound sincere and simple. "I don't like dishonesty. Look, you can tell me if I'm out of line. I'm not pressuring you or anything. It's just well, I like being with you." He said this like someone making a confession long overdue. "I like it a lot." It was the kind of thing Peter would say; had said, in fact, a long time ago. Had he said it to Maggie, too? Did she pause and glance away because it sounded like an echo? He covered the hand he held with his other hand. "Let's relax, okay? We're two people who like each other, and we've been friends a long time. It's lovely here. We'll find a fireplace or a game of Monopoly in the game room, and then tomorrow we leave and by then, we'll know something." He could tell that "something" disappointed her; she was a concrete person; she liked to know exactly what was being proposed.

"Playing games sounds so symbolic," she said.

"We can read a lot into it, then. But as long as one of us wins, it can't be all bad, can it?"

$\mathscr{M}$onopoly was taken in the game room, so they played checkers for a while, but in fact they couldn't concentrate and started jumping each other's tokens randomly. So they went to dinner, ordering one bottle of wine and then another. They hadn't finished the second bottle by dessert, so they took it with them to Bob's room.

By then Maggie was giggling. Bob kept her glass full. She lolled around, her head flopping gracefully to left and right, her eyes bright but her lids heavy.

"If you could have anything you wanted right now," he said as she frowned, trying to pay attention, "what would it be?" Her eyes looked around the room, glancing off the furniture and then stumbling back to him. "I'd like to be hugged," she said finally, triumphantly, as if she'd discovered something.

"Oh, that's so easy," Bob whispered, and he slid his arm around her, hugging her close. He settled against her, enjoying the sheer physical closeness of it. He had always loved being hugged, as a woman, the sensation of being encircled and enclosed was delightful; now he found the reverse—to enclose, to hold close, to wrap—equally enticing. He hugged her harder. He felt her bones adjust to him.

"Feels good," she mumbled to his chest.

"Feels very good," he said and he pulled her head up to kiss her. Her head drifted to his shoulder as she kissed back, her lips burrowing into his.

She reached her hand up to his head, drawing him closer, and he eased her down on the floor, holding her, rubbing her back with one hand while the other kneaded the nape of her neck, gently, experimentally. Her hand slipped to his waist; his hand slipped to her ribs and then crept to her blouse, probing below it, finding her breast.

Maggie was tipsy, making small alcoholic moans, her eyelids fluttering. Bob wanted to undress her carefully but he found himself rushing forward, wanting to touch more and more of her. These were the breasts that Peter preferred to Alyson's, and these breasts leaned, gently weighted, into his hands, small buoyant breasts. He fondled them, rolling them around in his hand, bending down to suck at them, loving the resilience, the play of them. He had as his template the way Peter had made love to Alyson, but even as he started with that he found his own way, listening to Maggie's indrawn breaths as well as to his own inclinations, and the more they moved around and thrashed and arched and rubbed, the more he gave way to the need to push and thrust. It was a new way of making love for him, more specific, more focused. He wanted her to touch his penis, his wanted his penis inside her, his body seemed to be pent up in a more defined way than he was used to—and then their clothes were off or mostly off and he was inside her and he moved a little to the side and nearly slipped out again until he found a rhythm and quickly (too quickly) he burst beyond himself. He fell on top of her, his hand stroking her until she relaxed with a little sigh and they settled peacefully together.

Later, as Maggie slept in his bed, Bob got up and looked out the window. It was a clear night (new moon? full moon? he hadn't a clue) and the silence was frozen outside into shadows. Some restlessness

Karen Heuler

overtook him, and he searched the landscape, expecting to see a squat figure standing in the middle of the ice, a figure whose hand would rise and salute him.

He saw nothing. Was he disappointed? He looked at Maggie, sleeping all rolled up in the blankets, and he imagined telling Peter about it. He didn't feel any anguish about Peter anymore; what he felt was cold and deliberate. He looked at Maggie objectively: he felt a kind of affection for her, he decided. He tested his emotions a little more and realized that the affection was more like a small sense of gratitude for getting away with screwing her. He could walk away from her without a problem, something Alyson had never been able to do with a bed partner. If this was revenge, it was going to be easy and it was going to be sweet.

Chapter 16

"*This* campaign," Bob said to Madame Hope. "Is there any way to jazz it up?" He was sitting in her storefront, tapping his fingers on the same table that, three months earlier, had sealed his fate.

"What did you have in mind?" She selected a pipe from a mass of shapes located on a chair, and tapped it against the wall.

"A pipe?" Bob asked. "A pipe?" It was irritating, how she always managed to mix up gender stereotypes. He had never seen a woman smoke a pipe.

"You have something against pipes?"

He waved the question away. "Can you guarantee a good turnout, or good weather or something?"

"Good weather!" she scoffed. "Next you'll want me to do picnics!"

Bob's jaw clenched. "I'm not talking about a picnic. This is a make-or-break situation for me. I need a good showing for my career. Don't bait me."

"Oooh," Madame Hope said, filling her pipe from a pouch she found on the floor, "You've got a temper, too, now? Or should I say 'balls'?"

"That tobacco is sickening," he said as a terribly sweet odor filled the room.

"There's fresh air out on the street."

Bob took quick little sniffs of air, trying to avoid inhaling too deeply. "I was thinking of some kind of accident, maybe—nothing fatal, just showy enough to get attention. Something the Red Cross could handle, maybe. You know a bus skidding into a ditch or something." He shook his head. "Come on, *think*. You must have some ideas. My mind is empty."

He told himself immediately to watch the way he talked to her; he could see she was glaring at the tone of his voice. That dog, Imp, growled and hauled himself slowly through the doorway to snarl at him. The dog was huge; how had he ever thought it was a spaniel?

"Rock slide, avalanche, thin ice, slick roads, hotel fire, flash flood, food poisoning, bear attack, tornado, airplane crash, terrorist attack, Legionnaire's disease. You name it, it's yours. No extra charge." She wreathed her head in the cloying smoke, her eyes on him.

"I want something simple. Nothing faked."

"Faked?" Her lips curled back; the hair on the dog's neck bristled. "When have I ever done anything fake?"

"Don't get sensitive," Bob said uneasily. "I just meant I wanted a natural accident. I don't want to raise anyone's suspicions."

"Do you think you're talking to an idiot?" She stroked the dog slowly. They seemed to be on better terms now.

Bob flushed. "I didn't mean it personally. I was really just thinking out loud. I need your advice," he said, changing his tactics. He eyed her warily.

"We could have an accident," she agreed finally. "And I suppose you want to be the hero?"

"No. That's not necessary. I just need a successful event."

"You could be the hero," she repeated. Her eyes were gleaming, half-closed. She was enjoying herself.

"I'm talking about getting good publicity," he said, once again impatient with her. "The sponsor has to be the hero, not me. That's how it works."

"Temper, temper," she said, suddenly soothing. "I know how it works. But, let's face it, there's nothing wrong with a little fantasy coming true, is there? You could rescue a blue-eyed child, you could warn some honcho about a jewel heist. A sudden flourish won't do any harm." She grinned at him. "We can arrange things any way you like."

"Should we draw up a contract?" He snapped the words out and they lay there in silence for the space of a minute.

"You can trust me," Madame Hope said finally. "You've gotten everything you've wanted so far, haven't you? There will be an accident," she said, almost disinterested. "We'll settle the details later." She tapped her pipe into an ashtray, dismissing him. "I'm expecting a customer," she said.

Bob passed, on his way out, a thin young man who stood hesitantly at the door.

He saw Maggie two or three times a week, often at his apartment. The mattress on his bed bore a record of stains—once his and Peter's, now his and Maggie's. When he changed the sheets he had felt compelled to rub them, these faint marks, these records of his true transformation. Like those microscopic beasts that lived in one's eyelashes, was there a nation of wriggling vermin swarming in each fragment, each molecular pool?

He found himself thinking about his own indifference, sometimes. He liked being with Maggie; he particularly liked making love with her. But warmth, affection? No. He had never known how erotic it was to be on this edge of contempt, how his own mood shifted quickly from liking her to looking forward to her comeuppance. It was a strange, twilit world. He thought of her often, but it was most often sexual; pornographic, even. When he imagined talking to her it was merely to keep her interest or to find out something about Peter; it was never to find out anything about her. He lacked tenderness; and he missed tenderness; but it wasn't going to happen with her. The first few times he had climaxed quickly, unused to the variety of sensations, the differences. As a woman, he had had to learn to let go; as a man he had needed to learn to hold back. It was true that his most pleasurable moments had been with his eyes open, rolling his rump, watching

Maggie's face, her mouth open, her eyes almost liquid. He knew how to please her—the small gifts, the bursts of well-thought-out consideration. Peter was good at such things, too, but only when he concentrated, and he was so easily distracted. Whatever Peter was doing, Bob could beat him at it, because Bob had a better plan.

So, as far as Maggie went, he was succeeding. It was even easier than expected. He said just enough to keep her wavering, quivering on the edge of indecision. She had an image of them as star-crossed lovers, and he encouraged it.

"I'd know your hands anywhere," he said. "I'd know your fingers anywhere, even if I found them by the side of the road."

She laughed. "That's what I like about you. You shock me; you look so innocent and you say the damnedest things."

He smiled and kissed her fingernails. She sighed. "This isn't right, you know. I should tell Peter."

He ran his hand over her head, moving it gently from side to side. "Things have a natural way of working out. Who knows? Maybe he'll grow tired of you. Then you won't have to break his heart."

She scowled. "You don't worry about him? It doesn't bother you that I'm sleeping with him, night after night?"

He knew his cue. "Bother me?" he said coldly. "I think about killing him. I think about killing you. I hate the two of you together." She looked gratified and squeezed his arm, and he glared at her, a jealous rival.

He was becoming cunning, cocksure, adept at lies and pleasing deceptions.

He would have been shocked at himself if he were Alyson, and at times he tried to imagine being shocked at himself. Where had Alyson gone? How many limits would he exceed before he annihilated what had been himself? Herself? And why did questions still plague him—why did he keep thinking about what he was doing? Surely his soul would not be saved by a quibble? And if his soul was lost what did decency or honesty matter? The only thing that mattered was to get what he deserved. He played it through again and again: seeing Peter and Maggie in the taxi;

hearing Peter say he had tried to love Alyson, but couldn't.

He got some degree of comfort from spending time with Anna, where he felt at peace. He even felt genuinely kind towards her, and felt a real warmth returned. Her belly was growing, ever so faintly, and he liked to rub it. That baby had been known to him from its inception; it was almost his. Weekends with Anna were so domestic, settling into a familiar pattern of meals and shopping. They leaned against each other comfortably as the TV blinked at them. His eyes traveled over the walls, over the furniture. He knew when anything was moved. He offered suggestions at new arrangements.

He was now in the habit of occasionally sleeping at Anna's, as yet chastely. It had grown late once, and neither of them had felt like parting. It was so much easier just to continue. Anna fell asleep and he stared at her thoughtfully, before finally waking her.

"I'm sorry it's so late," he apologized. "I didn't feel like moving."

"Neither did I." She yawned and stretched. "But I've got to get some sleep."

"Can I stay?" he asked hastily. "I won't bother you. It will be nice."

She laughed sleepily, tolerantly.

"We can cuddle," he offered. "We both need that."

"We do," she said. She hesitated and then shrugged. "I guess so," she said. "But no experiments."

And so he had stayed, and they had fit into a spoon, Bob pressed in his underwear against Anna in her cotton nightshirt, relieved for once to have no agenda.

He had kissed her in the morning and made breakfast, cheered by the routine, comfortable pleasures.

"This is a good arrangement," he said over toast.

"It has its points," was all she'd admit.

After that it was fairly routine to stay there Saturday nights. He was tempted to increase his visits, to come over during the week, especially when his edgy triumphs over Maggie made him want to bask elsewhere. He told himself—he even believed—that he was honest with Anna, that he was "himself" with her, free of manipulation.

But it was gratifying to know he had her in reserve for the future. Anna had been Alyson's closest friend, after all; she had never betrayed her. She was honest and trustworthy and maybe a little too focused on the baby to be much fun at the moment, but sometimes safety and comfort rated higher than revenge and fun; and Anna satisfied those cravings. And, too, he was sure he could have her sexually. There was no need to rush. His hand could lay on her breast now as they slept. He rubbed her stomach and his hand, in its cunning circles, crept down to her pubis, teasing her gently. It was a matter of time.

On the other hand, why settle for Anna? The world was open. In three short months he had managed to collect two women. What more was ahead? There was no reason to limit himself. He had changed overnight from the handicapped to the privileged, and privilege had charm. There was no need to ruin it; there was no reason to exclude any part of his future. He could have anything he wanted. It was too soon to decide what it would be.

$\mathcal{B}$ob studied himself in the mirror. It was impossible to keep from grinning. He was used to his face now—he thought, all in all, that it wasn't a bad face. His jaw was firm; he had grown a little stubble, then shaved it off and grown a little mustache. His fingers smoothed it automatically. He had good eyes; and he looked forthrightly at the mirror. He no longer had a soft look; he could meet anyone's eye; he liked to do it, even. There was no doubt about the hair; that was slipping away. An annoyance; he should have been specific about the hair. That had definitely taught him a lesson about anticipating details, but it also taught him that other people weren't clear about consequences either. He grinned again. It was incredible to be so in control. He felt an adrenaline high; his pulse might be fast, but it was anticipation, not fear, that raised it.

He checked his watch and washed his hands. Peter should arrive in thirty minutes. It was odd. As a woman he had been totally in Peter's power; there had been no restrictions. It had seemed heady; it had proved disastrous. At one time life without that kind of obsession had seemed worthless. But now he had power of his own, and he was proud to be free of constricting sentiments. Even his groin admitted it, throwing a little pulse of its own his way.

He had told Peter to meet him for a drink; he had already asked Maggie to meet him at the same place.

Bob stepped out of the men's room and saw Maggie at their table. "Dear Maggie," he thought, warming in anticipation. He looked at the door to the restaurant. He had chosen the table well.

He was still grinning when he sat down again next to Maggie. He lifted her hand and then kissed it.

"I wish I had a camera," he said. "I wish I could keep you forever the way you are tonight."

"What's special about tonight?" she laughed. Her eyes, too, showed a strange excitement. She had caught his mood; that was obvious. What did she expect to happen?

"It could be a very special night for us," he said warmly, still stroking her hand with his thumb. Her face kept opening up to him, unfolding, fluttering. He could read her expectations around her mouth, in the fine lines under her eyes. She leaned closer, her shoulders hunched together, shivering pleasantly.

"I never thought I'd be so in love," he said softly. He put exactly the right amount of emotion in those words: pleasure, pride, awe. What wonderful words for a woman to hear! They even thrilled him, nostalgically. If he wasn't careful, he would get moist-eyed.

He was leaving pauses everywhere, and it seemed to intrigue Maggie, as if she were watching a man who might, indeed, fall from his side of life over to hers.

He kissed her hand again, seemingly overcome by emotion. Maggie's lips were slightly opened, she was breathing through her mouth, little forced gasps, waiting for the hook.

Carefully, he kept his eyes on the door while he replayed the memory of Peter and Maggie getting into the cab together, the terrible jolting of the universe he had felt as Alyson. He remembered Peter saying he had tried to love Alyson, but just couldn't. And he was ready.

He had shifted his chair slightly when he sat down. As Peter came through the door, first glancing along the bar and then from table to table, Bob said, "Will you marry me, Maggie?"

All his senses were tuned to Peter, turning slowly toward them, his eyes scanning the restaurant. Bob had to remember to keep the pressure on Maggie's hand, to keep his face taut and expectant. He heard Maggie's sigh; he had expected Maggie's sigh, just as he had expected the color to start to her face, the eyes opening and then, briefly, closing, the pull of satisfaction at her mouth.

He expected her to say yes, and she leaned forward to him, whispering, "Oh Bob! Marry you!" but he wasn't paying attention to her. Out of the corner of his eye he could tell that Peter had seen them; that he had frozen stiffly at first and was now walking towards them, his eyes alert.

"Oh, Maggie, I love you!" Bob said, anticipation making the words quiver, so that she took her hand out from his and reached up to his chin. She looked at him briefly—fleetingly—Bob could feel how close Peter was to them, now—and she kissed him, slowly, happily. "I love you, too," she said, "but what can we do about—"

"That's nice."

Maggie whipped back in her chair, grimacing with shock. She faced Peter.

"That's nice," he repeated. "Working hard, you two?" His jaw moved tightly, the words spitting themselves out.

"Why don't you join us?" Bob said, grinning. He hoped it was a relaxed, superior grin. Peter looked like every muscle in his body was ready to snap; Maggie's face had lost all color and she sat open-mouthed and bleached. Bob was strained with hope and expectation—this was the moment he'd been working towards.

Peter refused to sit. His hands were clenched.

"I just asked Maggie to marry me," Bob said. He had to keep himself from laughing out loud, he felt so jubilant.

"Peter, I'm so sorry," Maggie said quietly. She held her hand out to him, but he refused her touch.

"It was a joke, really," Bob continued, watching Peter's face. It fascinated him. Peter in a fury, Peter bested; Bob continued, ruthlessly, pointedly. "I always propose to the women I've been sleeping with. It's a habit." He had rehearsed the words, and even as he spoke them they sounded borrowed. But they had the desired effect: Peter stepped back and his hands opened in a brief flutter of surprise. The impact of the information hit him hard.

"What?" Maggie gasped, turning to him.

"It's just a little game we all play, isn't it?" Bob continued. "Like cheating on the woman you live with, or screwing with your friend's lover. But don't worry, Peter." He patted Maggie's clenched hand on the table. "I'm dumping her. I don't want her. It wasn't hard, either, getting her. Maybe the two of you are shallow." He made an exaggerated frown. "Maybe that's why you keep falling in love so much. What do you think?" His heart was bouncing around in excitement; he was trying hard to keep his voice level, but it was a struggle. He wanted to giggle; he'd done it!

"Stop it," Maggie cried. She put her face in her hands.

"It's true?" Peter asked her, and Bob reveled in the glance they exchanged then, which was angry and shocked and humiliated.

Maggie seemed unable to answer. Her eyes swung back and forth between the two men, but her mouth merely moved without any sound.

"I guess she's gotten tired of you already," Bob gloated. "Maybe you're not as fascinating as you think? What is it, less than four months and you've already begun to pall? No, wait—less than three months? Let's see," he turned to Maggie, "the first time we slept together was over a month ago, wasn't it?"

"Why are you being such a *prick?*" Maggie cried, but the question was lost as Peter lunged for Bob, dragging him out of his chair. Faces had already been turned to them in the restaurant, and Bob was suddenly aware how quiet it had grown. A waiter was making his way cautiously towards them, stopping indecisively as Peter grabbed Bob.

He felt almost giddy with pleasure. Peter was flushed and ugly with anger, Maggie's head was lowered and her face hidden. He was paying them both back for the misery they'd caused—he'd done it all and it was splendid.

"You—you—" Peter choked out the words. He held the front of Bob's jacket in his left hand; his right hand, clenched, seemed to wander in the air looking for a target.

"Be careful, Peter," Bob said, baiting him, rubbing it in, "you don't want to make a fool of yourself in public as well as in private."

Peter swung at him, but Bob moved, pulling Peter off balance. He snapped back, his heart leaped, he slapped Peter and saw the surprise on Peter's face. A *slap*! he thought in exasperation and then hauled back, clenching his fist, remembering not to tuck his thumb inside, and aimed for Peter's jaw. It was fast, instinctive, an action loaded with adrenaline, and one that he had longed for. But he struck weakly, enough to hurt but not enough to stop, and Peter frowned and struck back.

People had jumped up from the tables close to them, which was lucky because Peter's punch landed with decision and Bob toppled backwards, sprawling against another table. He got up and started to lunge again towards Peter, but a man grabbed him from behind, shouting, "Enough! Stop it! I'm calling the police! Get out of here!"

Then Maggie started screaming. "What are you, some kind of lunatic? You set this up! Peter," she cried, "he did it on purpose!"

Peter, panting, disheveled, glared at her. "Slut," he answered, his lips taut.

"And what does that make you? I wouldn't have dumped you the way you did with Alyson. You and your stupid dog!"

"Dingo? What's stupid about Dingo?" Bob asked. The three of them were grabbing their clothes, straightening their chairs, none of them looking directly into anyone else's eye. They were all anxious to get out quickly. It was over; there was a real sense of anticlimax—and had that waiter said he was calling the police?

In his imagination, it had always ended with a stunning

denunciation, Peter knocked out cold, with Maggie begging for pity.

But it wasn't like that—it was a burst, a scuffle, a bout of indecision, and a self-conscious hustle out the door. They stood outside, together, and it was just flat, like a hangover. And like a hangover, it tarnished the earlier events: had any of it been as satisfying as he'd thought? And what about this pain in his jaw?

He stole a glance at Peter. His shoulders were hunched up around his neck.

They stood outside, still getting into their coats, straightening their clothes. A waiter watched them through the glass.

"Peter—" Maggie said tentatively. "We've got to talk."

"Not now," he said gruffly.

Bob had an odd impulse to buy them drinks. He no longer felt the pinch of anger, of vindictiveness. In fact, he felt expansive. It might not have gone the way he imagined, but it was far worse for them—and he'd done it.

"Where are you going?" Maggie continued. She kept putting her hand on Peter's arm, and he kept stepping away.

He sighed. "Leave me alone, Maggie. I've got to think." He started to walk away, and she took a step to follow, until he snapped, "Leave me alone!" He held his head stiffly up; Bob believed it would be lowered as soon as he was out of sight.

"Aren't we supposed to shake hands now?" Bob called as Peter walked away.

He watched Maggie's face. She bit her lip, she ran her hand through her hair. She began walking slowly in the direction Peter had taken. Bob followed her.

"Maggie, Maggie, will you marry me?" he laughed, and he didn't try to hide the mockery in his voice.

He watched her brush at her cheeks, but she wouldn't allow herself to cry. She stopped in the street and drew in her breath. When she spoke, little white clouds of steam floated out of her mouth, as if the words themselves were loaded with heat.

"Look," she spat, "get it straight. You were a brief diversion. I was feeling low, and it always cheers me up to be in a flush of love—or sex—or whatever. Anyone will do. You were already wearing off; I just needed to feel attractive because Peter was being distant. He's the one I care about." She drew in her breath again. "You're scum. Simple scum. Worse than dirt." She shook her head. "What a hypocrite. What can you possibly get out of it? We both hate you now." Her feet had picked up their pace; they were walking briskly along the avenue. Bob could feel goosebumps on his scalp where the hair had fallen out. In a month it would be spring, but right now there was a cold damp wind blowing and his ears were beginning to ache.

"I get satisfaction," he said. "I did it for Alyson. Don't you think it worked beautifully?"

"You forgot one thing," she snapped. "Peter loved me when he left Alyson. The only thing I feel for you is disgust."

"It might work out just the same, don't you think?" he answered genially. "Will Peter forgive and forget? He's the brooding type, you said so yourself."

"He'll forgive. He'll forget," she said, swinging her earrings, flashing them in the streetlight. "He loves me."

"Isn't it wonderful how fast that can change?" he mocked her. "I mean, ten minutes ago you loved me."

"Go to hell, Bob," she said, and hailed a cab speeding towards them.

"It must be female intuition," Bob muttered to himself as she slammed the taxi door. He was alone now with his triumph, and it was already starting to fade. Go to hell, she'd said, and he had to admit that if this was all the payback he'd get for going to hell, it was pretty paltry. He looked restlessly along the streets. Madame Hope? She always showed up after scenes with Maggie or Peter. Where was she now? Was she bored with him?

He could call Anna. He could even go see her. He started toward a telephone, and found himself relieved when it didn't work. He didn't want to see Anna; he couldn't talk to her about all this.

He suddenly made his mind up and took a cab down to the gypsy's storefront.

The lights were out. Frowning, he checked his watch. Nine o'clock. Was she asleep already? He rang the bell, knocked on the door. And knocked again. He thought he heard something. The fortuneteller's dog? He knocked harder.

Finally, a light switched on and steps shuffled to the door. He heard the gypsy unlatch the chain, open the door a crack, and mutter, "Oh, it's you. What do you want?"

"I want to talk to you, of course," he said impatiently. "Where were you? Don't you know what's been going on?"

"I was taking a nap," she said defensively, opening the door.

He could see that. Her clothes were rumpled; she had a crease mark on the side of her face.

"I know, I know," she grumbled. "You didn't know I slept. Well, I can tell you, I get tired too. Damn hard business it is. Damn hard." She rubbed her eyes. "So all right. Tell me how it went."

"This is very annoying," he said stiffly. "How can you just nap like that—as if what happens to me isn't important!"

"Why do you need an audience?" She yawned, let him in, and then shuffled into an easy chair.

"*Everyone* wants an audience," he objected. "How else can you tell if you've won?"

She shrugged. "All right. You've won. Feel better? They were bad, those two. They lied to you and hurt you. Scum of the earth! But *you*," her eyes glinted and she smiled, "you lied better. Poor fools! They probably didn't even mean to hurt anyone when they started out. Poor planning! Not like you." Her teeth bit on her lower lip.

Despite himself, Bob was beginning to feel slightly ashamed and she could probably see that. Maybe she was trying to *make* him ashamed. He shrugged defensively. "That's different. That's revenge."

She snapped the objection away. "Everyone's taking revenge on something. You're just talking about motivation and *everyone* has motivation."

"Well, they motivated me all right," he said. "I did it because of

Karen Heuler

what they did to me."

"Well, of course that's better than being unintentionally cruel. Why bother trying to justify yourself? What does it matter? Are you still bothered by good and evil?" She eyed him humorously. "That old itch?"

"Perhaps," he said slowly. Then he shook his head. "No. I don't care about that. I care about success."

"That's good."

"But have I succeeded?"

"Very likely."

"I don't like your 'very likely.' It's not satisfying."

"Are you looking to me for satisfaction?"

"We have a contract, remember."

"So far, I've held to my side." She struck a match and it flared. She pulled a cigarette from her pocket.

"I seem to remember that you said I'd be happy."

"Not happy." She inhaled and the tip of her cigarette flared. "I said you'd like it. Look at your life now. You have to admit you like it. Intrigues. How did you feel when Peter saw you and Maggie together? When he understood?"

"It felt good," he admitted. "But it passed. It ended. I wanted more."

Her eyes gleamed and she stroked her dog slowly. "Nothing has ended yet. Nothing ends in one scene." Her voice was lowered; soothing, gentle. "You'll have everything you want. As much as you can take. This is what dreams are made of."

Chapter 17

$\mathcal{B}$ ob didn't hear from either Peter or Maggie. That wasn't unexpected, but it made working out the last details of the promotional campaign—just three weeks before the event—difficult. He relied on her to handle the details; he had seen himself as the creative end, and Maggie as the efficient, professional aide. Like a secretary, in fact. Since she refused to return his calls he had been forced to fudge questions.

"What's the latest count on participants?" Pierre had asked.

"Something over 600," Bob answered automatically, although he had no idea if this was true or not. Maggie had the figures; she was the one who got the mail and sorted the applications. From there she forwarded the hotel reservations, and made a copy of every name for the subscriber list. *Adventure* paid a fee based on the amount of names they got, and Bob had delegated the whole business to Maggie's office. She now had the only accurate list of applicants.

"How many new subscribers?"

"It takes six weeks to filter out duplicates. The last tally showed close to a thousand."

Pierre nodded. "Not that impressive. We'll have to rely a lot on publicity. How's that going?"

"All the local stations, of course. Plus we're alerting radio stations in the major cities, based on participants. You know, local boy takes a run at the prize money. We've got two TV stations sending cameras. AP will be there. We've sent press releases to all the papers, with a follow-up scheduled the week before."

"Anyone interested?"

"A few. It will depend on whether it's a slow news day or not." Bob wished he had accurate figures on hand; or at least some names. Maggie would know, of course.

"Let's sit down early next week and go over it. Tuesday all right?"

Bob was flattered that it was a question, not an order. "Tuesday. Eleven?"

Pierre nodded.

By the end of the week Maggie still hadn't returned any of his calls and he went over her head to her boss, making him understand firmly that Maggie needed to be at the meeting with all the latest figures.

He missed having her feedback. Pierre had asked about the next competition, and Maggie would have been the one to discuss it with. She was an organizer. He had ideas, but he needed a sounding board, and for some reason he didn't think of Anna. There was no doubt about it, Maggie was still necessary. Where was his sense of timing? Surely he could have waited another month, gotten all his triumphs in order?

And just what, exactly, was happening with her and Peter? Silence led to endless speculation. He imagined tears, shouts, slammed doors; Maggie wouldn't give up without a fight—unlike Alyson, with her fatalistic passivity, her collapse at the news of Peter's departure. He had come to think of Alyson as another person; he was getting more objective about her. Alyson should have fought back.

He imagined Maggie and Peter fighting—Peter's face sullen and threatening, his shoulders crushed tight against his neck so that you could feel the tension. Or would he just turn around and leave, as he had with Alyson? What would Maggie do? Plead, argue, beg forgiveness, point out that Peter, too, was capable of infidelity—though that would hardly aid her cause.

It maddened him not to know what was happening, it drove him into a frenzy to think that, even now, the two of them might be reconciling, be swarming over each other with hideous excitement.

Maggie wouldn't back down; she was used to getting what she wanted—and, actually, of deciding what she wanted. Not that Peter was a fool, either. He wouldn't like how Maggie's deception mirrored his own deception. Good. Would it occur to them that, indeed, Bob had manipulated the two of them, setting it all up from the start? They wouldn't know it was the same triangle—Peter, Maggie, Bob/Alyson—but the similarities were all too obvious. Would they unite against him?

By the end of the week he was thinking only of how to find out about Maggie and Peter, because knowledge was the cornerstone of his revenge.

He rented a car on Saturday and parked it down the street from Maggie's apartment. He brought newspapers, coffee, an empty bottle to pee in. There was a grocery on the corner where he could get sandwiches, even a small bar midblock where he could get a drink and watch. He had had to get there early in order to get a parking spot. There was a southwest wind blowing—false spring—but he had dressed warmly, even wearing a cap. Lightly tinted glasses, he hoped, would be an additional disguise. He moved to the back seat of the car, since other drivers, seeing him at the wheel, pulled up next to him and honked, asking if he was leaving so they could get his spot.

Despite the coffee, he dozed off for a while, not sure for how long. He was convinced he had missed something, but less than an hour later he saw Maggie and Peter leave the building. They weren't holding hands, he noted, which was something Peter liked to do. But they were together, and they were talking to each other. He watched them over the top of his newspaper. Peter's walk was relaxed; Maggie said something and touched him on the arm; he nodded, and they walked on.

So they were still together. Bob found himself grinding his teeth, and then told himself to be reasonable. They didn't look very much in love. They looked like people who were in the middle of a steady disagreement.

He wasn't satisfied, however, with this glimpse. He decided to watch their comings and goings for a day. He checked his watch; it was 1:30.

They might be going for brunch. Maybe an early movie. Peter didn't like to sit around on weekends. They would have to be back to walk the dog, anyway. Bob's heart thudded; that was what he had missed. One of them had walked the dog while he dozed, perhaps even passing right by him. He could visualize Dingo lifting his leg on the wheel of the car.

He wanted, very much, to see the dog.

They didn't get back until close to eight, laden with shopping bags and brown bags of food. Fifteen minutes later, Maggie came out with Dingo. She stopped once and checked her pockets. For money? Bob wondered. Had she forgotten something?

Maggie walked on the other side of the street and turned the corner. Bob opened the car door cautiously and slid out. He kept as much to the shadows as he could—not easy with everything lit up. He kept far behind her.

He was, quite simply, overjoyed when she tied Dingo to a No Parking sign and went inside a vegetable stand.

Bob cautiously moved forward. Dingo sat at the curb, his face patiently watching the doorway. Bob got a glimpse inside the store. It was small and densely packed with goods. Maggie had her back to him, picking through lemons. She already had a lettuce in her hand.

With sudden decision he walked forward smoothly, unhooked Dingo's leash, and turned back to the car. The dog whined and pranced around his knees. Bob ignored him. He didn't want to attract attention.

He got into the car, started it, and pulled out quickly. He waited until he was at least five blocks away before he parked in a bus stop and hugged Dingo. The dog was teary-eyed with pleasure.

"Good dog, good dog, good dog, Dingo," Bob crooned. "We're together again." Dingo's tongue, snaky and tinted brown at the edges, flung itself all over Bob's face, stupid with happiness.

"Enough," Bob said finally, "sit!" Dingo sat next to him, his tail wagging, one paw scratching at his arm.

"Leaving a dog tied outside in New York," Bob said self-righteously. "She deserved to lose you. Thank God I was the one to take you! You

The Made-up Man   169

and me, Dingo," he said happily, the simple straightforward audacity of his act striking him at last. How marvelous to do something without hesitation, to do something good—for he had no doubt that it would be good for Dingo to be back with him, since Maggie was not caring enough. And it certainly was good for him.

He spent the evening with the dog. He got dog food, toys, a brush, and he brushed him for half an hour, then played "pull" with a toy, then took him for a long, long walk around the neighborhood. Dingo bounded and bounced, marking his old favorite spots, chuffing with pleasure.

"I could have done this long ago," Bob thought. "Peter will never figure it out. He doesn't come here anymore."

And how would this new development sit with Peter? His dog stolen because of Maggie's carelessness? Peter knew what happened to dogs lost that way—sold to laboratories; tortured for what was left of their lives in some useless experiment. Peter wouldn't forgive Maggie on this one.

Having Dingo back made him feel steady again. Those beautiful dog eyes, that beautiful dog snout, the panting, the tail-wagging, the utter joy of being recognized and loved. Dingo was the only creature who knew him for what he was, who did not discriminate between Alyson and Bob.

So he sunk himself in the dog over the weekend, not even realizing that Anna was probably expecting him, that the least he could do would be to call her and let her know that he wasn't coming over as he usually did. He was too wrapped up in Dingo.

On Sunday he asked around and found a boy who would walk Dingo after school. Then he took the dog for a walk in Tompkins Square Park, letting him off the leash for a bit, watching him run.

It wasn't until he was heading for work Monday morning, as he thought of telling Anna (he would tell her the truth; she knew about Peter and Maggie, and it would be good to have her involved in the secret; she would be so much more on her guard if one of them showed up)—when he realized, with a start, that he hadn't even called her.

It was not intentional: at least he hadn't deliberately decided not to visit Anna that weekend. They had an unspoken agreement. She expected him; she made dinner on Saturday nights even though they both maintained that his arrivals Saturday night and his departures Sunday night were entirely unpremeditated. They counted on it anyway.

He was happy to be with her, serene, domestic, helpful, compliant, and occasionally spontaneous. He brought her flowers, stacks of flowers, and they filled vases and juice jars and laid them everywhere, on the tables, on the floors.

He brought her out-of-season fruits, raspberries like candies, kiwis somehow suggestive of sex, globes of grapes that split open before they even met a tooth, and then strange mushrooms, enoki and morel, and slender, velvet-tipped asparagus, and together they eyed these things, white and green and brown, quivering on the verge of discussing their suggestiveness, looking at them out of the corner of their eyes, furtive, sly grins shaping their mouths. They ate a lot of them raw, nibbling first at the fungusy heads, inserting the stalks into cream-colored dips or pale pink dips, licking industriously, slowly, their tongues sliding back and forth.

Anna kept the lamps low, and they sat on the floor with the bowls and platters spread on the coffee table, moving slowly, languidly lifting a wrist or uncurling fingers, delicately touching the fresh-washed produce, drops of water beading like dew; they were almost humming, half-lidded, lips moist with their nibbling.

Sometimes they listened to music. Chopin was Anna's favorite, she played the Nocturnes relentlessly. Bob preferred Beethoven, but he would listen to anything. They licked their fingers and a record dropped and some inhuman sound drifted around them like a fog, and Anna or Bob would shift a leg in slow motion, as if drugged. They drooped towards each other as the hours passed, spent from the endless licking and sucking at their fingers, folding together closer and closer.

They murmured softly together in bed. Their modesty had slowly slipped aside, and they lay together unclothed. Anna's breasts were like speckled pears, her nipples brownish-red dropping lower and lower to her belly. His balls were like Redouté's nectarines, firm and fresh, hanging cheek to cheek. He maintained a fiction of sexual confusion, a sort of sexual middle ground, and she accepted it.

He felt at times overflowing. It seemed indecent not to make love fully. But any touch or move that went beyond Anna's arbitrary limits made her back stiffen in indecision. He had been aroused and fully erect a number of times by now, but Anna had told him she didn't want sex based on indecision, and he had respected that. He took himself off to the bathroom, panting discreetly while he relieved himself, watching his ejaculate hit the wall and then wiping it off. This repulsed him. He learned to place condoms in her medicine cabinet, and he covered himself from then on to be neat.

"Have you ever thought of having a child of your own?" Anna said quietly once as he slipped back into bed beside her.

"I've thought of it."

She laughed, slightly embarrassed. "You can donate to the sperm bank, you know. Save it up. For the future. In case someone agrees to have your baby."

He touched her arm lightly. "Have you ever thought that maybe *we* could have one together?"

She was silent for a moment, then nodded. "I have, but there's a lot happening before that question comes up. You should save your sperm." She hesitated. "And we could have it tested." He removed his hand, and lay on his back, staring at the ceiling.

"Sorry," she whispered.

"Of course you're right," he answered carefully. She turned over and put an arm around him.

"Sometimes you have to face reality."

"Funny. No one ever mentions reality when it's good news."

He thought about her suggestion however. Semen seemed to fall from him like a golden natural resource. He didn't think that each pool held a humunculus, a private small replica of himself, but it contained an emotional wealth worth something in the long run. From then on, whenever he felt like it, he neatly folded his condoms and placed them in a plastic bag in the freezer and took them home with him the next day.

He never told her he wasn't gay; Madame Hope had planted it in her mind and there was no easy way to change that, other than by doing what he was already doing—say he was reconsidering his sexuality; stay by her side and be attentive. He liked being with her and talking to her, listening to her. What they had was friendship plus these demanding physical promptings which he really believed would work out for them eventually.

But the fact was that he hadn't even called her that weekend, and he immediately felt defensive. He frowned. Maybe it didn't matter; maybe she had simply shrugged her shoulders, tapped the arm of her chair, and gone to a movie.

It would be awkward if she were annoyed. Why should she be? Had he made any promises? All right, they had a habit of getting together— but no promises, right? Could she blame him if he hadn't promised anything?

He hadn't said he would go, so he was technically in the right. That suited him. He had a better understanding, now, of freedom—of the potential in all sorts of situations. He had enjoyed pursuing Maggie, for example: not her personally, but he had set out to seduce her and he had succeeded. He had never before succeeded in controlling anyone, and control, when you finally got to taste it, was heady. Women can manipulate, too, but they lost, subtly, each time. In this day and age a woman who screwed around too much still lost status; a man gained by it. Unfair but true. He would never need to be embarrassed by Maggie: she had been used, and by definition she was devalued. He wasn't.

The smug smile that flirted with his lips wandered away.

It was strange to catch himself thinking this sort of thing. Not exactly feminism, was it? He was quiet for a moment, testing his own reaction. Did his attitude about women matter? Not really. Not at all. He could pick and choose—champion liberation when it benefited him, and still rely on the old double standard to get him through. He had decided not to be a woman; other women could do the same if they hated powerlessness. They could choose to be strong.

It was odd, too, how he had wanted to get even with Maggie even more than with Peter. He had wanted to hurt Peter and obliterate her.

Well, he had probably done that. First screwing her and then stealing the dog. Maggie was in for a hard time. Peter would be pushed beyond his limits. Peter liked to pretend an easy attitude towards life. "Keep it untroubled and clean." Hadn't he once said that, smugly, about his music? And didn't he always think that was his aim, no matter how convoluted his life got? If nothing else, he would be forced to acknowledge he'd been had. He would hate that. It had never happened to him before. It would be obvious that his life had turned to shit after leaving Alyson. As well it should.

But, still, he would have to approach Anna wisely. He liked her; they were compatible. She was his long-term plan. If he wanted a baby of his own, she could turn out to be handy. A baby might be a nice thing. He could imagine holding it, crooning, watching its delicate deep eyes learn to focus, stroking the smooth refinement of its skin. And Anna would take care of all its messy, demanding needs. So many women hesitated about giving up their lives to be controlled by a howling fury. But when they did, an amazing thing happened, they were totally taken in, their ears were constantly listening for the baby's cry, the baby's laugh, and the rest of the world lay discarded like an outgrown toy.

He wouldn't have to be so circumscribed. Maybe he would miss out on that obsessive bonding, but then again, he was perfectly free to take as much of it as he desired, and escape whenever he wanted.

To be honest, Anna had no great emotional hold over him. That, too, could be an advantage. He liked her, he could talk to her. And never again would he lose his own boundaries, overflow into another person. It was much, much better not to.

Actually, if she turned out to be jealous or annoyed because he hadn't called her, that would be a good sign, it would indicate that he mattered. He could make it up to her. How had Peter always done it? Not flowers, never flowers, it was too embarrassing a cliche. Paying attention, being solicitous. Dinner to make amends and get confidential again. And then, a day or two later, a small, impulsive gift, either silly or small and delicate. Never anything large. Something that could be hidden in a pocket and brought out at the right moment. A pin, a scarf, a book, something personal. But whatever it was, it had to be small.

Chapter 18

The meeting consisted of Maggie, Bob, Pierre and Eliot.

Maggie came armed with all the figures, neatly arranged in a series of folders. She was carefully dressed in a turquoise skirt and jacket. Low heels, a white pleated shirt with a marble pin at the throat. She kept her eyes firmly on Pierre or her notes.

"How are things, Maggie?" Bob asked as he took her coat and hung it up.

"Fine," she said curtly. "Your little joke was a success."

"Which joke was that, Maggie?" he asked softly.

She gave him a single, wary stare. "Just how many did you pull off?"

"Sometimes I lose track," he answered sweetly.

Two little spots of color appeared on her cheeks.

Pierre picked up on Maggie's mood immediately and used his high-powered smile, looking at her intently, complimenting her. He tossed a quick amused glance at Bob, who raised his eyebrows in mock helplessness. Maggie caught the look; Bob meant her to.

She had, however, done an impressive job. She had interviews lined up for the contest winner on the local radio station and spots for TV stations, including one from New York. Bob was surprised to learn, as well, of the magazines and newspapers who had given promises to mention it. Obviously, Adpub had good connections; he should have guessed that.

There were 600 registered and paid contestants. The winner's purse now stood at $1,500; the Red Cross had been promised $5 per entrant as a charitable donation. The Red Cross was setting up a number of emergency stations, most at the starting line, since they had demanded the right to start the race. The last-minute clues were to be given only by their representatives, who would precede the instructions with a lecture on proper disaster protocol.

The numbers, it was agreed, were low. But Adpub was placing public service ads in publications all over New York, New Jersey and Connecticut in another week, and they would pick up a respectable number of last-minute participants.

"Of course the lead story for our next issue will be on the event," Pierre noted. "I admit I'm very excited about it myself. I imagine the two of you will have to pretty much camp up out there now? It will be difficult to spare you, Bob." He grinned decisively. "That's one of the reasons I thought a meeting was in order." He cleared his throat self-consciously and continued. "I like what you've been doing. You've shown a great deal of ingenuity and creativity. I don't want you to be bogged down in the day-to-day editorial processes. Eliot can handle that." Bob glanced quickly at Eliot, who succeeded in looking satisfied and meritorious. "Beginning with the next issue you'll be a senior editor. I can hire some more staff if Eliot can't handle the work, but I want you involved more with planning. Speaking of which, what's the next event supposed to be?"

Bob's eyes moved from Eliot's face, which had frozen into blank shock.

"Bigfoot," Bob said automatically. "I haven't discussed it with Maggie yet. I was going to suggest the Wildlife Fund or one of the endangered-species groups as a sponsor. There are more sightings in early summer." He glanced quickly around the room. He had sprung the idea without trying it out on anyone.

"Bigfoot," Pierre said quietly. He tapped his finger on his desk. "I've always wondered about that." Again he trailed off, thinking. "Of course, if we found him. . ."

"Someone always finds *something*," Bob assured him.

Pierre wagged his head. "I think you've got it now. It's definitely time for another Bigfoot story. The media would love it. Will love it." His voice gained assurance. "It's a great idea. This one will really fly." He turned to Maggie. "Don't you just love it?"

"It's thrilling," she said unemotionally. "But I'm afraid you'll have to get through it without me. Someone else will be taking over this project."

Everyone looked at her expectantly. Bob assumed, of course, that she was about to say she refused to work with him. But would she say why? And if she did, would it matter? He looked at Pierre apprehensively. Of course it would matter. Pierre was a businessman. You can flirt, you can romance, but never ruin a business relationship while there's still business to be done.

"I handed in my resignation this morning."

"I'm sorry to hear that," Pierre said promptly. "A better offer?"

"I'm giving myself a sabbatical. I have some personal business to take care of. But I wanted to make sure all the loose ends were tied up before I left." Her eyes strayed briefly to Bob. "I'll be working for a few more weeks, and of course I'll be available for any questions." She gathered her folders together and stood up.

"I think everything will go well—very well. I think you have a very good idea. And you certainly have someone capable of seeing things through. So," she took a self-conscious step towards the door, "if there's nothing else, I'd just like to say thank you. It's been an invaluable experience."

Pierre shook her hand, adding a compliment on her work. They stopped at the doorway; Pierre waited for Bob to take over.

He walked to the closet with Maggie and took out her coat.

"What are you planning to do?" he asked. He noticed that he even felt sympathetic. Is it so much easier to feel sorry when you know you've won?

She shrugged his question off. "Never mind that. I have to talk to you. Alone."

He withdrew his sympathy immediately. He should have known Maggie wouldn't let him off easily. Unconsciously, he took a step back.

"Don't be afraid," she sneered, "I'm not going to smack your wrist. There's something I have to tell you and I can't do it here."

"All right," he said reluctantly. "Do you want to meet for a drink?"

Her face flushed. "No. And no more surprises. I'll be at your place at eight."

"That should be fun," he said wryly.

She gave him a long, withering look and took her coat from his hands. He hated helping women into their coats, anyway. He never needed help getting into his.

*H*e thought, at first, that he would keep Dingo with him when Maggie came. But then he envisioned consequences. Maggie would tell Peter; perhaps having a common enemy would unite them. Maybe they would even manage to steal Dingo back again. He couldn't just claim that the dog had wandered home; if he did, then Maggie could take Dingo back to Peter. From their perspective, Bob had no right to the dog anyway.

No, it was safer to hide the dog. He asked Anna as soon as he thought of it. "Of course," she said quickly. "He's safe with me. Does he know any tricks? Or do I have to entertain him?"

"Just scratch his ears and tell him he's a genius. He falls for it every time."

"It's a male trait," she agreed.

"I'll bring the dog around seven. Maggie's coming at eight."

She came exactly at eight. Bob was unsure of the attitude to strike. Should he offer her a drink? Should he appear cool and unconcerned, or sarcastic and cruel? He tried them on mentally, in turns, but his difficulty was that he didn't know what she wanted, and that made it hard to prepare his role.

He straightened the apartment quickly, making sure the bed was made, the dishes done. He looked at his rooms with a critical eye. Who lived here? Bob or Alyson? He hadn't made much of an imprint of any sort, content to live with what remained when Peter left. There were pictures on the wall, of course; those he had never taken down. But there was little of his new personality in evidence.

It was supposed to be a sublet anyway, he argued; there was no reason to worry about what anyone would *think*, although it was just as well not to give your enemies room for speculation. And he supposed Maggie was an enemy.

She certainly came in with her jaw set. And she refused to give him her coat. "This won't take long," she said firmly. It looked like she intended to make a quick exit.

"Should I offer you a glass of wine?" he asked formally. "Or would you prefer a gun?"

They took seats opposite one another. Bob felt that he should have been wearing a smoking jacket or some striped silk robe. And Maggie should have worn more jewelry.

"No wine," she said. "In case you're wondering, you've been successful. Peter has left me. I don't know where he is." She raised her hand. "No, wait. Let me finish. I don't know all the details of your plot. That's why I'm here. Peter left because I'm pregnant."

Bob's mouth dropped open, and Maggie eyed him with a kind of triumph.

"Exactly two months' pregnant," she said. "And as hard as I tried to work it out, I can't swear it's Peter's child. The timing is too close. Of course, he says it isn't his. He says a lot of things, none of them very nice. He won't live with a woman who's having someone else's child. When I told him it was his, he laughed. He's barely spoken to me, anyhow. He walked around all hard and cold for a few days, then told me he was leaving." She bent her eyes to her hands.

"Can you blame him?"

"Of course I can," she said firmly. "He didn't care for me enough. He never paid enough attention. Why else did any of this happen? I didn't want it to."

She gave her defense without any sense of self-consciousness, as if it were enough. Bob snorted. "You sound like a child. You were never responsible for anything, were you? Not for getting involved with Peter when you knew he was living with Alyson; not for getting involved with me when you were living with Peter."

"Oh, we'll talk about responsibility in a minute," she said, her eyes glinting. "But right now, aren't you painting things rather black and white? People make themselves into victims. They have a responsibility, too, for being aware of what's going on, for taking care of business. In this case business is who you're living with. If you fail, you get fired. It's how the world works. But don't start mouthing at me about love and loyalty. I know all about it: those are the words people use when they've lost what they took for granted. I know," she said, setting her mouth hard. "I just used them the other day. With Peter." She grew quiet.

But Bob had stopped listening to her. What she'd said was finally hitting him. She was pregnant. At first he was simply surprised, then he thought it was a trick, and then he began to consider it.

"You're really pregnant?" he asked.

She nodded, her lips pressed tight.

"And you think it's mine?" He was stumbling mentally. He wished he had more time—time to think about this in private, to figure out what to do. A child.

"I'm clear about dates," she said. "The laws of probability are on your side." She leaned back in her chair, spreading her hands out on the arm of the chair, watching his confusion. "A kick in the pants, isn't it?"

"I've been thinking about having a child," he murmured. He closed his eyes for a moment; when he opened them he saw her looking at him with victory.

"You can go on thinking about it," she said. "Do you think I'd have a child of yours? If I knew it was Peter's, I'd have it. But I can't take the chance. It's yours, I know it, it's how this whole travesty *would* work out. Your child! Do you think I could go through with it, thinking it was yours? Deluding myself that maybe it was Peter's child, *maybe* I was wrong. And then, every so often, seeing something in it that reminded me of you?"

"How can you get rid of it? It's my child too," he protested.

"Is it my turn to talk about love and loyalty? You used me like a stick of wood you picked up to wipe shit off your shoes. I don't know why—I don't know how you became Alyson's personal avenger—but I never set out to hurt anyone, and you did. You see, even I have some moral standards. And one of those standards is not to bring more evil into the world." She paused. "Any child of yours would be evil."

Bob's face contorted; he thought instantly that she had found out, somehow, about his pact with the devil. But she glared at him spitefully. "I suppose you'll refuse to pay for the abortion, too, out of some sort of righteousness? Well, I'm not asking for money. I think I'll even get a certain pleasure out of it."

He leapt up and she flinched. "That's disgusting!" he hissed. He felt a shiver go through him. "You'll be killing my child."

"Yes." She said it coldly.

"Maggie, please. Whatever you think of me, it's your child too. And you can't get by with the arguments you're using. There's no terrible infection from me—no mystical scourge to pollute the generations. It's just a child. Think about it. And what if it isn't mine? What if it's Peter's child?"

Her mouth twisted. "Either way it's not going to get much for a father, is it? No. I won't do it."

"Maggie, I'll support it. I'll sign paternity papers. You know you want a child. We talked about it."

Her face clamped shut, tight and suspicious. "When did I ever talk to you about that?"

"We were talking about growing older," he said persuasively, "about what we would have when we're forty . . ." He stopped abruptly.

She eyed him. "That wasn't you. That was Alyson." Slowly her hand reared up and brushed her hair behind her ears. "So the plot thickens. Alyson told you that. Why would she tell you that? Do you see her?"

"No. I haven't seen her since she left."

"Still. You're not all that honest, as it turns out. So maybe you and

Alyson are an item." She considered it. "It doesn't make sense." She began to button her coat. "That's the problem with secrets, after a while they're too much trouble." She stood up. "Maybe all men like to forge secrets. Maybe they fill their lives with them. I don't care anymore. You can have your damn secrets. It's too much." She laughed. "That shows me something. I thought you were basically honest; I thought Peter was too." She turned to the door.

"Where is Peter?" he tried to ask the question idly, but he wanted badly to know.

She suddenly became alive. "Don't you mean who is Peter with? He's not the kind to lick his wounds in private."

"All right," he said. "Who is he staying with?"

"It's a good question. I've thought it over. He wouldn't tell me when he left. I have an idea, of course; actually, one or two. But you can't exactly call a friend up and ask if your lover is sleeping there, can you? There is a protocol. But don't you think it's a little—oh, I don't know—crude—for a man to plead his love to so many women in so short a time? I mean, why bother zipping up? Maybe he's cooing to some other fool. Why not? Right, Bob? It's only words, after all, and words don't count. You could say you loved someone, too, and not mean it? Couldn't you?"

She glared at him with such pointed hatred that he felt his face grow hot. Of course it was different for him; of course she deserved what she got, but still, the white-hot contempt, the belittling, raised a welt in his pride.

"I would never," he said slowly and carefully, "make love to someone without knowing exactly what I was doing."

"Of course. You wouldn't be cruel accidentally. I don't know which is worse. People who pretend to be innocent or the ones who want to teach you a lesson." She reached the door. "Still, I suppose the difference doesn't matter. It's the kind of stuff you flush away." She opened the door.

She was taking his child with her. "Maggie—wait! We have to talk! The baby—I want—"

"You got what you wanted," she spit out. "You got a scene and vengeance for God knows what. The rest of it has nothing to do with you. Because as far as I'm concerned, you're dead!"

She slammed the door, leaving Bob standing there, frozen. He remembered saying the same words to Peter. And Peter was now alone.

What did it matter if Maggie thought he was cruel or vicious? How could it possibly matter what that cheap, double-dealing bitch thought? He pushed the idea aside, his fingers flicking an invisible, minute Maggie away from him, like a gnat.

The mother of his child, however. Where was Madame Hope and what was she doing about it? He got up and put on his coat, his forehead wrinkled with a line straight across it. The more he thought about it, the angrier he got with the gypsy.

"*I* don't make babies," Madame Hope said gruffly, clamping down on her cigar when Bob approached her. She leaned against a flimsy counter she was making in the front room. The framework was already done; the gypsy was nailing plywood over it. She took the cigar out and stuck nails in the side of her mouth.

"Of course you don't make babies," Bob said shortly. "But you can cause them to be made, so to speak. And anyway, that's not my point."

"Your point is that you don't want Maggie to have an abortion. Even more, you don't see how I could *allow* her to have an abortion, since *you* don't want it."

"That's right." He stood as straight as he possibly could. He could feel his mouth heavily weighted down with a cold, impatient frown.

"Well, let's look at this," the gypsy said with a bright, clever tone to her voice as she drove a nail in. "Did you use contraceptives?" One eyebrow was raised, giving her an arch, maternal look, unsuitable with her cropped hair and cigar voice.

"No," he said impatiently. "I assumed Maggie—"

"Hmph. Typical. So, let's put it this way—you gave the responsibility whether to have a baby or not—completely to Maggie."

"I didn't *give* it to her!" he protested. "I forgot about it, that's all."

She laughed. "It came to the same thing, didn't it? And now you want the responsibility of whether or not she'll have a baby. The horse has rather bolted, hasn't it? And besides, I don't remember any particular agreement about it. You did say you wanted a family—you didn't say whose, you didn't say when. And what about that other one— Anna? How many wives and babies do you plan on?" She laughed and gave him a shrewd look. "Don't worry so much. You don't know what'll happen next. Funny she didn't come and tell you she'd already *had* an abortion, isn't it?"

"She wants me to *feel* it; she wants me to pay for it emotionally."

"Still, you never can tell with a thing like this, can you? She may change her mind." She hammered another nail in. "How do you like my counter? I think I've got a natural talent for carpentry, don't you?" She surveyed her work with pride.

"What's it for?" he asked, suddenly noting that it was an odd thing for a fortune teller.

"Mineral waters," she said. "With properties. For energy. For prowess. To quit smoking. All kinds." She harrumphed. "They'll have different labels."

"What for?" he cried. "Can't you find anything better to do?"

She took the remaining nail out of her mouth. "I expect to get a following. You see, they *will* have properties. I've always dealt with individuals, one at a time. That's too slow. There are too many empty hours. I don't feel at the top of my form. It occurred to me that a group would be a nice change. Oh, they'll like these waters, and they'll come back, and then they'll want to chat—quite curious at first as to why anything should work, in New York of all places! A magazine article or two, maybe a TV appearance. And I'll have friends—even if they're only those who drink my water. Maybe I'll be invited for dinner, maybe I'll run for office—local, you understand, something minor, at least at first. Parties! Benefits! That sort of thing could be fun.

"To actually be in the middle of things instead of just whispering into someone else's ear. Ah!" she sighed, "bribes. How I would love a bribe."

Bob exploded. "Concentrate on me! I don't want anything else slipping through my fingers because you're busy! You're like the super in my building: you always show up when the rent's to be paid, but where are you when the faucet leaks?"

"That's good!" she cried. "I like it! You're right, you know. A leaking faucet! A baby on the way! A sudden wrench and there goes the leak!"

He turned in disgust, slamming the door behind him, shutting out her final words: "And don't forget the rent! I'll see you when your lease is up!"

Chapter 19

*I*t came out of nowhere. All at once Bob looked up and a large black blur raced across the field, dragging a female shape in the snow. An excited, inarticulate roar burst from the crowds of men just spreading out from the starting point set up by the Red Cross.

Bob, startled by the sight, shouted "No! No! Let go! It's got her!" He was pointing wildly, and he sounded panicked. He wasn't panicked; it was sheer annoyance. It had taken over an hour for him to plant that dummy in the cliffs and hide his tracks in the snow. And suddenly he felt the whole contest collapse around him. How could anyone rescue a hidden "victim" if the victim was dragged out in front of everyone's noses?

It was a black dog, moreover, a familiar black dog, loping and insolent.

Pierre's profiles had been right; all the contestants were men, not a woman among them, and they'd divided themselves into groups dressed in red plaid jackets, or ski jackets, or skin-tight rock-climbing gear.

But there was blood in the air. It was the plaid-jacketed men who raised the loudest bellow. Their arms raked the air, deprived of guns, but Bob could almost feel the leap in their hearts. Maybe there would be blood after all, they thought, and their teeth showed between parted grins and they took off after it, whatever it was, "A wolf. A bear. A mountain cat." There was the smell of animal heat.

The dog disappeared quickly, its loping footprints burning deep into the ice and snow. Bob started after it half-heartedly. He had to elbow his way through a sudden surge of hard-breathing men and he fell behind almost at once. There was no reason to rush to the front. All his plans were ruined, totally ruined. He might as well call Pierre right now and resign. And what if those rushing, panting men turned on him, demanding money back, compensation for wasted time?

The men started dividing to left and right when they reached an outcrop of bushes and rocks. Bob heard their excited calls:

"I saw it go to the right."

"No! To the left!"

"It went up the mountain!"

Rock climbers were finding toeholds in the sheer face of the cliff, and cross-country skiers were taking the seemingly long-way around the outcropping to the fields and frozen lake beyond.

Just as he'd planned.

He stood still, looking carefully around at all the excited, purposeful, stalking men, some of them already running or skiing or simply ducking out of sight.

Where had the damn dog gone? He scanned the horizon and there, to the right, on a low hill, he saw a squat figure, almost as wide as tall, and even at this hour with a cigar in her mouth (of course it could just be her breath; everyone breathed steam here). He was sure it was Madame Hope, and that meant the dog (*her* dog, that hostile, glaring wretch, grown huge with a winter fur coat, a snow beast's coat)—the dog was a plant.

He walked back down the slopes to the lodge. He heard the ring and call of voices, farther and farther away. Along the highway, there were waiting ambulances with flashing lights, there were news vans and stamping, chilled, microphone-holding reporters taking turns laughing and being stern, training their cameras on dozens of disappearing backs, passing the time with stragglers or those already quitting because of the cold or twisted ankles or forgotten packs of cigarettes. The Red Cross set up its vats of coffee and rows of donuts. The snow was being trampled into slush. And, as far as Bob could tell, everything was going well.

He went back to his room at the top of the lodge, where he could get a better look. He felt like the king of his own mountain, he realized, as he focused his binoculars on the white and gray world in front of him.

The men had spread out in every direction over the living map in front of him. Bob could see the bumping black speck that was the devil's dog crossing back and forth at intervals, sometimes even doubling back behind a line of men, confusing their footprints.

And to the right, on her own small precipice, arms crossed, head turned, standing smug as a rock, the fortuneteller nodded contemptuously, rolling her cigar back and forth on her tongue, or so Bob imagined. He phoned for coffee and stood at the window, watching, until it came. And then he stood and watched some more as he drank it. The dog finally ran out of sight and when he looked again, the figure of the fortuneteller had gone.

And then, suddenly, two commotions began from two opposite directions. Bob saw figures running and gesticulating wildly at the finish line, and then the Red Cross began to scurry and the ambulances turned and pulled closer, and the camera crews flashed and raced out.

Bob grabbed his jacket and ran down the stairs, puffing wildly. He pushed his way through the dawdlers to one of the Red Cross tents. "What is it?" he barked.

"A child. They rescued a child from the water. Submerged, I think."

Bob continued to push, listening to the snatches of talk.

The child was in the ambulance, and breathing on its own. He got close just as the ambulance took off and the TV reporters spoke seriously into their microphones. One of them even grabbed Bob for a statement.

"I don't really know what happened," Bob said, blinking into the camera. "But my god how lucky we were to be here." He shook his head momentously, and then he moved on to the main tent, where two men were the center of attention. They were being slapped on the back and offered coffee; they lifted their chins stonily, looking people in the eye, as if to convince themselves they had really been heroes. Bob went over, congratulating them.

"I don't know," one man said. "What was a kid doing there like that? I mean alone. What was he—eight, nine? Where were the parents?"

"Scared the shit out of me," his partner agreed. "Thought it was that dummy with its hand sticking out of the ice. But it wasn't." His head wobbled, still amazed.

"Damnedest thing."

"Damnedest. You said it."

Bob walked away. His steps led over to the finish line, where, almost unnoticed, the winner stood being photographed with the dummy in his arms.

The reporter looked very young and clutched a tape recorder.

"I don't care," the winner said stoically. "I don't mind. I'm the one that gets the money anyhow. They can get all the publicity they want. It was a damn fine thing they did, saving that boy. I would have done it myself, any full-blooded American would have done it. Good for them, I say. But I get the money." He grinned into the camera.

Bob stepped forward, reaching out his hand, and the camera snapped again.

"An exceptional job," Pierre said, beaming, as he came towards Bob, his hand extended. "Better than anyone could have hoped. We've got interviews lined up, the phones have been ringing like mad, TV spots and front-page photos. Thank God, it was a slow news day." He laughed. "Slow! The rest of the world must have been asleep, we got so much coverage."

Bob nodded. "I managed to get things put on hold for a bit."

Pierre laughed. "Too much confidence can get you hanged." He stood, squeezed Bob's arm and let go. "But that might not be bad for circulation either."

"There's a part of me that isn't a company man," Bob said. "It's concentrating hard on not being hanged."

"Fine, fine," Pierre said. "We'll have a celebration at lunchtime. The whole office. I've ordered food, even champagne. A small speech would be nice." He sailed off in his smooth, happy walk.

Bob was thumbing through a pile of letters absent-mindedly when Anna came in.

"Welcome back." She leaned against the wall comfortably, the toe of one foot hooked behind the ankle of the other. "You've had it tough," she grinned. "All that adulation. All that success. I kept switching the channels but there you always were."

He sat straight up. "You kept switching the channels?"

"Well, I was annoyed, you know. Maybe even bitter. Certainly resentful. They wouldn't even take messages for you at that hotel, you know. Not after the race. Apparently everyone who wanted to get in touch with you claimed to be a 'very close personal friend.' " She lowered her eyelids lazily. "I hate competition."

He was settling down happily now. "There's not much competition, really. So few of the others are pregnant. And none of them were taking care of my dog."

"He snores," she said. "He chuffs and mutters and makes yipping sounds. Either he misses you or he has a guilty conscience."

"He misses me."

"At first when I mentioned your name he whined and wagged his tail. Yesterday he sneezed. I think he's over you."

"Maybe you're a little jealous," he smiled.

"Of your dog?"

"Of my success."

She shrugged. "You've been heading for success on a collision course. Even I could see it. It was just a question of time." She smiled. "Actually, I'm enjoying your success. It seems so strange when you know the person involved. Don't you think so? I mean, don't you feel just a little bit like you might be unmasked at any moment, that they'll see it was just an accident, like winning a lottery prize?"

"A five-minute wonder?"

"I mean, what happened? The contest would have been forgettable—a good idea, but there're lots of good ideas around—except that a child almost died."

"Yes, that was the turning point," he said slowly.

"He had a test and cut school. He found a thin spot on the lake. It happens. I won't hold it against you." Her smile seemed mischievous, even knowing.

"Hold what against me?"

"How fortunes change. I've decided to take the good with the bad, for better or for worse. I've heard that the good is the hardest part, anyway. But I think I can keep you straight. So to speak. If you want."

She continued to grin at him, steadily and consciously. He creased his forehead, puzzled.

"You goon," she said affectionately, "you slow lughead. I'm asking you to marry me."

His mouth dropped open.

"It was your idea, you know. I've just thought it through for a long time. It makes sense. It's not a capitulation of any kind. It's an economic and parental partnership. We like each other and we'll love the baby." She patted her stomach gently.

"You're starting to show," he said.

"I am," she said with satisfaction. "I even jut myself out for effect. I'm going to announce it today. I'm going to tell all the egos here that I am with child. They'll pretend to be pleased for me and they'll think maybe they can get someone prettier and more accommodating to replace me. I'll tell them I'm coming back after the baby is born and they'll think I won't. But I don't care. I'm having a baby and I believe everything will work out. Are you taking time to decide?"

His head snapped up and he smiled slightly. "You've changed my train of thought entirely."

"Well, will you?" A slow flush was edging from her cheeks outwards. Her smile was stuck hopefully on her face, but her eyes had lost some of their glitter. She had shifted her weight away from the wall; she was ready to flee.

"Yes," he said casually. "Yes." He paused then added, "I want a child." It was almost as if he were thinking out loud.

"The next one can be yours," she promised. "Maybe we'll shoot for twins. You're on a roll."

$\mathcal{T}$he food at Pierre's party was molded, not simply spread out in overlapping circles or heaped in mounds. The pâté was in the shape of a dog; there was a pudding "lake" covered by white lemon icing and ringed by mountains of meringue and whipped cream.

It made Bob uneasy because he had never thought Pierre capable of bad taste, and this was bad taste. There was too much food—too much potato salad shaped like a mountain, with parsley bushes and celery trees, and sun-dried tomatoes in the shape of a red cross; too many rolls heaped to look like an avalanche down a mound of stuffed endive. All this was in the middle of their overcrowded office, spread out on folding tables covered by rented linen tablecloths. Anna murmured in disbelief, "This cost a fortune. We could have eaten out!"

But Pierre gleamed. He showed no self-consciousness, no embarrassment. He laughed at the molded foods. Was this irony? Was Pierre making fun of catered luncheons? Bob couldn't figure it out.

Pierre uncorked the first bottle of champagne. There were real glasses, not plastic, and cloth napkins, not paper.

"Less than a week ago," Pierre announced, "we were a name that had never been mentioned on air, we had a face that no one had seen, and a product without an edge in a very competitive market." He paused to look quickly around the room in a friendly and encouraging manner. "We knocked ourselves silly. You all did an incredible job. And we would have made it, sooner or later, just because of the great drive and creativity of all of you. If we've made it sooner than anyone had a right to expect, it's because of one person in our organization." He raised his glass. "To Bob," he said. "Huzzah."

Everyone murmured congratulations and drank their champagne. "Thank you," Bob answered. "Of course I owe my success more to perspiration than to inspiration, and more to luck than anything else.

But I'm grateful to Pierre—who gave me the chance to try something out—and I'm glad, completely overwhelmed, that we were lucky enough to be there when a child needed us to be there." He raised his glass briefly and then drank.

Pierre patted him quickly on the shoulders. "And to continue on that note, we've started a small fund for that child. I'm sure you're all aware that he suffered some brain-damage and will require a lot of rehabilitation. The magazine will set up a running medical fund for him. To his health and recovery!" he cried and everyone drank, Bob slowly and stiffly, with his eyes focused blindly off to the distance. Would that child have been there anyway? he wondered. He forced himself to picture it over and over again, until he could think of it without his heart thudding.

Eliot stood off to one side, impeccably dressed, sneering to himself. After a few moments, as people hovered around the food, Bob became aware of him. He disliked the look on Eliot's face; he disliked how well Eliot managed to hold on to his contempt, as if Bob's success could be outwaited. He watched as Eliot stepped up to Pierre and said something to him in a low voice. Pierre laughed and Eliot's eyes darted over to Bob to make sure he was watching. He felt the beginning of a flush rising from his neck. He tried to waylay it by drinking his champagne quickly and pouring another. He ended up next to Anna. They were within Eliot's earshot if he spoke loud enough.

"You're not drinking?" he asked in a stage whisper.

She shook her head. Eliot's eyes settled on them. Bob imagined him thinking, "The fag and his buddy." Eliot's fingers groomed his mustache carefully. Bob mimicked him, rubbing his upper lip. He leaned closer to Anna. "Now?" he asked tenderly.

She grinned at him, her eyes twinkling. "I think you're going to enjoy this even more than I am."

"I think you're right." He squeezed her arm, taking hold near the wrist. His other hand still held champagne.

"There's another announcement," he said, raising his voice. He tightened his hold on Anna, pulling her slightly forward.

She cleared her throat with a quick hum and stuck her chin up. "I'll be taking some leave at the end of the summer," she said in a voice that shook slightly. "Maternity leave." She laughed in an undertone and looked around, quick, to catch expressions.

Pierre's smile had spread wide; it was the smile he reserved for clients. Eliot was watching carefully.

"And sometime soon, in a whirl of passion, Anna and I will get married. Happily married." Bob stared directly at Eliot.

"On skis?" Pierre smiled, stepping forward to shake Bob's hand. "The magazine would pay. It might make a story." He added the right inflection, a touch of something slightly mocking, leaving them free to take it as a joke or not.

"I can't ski," Anna said flatly.

"Bob!" someone yelled. "Phone!" And as he turned away to pick up the line he heard Pierre's voice asking, "What can you do, then? I don't suppose you skate?"

He was laughing to himself as he picked up the phone, but that changed as soon as he heard Maggie's voice.

"I have to see you," she said. "It's important. Everything's changed. Can you meet me tonight at eight?"

"Tonight?" he repeated.

"I think you'll be interested. I'll come to your place."

"Okay," he agreed. "My place at eight," and before he could ask anything, she hung up.

He turned to find Eliot standing at his elbow. "Another announcement?" Eliot asked wickedly. "We're all dying for an encore."

Chapter 20

$\mathscr{A}$nna was disappointed rather than suspicious when Bob told her he had something lined up for the evening. A celebration would be better on the weekend, he said; they would have the fun of planning it. Just keep Dingo one more day, please; he had some loose ends to tie up. "It's just poor planning; I've lost control of my time. Tomorrow will be clear," he promised.

"No problem," Anna said. "He puts his head on my foot when I watch TV. It's like holding hands."

"Years of deprivation," Bob murmured sympathetically, "drove her to the arms of a dog."

He kissed her on the cheek when she left work and he headed back downtown. He was nervous; he tossed aside various explanations for Maggie's call. He stopped at a liquor store to buy a few bottles of wine; he picked up cheese and bread and grapes. "I'm being a hostess," he thought, but he went through with it anyway.

He grabbed the mail on the way up and dropped it on the counter. He put one bottle of wine in the refrigerator, then opened another and put it out on a side table. He put out three wine glasses—the third was merely for effect.

He was ready with time to spare, so he started glancing through the mail. There, hidden slyly between bills and magazines, was a letter from Peter. It was addressed to Alyson, with a note to forward it.

His hand shook as he opened it.

At first, Peter's handwriting looked abstractly familiar. Then it settled and became intimate, and he could hear Peter's voice as he read it:

I don't know what to say or how to say it. I've made a terrible mistake, but I guess you know that.

I was mixed up; I didn't know what I was doing. I guess I was afraid of being so close to one person (you) and I couldn't accept the idea that it would be for life.

I'm not afraid anymore, Alyson. I know what I want. In the process I've done terrible things. Some of them you know about, some you don't.

Can you ever forgive me? I know I love you, and I know I'll love you forever. I came across a photo of you when I was packing (I've left Maggie) and your beauty leapt up at me. Alyson, I just want to see you again, talk to you again. If there's any way in hell that I can convince you to take me back, I will. I'd do anything to be with you– to see you–to touch you. I'd give twenty years of my life–no, more, I'd give it all. I love you. Forever."

Bob closed his eyes and sagged against the sofa. The bell rang. It was eight o'clock. Maggie. He hid the letter quickly, sticking it under a cushion. He had a thick feeling in his head.

Maggie walked in the door quickly, not even bothering to take her coat off. She sat down on the same side of the sofa as she had the last time she was there.

"I haven't had the abortion," she said, smoothing her coat out. She leaned forward with her knees together.

"No?" He was determined not to indulge her. Interest, emotion of any sort, would gratify her. He could tell by her high color.

"It took me a week to get the appointment. A week gave me time to think. So I cancelled it to make it easier to think. And it's true, however you learned about it, the thought of a child has crossed my mind. I'm usually very careful. If I wasn't careful I have to assume it was for a reason. I must have wanted a child. And not just theoretically, but actually. That's why it was so hard to go through with an abortion. If I'm responsible, then I have to face that responsibility. I'm not sixteen, I'm not ignorant, I'm old enough to face the consequences of my acts, even if no one else is." She glared at him.

"You're having the baby," he said. He was trying very hard to pay attention, to keep his mind focused on what was happening in front of him. A baby, a baby, he kept reminding himself, trying to make it feel important, but his mind kept straying back to the letter under the cushion Maggie sat on.

"I'm having your baby," she said flatly. "Oh, it's yours. We can get some blood tests done if you want. I know you're the father, but I don't want any question. There's just one thing," she said, lowering her head to stare at her hands.

"Yes?"

"When you know it's your child, when you're absolutely sure, I don't want just paternity papers. I want the child to have every legal protection it can get. I want marriage. I don't care how long it lasts, as long as we make it till the baby's born. After that you can go your way. I want this child to feel normal. Divorce is normal everywhere now; illegitimacy still isn't and I'm not going to stick that on anyone. Get it?" she asked fiercely, her hands squashed tight into each other.

"Of course I'll marry you," Bob said automatically. He even managed a small smile. All he wanted was to get her out of there so he could think. There was too much happening too fast, and he couldn't deal with it off the top of his head. He needed to be alone, to re-read Peter's letter, to think. There was even a part of him that said marrying Maggie would be a good idea, certainly better than taking on Anna's child; of course; this was *his* child. And just think what a crushing blow this would be for Peter!

At that his eyes squinted. His face was frozen in a conciliatory grin as he escorted Maggie to the door, carrying on some kind of conversation, just filling in words. The picture kept changing in front of his eyes. It was insulting how Peter thought he could just write a letter and everything would be forgiven. As if Alyson would take any scrap of love from him.

On the other hand, Maggie was the kind of person who got what she wanted; she was pretty good at manipulating people. Peter was too romantic, that was it, lured away by fantasies. A little throb of tenderness pulsed in Bob's heart.

He picked up the letter, reading it distractedly, then put it in his pocket. If he went through with this—married Maggie, raised this child—then it was the final admission that his former life was gone for good. Well, you couldn't have it both ways, he thought reasonably. His former life *was* gone for good. He wasn't a woman any longer, he was a man who'd managed to get everything he'd ever wanted. Success, fame, even; marriage; children of his own.

His put on his coat automatically and went outside.

Everything except love, in fact.

And how important was that?

His stride slowed, he almost came to a stop, but then he began to pick up again. After all, he'd loved Peter, and that had brought misery.

Of course, if he were still a woman, Peter's return would be rather wonderful.

Maybe, if he'd stayed a woman and put up with these last dreadful months, maybe everything would have worked out in the end. Rather a sobering thought. Sometimes people needed time to work things out—needed, in fact, a substitution like Maggie, a sort of compare-and-contrast experience, something to cleanse the palate, just to reaffirm one's sense of taste.

At that he stopped walking altogether and he had a clear, piercing image of Peter opening the door to their apartment, the sound of his impetuous step, the feel of his arms, the way he half-swung her in a hug. . . . He was sobbing on the street. People were staring at him over their shoulders.

To calm himself he imagined Maggie with a small child in her arms. Or Anna with a child.

But Peter reappeared over their shoulders, and it became a kind of contest, a child's blank face vying with Peter's very real one. In his mind he kept straying to Peter's face, kept hearing Peter's voice. "Alyson? Alyson, please?" Peter whispered, and held out his hand.

It's no use, Bob thought desperately, I still love him, I want him more than anything I have, this has all been a charade, just a trick to try to keep myself from thinking about him. It doesn't matter—whatever I do, wherever I go, I can't put him out of my mind. Get even with him, get back with him, it's all the same. It just means he's the part of my body that's been ripped from me. How could I think revenge would cure it?

A tear snaked its way down his cheek.

I'd give anything to have him back, he thought. He laughed at himself contemptuously. He was the wrong sex now for *that*. What could he do? Go for surgery? It took years, and Peter was not known for either patience or concentration. He couldn't bargain his soul again, could he? With what as a bargaining chip?

His hand crept to his pocket, to feel it again. There it was, proof of love. He stopped twice under a streetlight to re-read it. He shook his head, he stamped his foot, he threw his hands up in the air melodramatically. What irony there was in it! What unappeasable irony! He couldn't even concentrate on it properly—his mind kept skipping around, considering all the possibilities. Anna and her baby. Maggie and his baby. Showing Eliot up, once and for all. Microphones pushed in his face, applause in his ears, a large black dog loping across a white frozen lake. And—he couldn't help himself—how wonderful it would be to be pregnant with Peter's child!

He had to find a way out, a way back. He'd been insane with grief, not rational, surely the bargain didn't count under those circumstances. He'd made some terrible mistake, that was it. Surely he couldn't be held to a mistake he'd made while completely insane? He found himself outside the gypsy's storefront again. His face was reflected back from the glass storefront, and he stood there, looking at a man, knowing in his heart he still loved Peter the old way, and always would. And then he smiled.

The street door had a sign that said Please Come In. The counter in the front room was finished. It was merely a long rectangular box waist-high with a single shelf. Dark blue felt was stapled down on it and then the various bottles were arranged by shape, with small hand-written signs propped in front of each group. The cards said Concentration, Success, Potency, Energy, Patience, Wisdom, Happiness. Even a quick glance revealed how poorly the counter was made. There was a nail sticking out at the side that already had a thread hanging from it. Unfortunately, too, it wasn't level.

The gypsy came hurrying through the doorway, rubbing her hands. She was wearing a long cotton multicolored skirt, gathered in many folds around her tubular figure, and an off-white ribbed sweater. She wore a blue plaid kerchief wrapped around her head, and the omnipresent cigar gave the whole outfit a false note, like an actor stepping out of character.

"I thought you were business," the fortuneteller muttered. "Can you believe it? The mineral-water craze is over. It's peaked. It was in the newspapers, that's how out-of-date it is! My timing's off. It used to be I was right on the money; I've let myself get distracted somehow." She shook her head. "Boredom. No challenge. I'm not active enough. Atrophy. The brain is a muscle. Or is that the heart?" She raised an eyebrow. "Do you know?" She sucked on her cigar.

"I had a surprise today," he said flatly.

"Let me see. Ticker-tape parade? A couple of marriage proposals? Buns in all the ovens? A red-letter day, I think. Better mark your calendar." She chortled, rolling her cigar between her fingers.

"I got a letter from Peter."

"A flutter of the heart?" she asked. "A cramp in the old muscle?"

"I want him back."

"Sloppy thinking!" Madame Hope snapped contemptuously.

"Maybe you haven't noticed the way things have changed in the past few months."

"I don't like the change anymore," Bob insisted.

Madame Hope snorted. "What a crying shame. And yet maybe you're not up to snuff yourself tonight. Maybe you're overlooking a few obvious things. You're making twice as much money as you were a few short months ago; you're a successful man—you're in the papers and on TV. You've got more women and babies than you know what to do with; you've got your dog back. And you can have more! More women! More babies! There's nothing to stop you! The American Dream come true!" She clutched her hands over her heart, eyes lifted upward.

"I don't want any of that," Bob said defiantly. "Not as a man. Peter wants me back. And I want him; I want him more than any of those other things I can have."

Madame Hope narrowed her eyes. "Tough luck. We have a bargain!"

"No," Bob said, shaking his head. "You didn't keep your end of it. I want out."

The gypsy rolled her cigar slowly and narrowed her eyes. She leaned toward Bob. "What are you talking about? I gave you everything I promised."

"I wanted to be a man."

"Check your pants pocket, sonny."

"Physically, yes, I'm male," Bob said earnestly. "You've got it all down right, I'm even going bald. But if I were truly a man I wouldn't care about Peter anymore, would I?"

"Preferential logic," the gypsy spat. "You've never heard of gay?"

"The bargain didn't include being gay."

"Didn't exclude it either," the gypsy shrugged.

"Oh yes it did. I said all the advantages of being a man. Being gay isn't an advantage, it's almost exactly as bad as being a woman. As a matter of fact you blew it by even letting *one* person around me think I was gay. And you did it with a whole office!" He clenched his fist.

Madame Hope scowled. "There are no loopholes. If you had any problems you should have raised them earlier. It's a little late now, after all the trouble I've been to—"

"I don't care about the trouble you've been to. You weren't doing it out of charity, and besides, you didn't do it well enough. You don't know how to keep the bargain, that's obvious. You don't understand the finer points. So forget it. No deal. Back to the starting point."

The gypsy's face had grown a dark, unpleasant red. She scowled fiercely, jabbing her cigar. "Coward. Little worm. So you won't stick to your word because you think you can get a better deal elsewhere?"

"Because you didn't keep your side of the bargain," he insisted.

"Bullshit! You got everything you wanted and more. You've got no concept of honor, your word doesn't mean anything, you want a look at the fine print, eh? You had secret reservations all along, you wanted a test trip, you never *really* thought this would happen, eh? I've heard it before!" She raised her hand to stop his protest. "Not really a man! Spare me! What do you think *you* know about it? You think it's like turning on a light bulb? It's got subtleties, complexities, ambiguities. You never heard of ambivalence? It comes with the territory."

"I want Peter. I still want Peter. That's the bottom line. And the only reason I bargained my soul in the first place was because I wanted Peter. So what really changed? Am I really a man? Or did you leave too much of Alyson behind? I want what she wanted and we both know that if I were truly a man, I wouldn't want what I wanted as a woman. So things haven't changed. So you have no right to my soul. And I demand that you restore me."

Madame Hope bit her lower lip. She picked up a bottle and rolled it in her hand. She seemed to be arguing with herself. After a moment her face relaxed and she smiled. "The contract is up at the end of your life," she said casually. "And I either get your soul then, or I don't. It's really kind of hard to judge whether you've had a satisfactory life or not until you're dead. Things can change up to the very last minute; pleasures are so erratic."

She began to pour water out of a pitcher into the bottles, filling up the rows. She took on the air of a competent shopkeeper, friendly but firm. "I don't have to do anything for you, except as it interests me. You see, you come at things from the wrong direction all the time. You could tell me that you've got a new spin, that your story as a man was falling apart, that there would be more intrigue if you were a woman again. I like a good soap opera myself, passions always perk me up. I'm reasonable, see?" she said, grinning wide enough to show all her teeth. She picked up a rag and began wiping the bottles. "And I've got to admit, I've got a weakness for star-crossed lovers. I keep cheering for them to get together again." She put down her bottles, sighed loudly and pleasantly, and patted Bob on the shoulder. "I like selling the joy jars the best," she whispered. "You know—Happiness, Love, Success." She patted her heart. "I was a regular Cupid when I was young."

"Does this mean you'll do it?" Bob asked. "I'll be a woman again?"

"I'm a sucker for this sort of thing." She took out a hankie from under her sweater and dabbed at her eyes.

Bob was suspicious. "No tricks," he said quickly.

"It'll be just like you never were a man at all. No one will even think about a guy called Bob."

"And my job?"

"Well, maybe your salary will drop a little. But the glory's still yours. You'll just be on your own from now on. If it's a flop, don't blame me."

"And Peter? Peter will still love me?"

"That's the whole point, isn't it? You two breathing heavily?"

Bob grabbed her hand. "That's it, then? No loose ends?"

"I can't think of anything," the gypsy smiled.

"Okay," he sighed explosively. "I guess I'm off." He waited to see if she had any final words.

"Give me a week," she said, walking him to the door. "Time to get everything in order." She laughed. "I can hear those wedding bells ringing! Name the first-born after me, now, won't you?" And with that she closed the door on Bob, waving at him once distractedly, and then turning back to her tilting counter and the ordinary water that she called happiness.

Bob found a stationery store on the way home and picked out a blank card with an orchid on the outside. He wrote the following note inside after he'd paid the cashier:

> Yes, we must meet again. Come over next Monday night at eight. Bob will be gone by then.

He mailed it immediately. He laughed as he walked down the street, with his head thrown back and his hand over his mouth, and he thought, "I'm laughing like a woman." He watched for glimpses of himself in store windows. He stopped at a boutique, greedily looking at the clothes. His hair—would his hair grow back? He would have to wear a scarf or a hat in the meantime. He would have to get some makeup, there was nothing at home.

And he wouldn't have to make any explanations to anyone. He could put off Anna and Maggie for a week—and all his promises would become nonexistent! He could peel off honeymoons for both women, swear anything, anything, big guy, fat cat, everybody's prince, make them happy for a while; and they wouldn't regret it because they wouldn't remember it. And in the end he would get his own fairytale come-true.

He fell asleep faster than he thought he would, although his head was filled with fast-moving images. As soon as he crawled into bed he curled up with his knees bent and both hands cupped protectively over his genitals.

The next morning he shaved off his mustache.

"Oh," Anna said, disappointed. "And you didn't tell me you would."

"I want to face the future with a clean slate," he said gaily.

"You look flushed. Are you okay?"

"Truthfully, Anna, I think I'm the happiest person on earth." He dragged one arm around her and squeezed.

"That's nice," Anna grinned. "That's very nice indeed."

"Let's go for wedding rings," he said. "During lunch."

Anna's eyes gleamed. "It's rather strange, being treated well."

He lowered his voice sympathetically. "Are you thinking of Jeff? Do you miss him?"

She tossed her head. "Him? I only hope he gets what he deserves." She laughed. "He's probably bald by this time," she said viciously. "I bet he's bald."

Bob fought to keep his hand from going up to his own thin hair. "There, there," he murmured.

"Sorry," she muttered sheepishly. "A stupid thing to say. I can't wait for lunch."

They found a small jeweler's booth on 47th Street that had exactly the plain gold bands they decided they wanted. Bob found a ring that fit, but none of them were the right size for Anna.

"It'll take a few days to get one," the jeweler said. "Maybe by Friday."

"We'll be back then," Bob promised.

They linked arms on the way back to the office, and Anna laughed joyfully at everything he said.

The next morning he called Maggie. "I've been looking at wedding rings," he said.

He could feel her surprise. "Rings?"

"I thought you might want to look at some with me."

"Yes," she said slowly. "I suppose we'll need rings."

He laughed softly. "Don't worry. I'm paying."

She met him for lunch and he went back to the same jeweler, who showed no trace of recognition. This time there was a ring that was the right size for Maggie. She studied it cautiously on her hand.

"You want them?" the jeweler asked.

"I think we want to look around some more," Bob said, raising his eyebrows quizzically at Maggie, who nodded.

"You never know," the jeweler said, winking at Bob. "Sometimes we get a run on these things. Sometimes everybody wants them."

Maggie stopped in the street outside and turned to Bob. "That was very considerate," she said formally. "Asking me to look at rings. I

Karen Heuler

guess maybe I don't understand everything you do, why you do it." She looked at her hands and then into Bob's face. "But I appreciate this. Thank you." And for the first time in over a month, she smiled at him, and then she kissed him lightly on the cheek.

Maybe he should buy them wedding dresses too, he thought to himself. But there probably was no time. Let them be happy for a day or two more, he thought expansively, before they forget they ever knew someone called Bob.

The office had Good Friday off, and by Thursday night Bob was feeling light-headed, giggly, wobbly and sore. He told Anna to stay away—"You can't come here. You're pregnant. What if you got sick and something happened?"—and Anna reluctantly agreed.

He found himself again dreaming of the cocktail party, but the mood had changed. The invisible guests told harsh jokes and made snide comments; they pinched and spilled hot liquids on him. He got up and walked the dog, buying a roll or a container of soup, but he could not remember the particulars of having done it. He washed his face constantly, but his vision was blurry and he quit trying to look in the mirror. He was sure, at times, that he heard Madame Hope's laughter, but when he tried to look there was no one there.

On Easter Sunday the sounds died away and each time he blinked his eyesight got stronger.

He put his feet down over the side of the bed and waited for the dizziness to pass. He looked up, and he saw his face in the bureau mirror. He stood, and dropped the sheet on the floor, and cupped his breasts with both hands, and then he felt his chin, which was hairless, and his throat, which was smooth.

Alyson found her old clothes back in the closet, and she put on a dress. She found makeup and tampons in the medicine cabinet, and she polished her nails and put on her highest heels, and took the dog for a walk as the church bells rang out the resurrection.

She swayed a little, and she listened to the sound of her nylon thighs rubbing against each other, and the swish in her skirt was certainly flashier than it needed to be. She smiled every time she saw her reflection.

She picked out the clothes she would wear when she saw Peter. Then she sat in an outdoor cafe and let the sun warm her face. And she thought about how good it would all be.

The next day everyone called her Alyson and no one was surprised. Anna came in to complain about loneliness and Eliot began to talk to Pierre about an important contact he'd made as they both headed for the men's room. Alyson tracked down some information about Bigfoot and contacted hotels to start negotiations. She scheduled a meeting with Adpub for later in the week.

She bought a bottle of champagne and flowers on the way home, as well as a scarf she had noticed the day before. She walked the dog, showered, let some cheese warm to room temperature, got out the good wine glasses, and selected records for the stereo.

At eight o'clock the downstairs buzzer rang and she stood by the door and listened to his footsteps running up the stairs. Dingo heard them, too, and he skittered to Alyson's feet, a low whine jittering from his throat, his head lowered to see under the door.

And then a knock, and she opened the door, and there was Peter. He seemed both fantastic and normal, standing there, his eyebrows raised. His eyes lit up to see her, and his mouth cracked open in his crooked grin, the dog went berserk, and he grabbed her and did his little half-spin, engulfing her and driving the dog crazy.

"Come in, come in," she said when she finally broke away. "Make yourself at home. You know where everything is."

He moved slowly to the living room, looking at things, even touching the wall lightly to re-orient himself. "You're back for good?" he asked finally, settling himself in his old seat on the sofa.

"For good or bad," she said firmly.

He looked down at his hands. She was still standing. "I've missed you," he said. "I can hardly believe how much I've missed you. I thought it would go away."

She sat down opposite him, feeling slightly formal and not yet pleased by his words. "You love me despite yourself?" she asked mockingly. She figured she might as well try for the sophisticated approach.

"The simpler I thought things were, the more complicated they got," he answered. "I don't enjoy being a heel, but it seems to happen automatically. I'm sorry." He looked unhappy as his eyes blinked rapidly.

"This isn't a very good start," she said, laughing nervously. She had pictured a different conversation entirely. Suddenly resolute, she moved over to the seat beside him and picked up his hand, stroking it tentatively. He closed his eyes and inhaled. "Oh God," he sighed. "I want to touch you."

"You can touch me."

Peter shook his head.

"Your letter last week," she said. "I understood from your letter that you were coming back to me. Did you lie again? Was that a lie?" Her voice was shrill; she clenched her hand.

"It was true last week," he said miserably.

"What's happened?" she cried sharply. "What could have changed so much in just a week?"

He blinked; his eyes seemed to overflow.

"Maggie's pregnant," he said and lifted his hands out and up.

"So?" she asked.

He looked at her with surprise. "It's one mistake on top of the other, but she's going to have the baby."

Alyson waited.

"And I'm going to marry her."

She almost said, "But you're not the father!" Instead she bit her lip and sat there frozen with realization.

"I even looked at rings for us," he moaned, "for you and me. I picked out rings."

Dingo sat at his feet and whined, staring at Peter, lifting one paw and begging.

Peter reached into his pocket. "I brought the rings," he said.

"I don't want to see them! Put them away!" Alyson cried.

He looked at her with pain on his face. "God, if only it hadn't all gone wrong," he moaned. "If only she wasn't pregnant! All I want is to be with you, to be free. Oh God, if only it were *your* baby and not hers."

Alyson winced visibly. "You don't have to stay with her. If she wants to keep it, let her."

"Alyson, I'm going to be a *father*. I can't just walk away. I'm responsible for another life. I don't know, I can't explain it, I feel I have to do this. I don't want to marry her, I want to marry *you*."

"Well then," Alyson said desperately, "then divorce her after the baby's born. Millions of men do it."

He looked at her angrily. "I hate myself over this mess, Alyson. I can't keep lying and breaking promises."

"Do you have to stop *now?*"

"I'm sorry. This hurts more than anything. But there's no way out now. This is it." He stood up. "I have to go."

She watched him walk slowly to the door then turn around. "Can I come and see the dog sometimes?" She lifted her head and stared. "Just a joke," he said quickly, then paused. "No, I guess not. I love you."

She could see the trail of one tear wet on his cheek as he opened the door and left.

*A*fter he'd gone, Alyson stared at the door with stunned abstraction. Her first impulse had been to rush to the gypsy and bargain, beg, cajole, or threaten her into a better form of living.

But she sat through that impulse, looking at what had already happened.

"What could I possibly do next?" she thought with alarm. The devil was always a step ahead of her, always able to find the detail Alyson forgot. It didn't seem much return for a soul, an entire soul, which Alyson was beginning to feel—and beginning to feel very strongly—was worth much more than the gypsy would ever agree to give.

Karen Heuler

Chapter 21

*O*ut in the redwood forest, on a mountain ridge that had not yet been cut down for export and ultimate conversion to disposable chopsticks, Alyson waited for the first of a series of interviews. She contemplated the scene with satisfaction. The entrants were an entirely different group from the last: everyone had cameras; many had backpacks and books illustrating the tracks of different animals. A large number of wildlife organizations had written about the search for Bigfoot, many of them noting that, as the forests disappeared, so would all the animals, documented or not, and all the mystery. The search for Bigfoot caught the public's eye. Even the general media caught on to it, often showing whole mountains stripped of trees as part of the story. This could be it, they said soberly, as we near the end of the frontier, the last of the wilderness; this might be your one chance to see a legend before the whole continent gets paved.

Even Pierre was astonished at the attention. "If someone does see Bigfoot, we could go down in history as saviors." His eyes glistened. "Think of the publicity."

"We could add another item to the Endangered Species list," Alyson answered drily.

"I'm beginning to believe in Bigfoot," Pierre answered. "I *want* to believe in Bigfoot."

"It would make a nice cover," she agreed.

"A cover," Pierre murmured. His teeth showed through his grin.

The rules of the hunt were simple: no one was expected to bring in Bigfoot, but the best piece of evidence would win. These included photos of the beast itself, or of its footprints; pieces of fur; scat; bones. The evidence would be evaluated by a panel which included doctors, veterinarians, a paleontologist, a photographic expert and, "for charm," as Pierre said, a poet. The contest itself ran a week in a wide area that provided campsites and inns. Each entrant had to wear a radio transmitter, supplied by a firm whose name was featured prominently. Portions of the proceeds were to be split between a number of local and federal wilderness and wildlife groups. By now, however, the money was secondary. Spinoffs in terms of new membership and press attention gave everyone an adrenaline high. The revenue generated by T-shirts alone would compensate the sponsoring groups for their involvement.

It was midweek. Daily buses collected entrants from the nearest towns. The weather was fine, and each day brought spur-of-the-moment participants, day-trippers only, with inadequate shoes and paper bags of sandwiches. They signed papers taking responsibility for themselves, swearing they would not leave refuse or pollute streams of water or burn open fires, but Alyson doubted they would all behave conscientiously. There were bets, she had heard, about the Bigfoot results. They were very uncomplicated bets, she supposed, since *Adventure* had been able to confirm that 'locals' had been caught creating footprints up in the hills. Pierre had decided to issue an announcement about it: "Adds spice. Definitely adds spice. And who looks bad? They do."

Two people had already come back with pictures of the false footprints—beautiful pictures taken with flushed faces. They were pinned to the board at the judges' booth. Newer entrants studied them carefully, along with an explanation of the obvious defects and a description of what to look for.

Alyson stood in front of the photos, looking around her at the vast extent of trees, the hills moving away from her, the busy hum of human life, listening to the high, excited calls and the rolling pitch of laughter. Camera crews had been staked out with an easy nonchalance;

they were there for the week even if nothing happened. Bigfoot had immense local appeal and had been revived nationally. Most stations had entered into the spirit of the thing by having daily bulletins. Alyson was scheduled for one of these, a quick update on a late morning news show, taped at the beginning of the day.

A group came towards her, carrying equipment. She straightened herself and smiled, automatically running her fingers through hair that had now grown long enough to reach her ears.

"Ms Salky?"

She nodded.

The reporter, an attractive man in, she guessed, his early forties, came closer. "Just a few minutes. A brief chat about developments. Any new specimens, a quick reference to the length of the contest and the rules about authenticity." He turned to the camera behind him. "Get the photos in." He turned back to Alyson. "Ready? Here goes."

Alyson studied him as he introduced himself to the camera, then introduced her.

"And this is, what, the third day of the hunt, now?" He smiled at her winningly, leaning his microphone towards her.

She nodded. "Four more to go. We've been averaging close to 100 new participants a day. Of course, a lot of them are here for the day only. Our current estimates are close to 1,000 for overnights or longer. A lot of those are experienced campers setting up their bases deeper in. They're the ones we think stand the best chance of a sighting, although," and here she grinned to show all her teeth, "there's no guarantee that going farther in will be an advantage. You can come across evidence anywhere. Sightings of Bigfoot have included sudden appearances in backyards or on highways. We assume whatever trails exist will be more perfectly preserved in the depths of the forest, but a sharp eye might be able to find evidence anywhere—maybe even close to where we stand."

The reporter turned to the camera. "Check your backyards, folks, though even if you shake hands with Bigfoot you've got to register first to get the prize money."

"That's right," Alyson said agreeably. "It's still possible to register and it's still possible to search. I'm going out myself today. It's too beautiful a day not to."

"So you're giving it a try?" the reporter said cheerfully. "Do you have any hints?"

"I've studied the footprints behind me." She turned and the camera followed. "These are false footprints planted by people with a small sense of humor. They were immediately disqualified by our board of experts—which includes paleontologists who can reconstruct whole dinosaurs from the blades of grass they stepped on, so don't think you can fool them—and even if I don't find Bigfoot, I think I'll find the spirit of this country. I can't think of a better way to spend the day than in these trees, here for centuries, in this good clean air." She turned to the camera and flashed another toothy smile. "But don't get me wrong. I plan to find Bigfoot—although it wouldn't count as a win for me, of course, since I'm one of the sponsors. It would be purely personal."

The reporter nodded and said, "Cut. Very good." He turned to Alyson. "You've done this before."

"And I'm getting good at it." She said it placidly and looked at him cheerfully.

"Yes, you are," he agreed. "Out for the day or staying overnight?"

"Oh, I think a five- or six-hour stroll will be enough for me. When night falls in the wilderness, I start to imagine things."

"That's why people build houses," he said. "Strong houses. How about a follow-up tomorrow? With or without Bigfoot. You can even get lyrical about birds and fawns. Good for tourism."

"Are there fawns this time of year?"

"Does it matter? Like I said, good for tourism. Tomorrow?"

She agreed.

She picked up the small backpack at her feet, hoisting it onto her shoulders as she watched him walk off. "I did get lyrical," she thought comfortably.

She signed herself out at the registration desk (where numbers were checked twice a day, so there was always a listing of who was still on the trail). She caught a ride a few miles down the road, hoping to give herself some distance from the starting groups.

They had had a week of glorious weather so far, and the forecasters continued to predict sun. She picked her way into the forest, walking slowly and looking all around. It was amazing how little she knew. What was this tree, this vine, this small plant at her feet? Insects flew at her face, not all of them mosquitoes. After the first fifteen minutes she no longer heard traffic on the road. Some birds sang: what birds were they? She stopped, listening, and followed one song to a small brown bird on a branch. "Sparrows, blue jays, pigeons," she said, listing the birds whose calls she knew. "Cardinals and robins. Sea gulls."

The slopes all looked gentle enough, but without trails the footing was rough. She came across thin lines, like narrow footpaths. Deer trails, she thought. The trees soared upward like fantastic, reaching hands. The sky disappeared somewhere up in the canopy, breaking through now and then where a great tree had fallen. The air was curiously still, though far above she caught the rustle of distant leaves.

Once or twice she heard an excited shriek or a break of laughter, disembodied voices that sounded like leftovers from history rather than searchers discovering and discarding their finds.

It was a fine day to stride in the woods, and she began to hum. She had felt, lately, as if she were harboring a constant, smug smile.

Suddenly, three months ago, when she'd discovered the plastic bags in the back of Anna's freezer, she'd achieved calm, a stable calm. Life had shifted into place again.

Something moved in the tree and she paused to study it. A possum, moving slowly. There was another yell far over to her right, and then a faint, answering response.

Her life was going well. Pierre was exultant with the Bigfoot search, had followed every development with a happy gleam in his eye. When he looked at Alsyon it was like he was looking at dessert or a good-luck charm. Though her salary had dropped when she turned back into a woman, Pierre had raised it only the month before. She now earned more than Eliot did, and she had an office to herself. Pierre checked with her first about ideas. She knew she was valuable.

Or does he see me as a performing dog? she wondered. It mattered little to her now, what Pierre thought. She hadn't been aware, during the first competition, how powerful it was to set all this machinery in motion. Now she could call hotels or anyone in the service industry, and she was recognized. People laughed indulgently, happily, when she spoke, their eyes watched her for cues. At this level, she thought—so long as she maintained this level—it didn't matter if she was a woman.

But she kept herself restrained. She evaluated the possibilities, she enjoyed the opportunities, but she watched. She had a sense, now, that she had more choice in life. The panic was gone, and in its place she was surrounded by opportunity. She was free; she could do anything.

Peter had fallen out of her heart, not all at once but surprisingly quickly. She looked back on loving him as if it were a journey that had gradually turned bad. It was so gradual that she hadn't registered it until it was over. She had hated the day when she'd thought of him and nothing in her heart had jammed. He still called her, but she was the one who no longer cared. It was odd and unsettling, to have stopped loving the love of her life.

What had changed? Revenge and despair were addictions; she could see that clearly now. She couldn't help but feel that the fortuneteller injected frenzy along with her bargains; she made sure that what you needed was hope, and more hope: never fruition, never satisfaction. She had miscalculated with Alyson; perhaps that's all that had happened. The gypsy had enjoyed one laugh too many, and turned into an obstacle. Now she only surfaced occasionally, nodding at Alyson from the center of a crowd, whispering things from a darkened doorway while Alyson walked Dingo. "My, my, what a juicy little dog," she'd hissed, twice.

Occasionally, when the phone rang and all Alyson could hear was a labored breathing, she thought it was the gypsy, and simply said "No" before she hung up. What could the gypsy offer, now, that she couldn't do on her own?

She had found a doctor willing to hold onto her supply of frozen sperm, and every month she went to have that sperm placed in her at the right time. When the Bigfoot hunt was over she would have another try.

She climbed to the top of a particularly steep slope and came suddenly on a view of the mountains that made her heart pound. All around her, in every direction, stood endless stands of trees linked up and down the mountains. Clouds passing overhead threw shadows like huge ships sailing over the forests, spreading and shifting and racing.

For hundreds of years these have been here, she thought; how many hundreds of years for these particular trees?

"Do you want these trees?" a voice wheedled at her shoulder, and with a sinking heart, she turned to see the gypsy there, grinning beside her.

"Consider the money you'd make," the gypsy chortled. "All those trees. The government charges about two dollars for each; you cut them down and sell them at what? Say ten dollars, a conservative figure." She swept her arm across the valley. "Can you imagine how many trees there are?"

"Cut them down?" Alyson repeated.

The gypsy looked at her with a sharp eye. "Or you could save them, of course, call a huge party and get the tree-huggers here. They can hug all they want, no damage done. You'd be a savior." She squinted. "There are owls here, too, you know. Spotted ones. Just say the word, it's all yours, from right here as far as you can see. Why, I bet you couldn't even walk it all in a lifetime. Too far to go and why bother anyway? A tree's a tree. But not a tree will fall without your knowing it, I'll take care of the details, if you say no then it will stand till the end of time, one very old toothpick. All this will be yours." She paused. "Not a bird will fall from the sky. I swear." She held up one hand like a boy scout, laying the other on her heart.

"No."

The gypsy bowed and scraped back a pace. "You're right, I forgot who I was dealing with. Forgot myself entirely. Of course you want love, what woman doesn't? What does it profit a woman if she gain the whole world but suffer the loss of her love? Believe me, I feel for you. I've made mistakes—I'll be the first to admit that I should have tightened up the show a little, covered some of the finer details. Though I think," she squinted, "you enjoyed the details quite a bit. But it's true," she cried, anticipating an argument, "I was going through a rough patch myself, not quite my usual speed—the last things that leave you, let me point out, are the emotions, the old swing-up, swing-down, wear and tear of the centuries. I look back and I can't forgive myself. You can't play with a soul like it's a mouse, can you? And everyone's so consumer-oriented these days, so insistent on their rights. What was I thinking of? But wait, there's a point here." She grinned and beamed and sucked in her breath, spilling it out again in a faint shower that Alyson could feel on her neck. "I can give you love."

One side of Alyson's mouth twisted.

"Real love, fundamental love, love straight down to your bowels, the whole joyride. Love thicker than time, crashing through you like thunder, oh! such love. Describe him to me, tell me what you want, I have the world to work with, I can find him with only the briefest sketch, just a few details."

"I did describe someone once, remember?"

"Don't be like that, don't hold a grudge. Just think, you've got experience, you know more about value now, I bet you can think of exactly the right ticket, can't you?"

"I don't want anything from you."

The gypsy frowned. "It won't work, you know. Frozen popsicles, eh? That was just a joke, my leaving them around, a little irony on my part. I confess I can't resist a joke. But, really why trust in miracles when I can give you anything you want in real terms? Your popsicles will run out, and then what?"

"No."

The gypsy seemed to relax, riding back on her heels and surveying the mountains. "I can't blame you, really. Who knows? Maybe some things *can* work out. It's chancy, but maybe you like chance now. Maybe you feel confident. Confidence is a wonderful thing. And you're riding high, a prominent figure now, lots of attention. I even saw you on TV." She stared thoughtfully at the distance.

"Yes," Alyson said cautiously, "I seem to be on a roll."

"Pity it will end," Madame Hope said easily.

Alyson, too, now stared into the green flow of the valley. Don't listen, she told herself.

"Power. Glory," the gypsy sighed. "It's more than a tickle, isn't it? Don't you love it? Doesn't it creep under your skin like a wonderful itch? People know you, respect you. With a little more success they'll hang on your every word, give you parades in the city. And applause! Imagine it. The rush of their ardor, their joy when they see you—leaping to their feet, clapping for you like a local wonder. And it can last—I can make it last. You'll be surrounded by eyes that judge how important they are by how close they get to you. Eager voices, hands reaching out to touch you, people who'll repeat your name—they saw you, you were this close!—because your name means success. The most important woman in your time! The woman who dared take on the wonders of the world, one by one, *real* wonders, *real* mysteries! How would you like to find Bigfoot? It's a start." Her voice dropped. "I know where to look."

Alyson had been listening despite herself. Success had a sweet ring to it, and failure had a sour taste. She knew she liked the ripple of excitement that touched her sometimes, and as yet she was just a tiny item of interest in a limited circle of eyes.

The gypsy watched her carefully as she considered. Alyson looked up to see her sharp eyes, her nasty smile. What she really longed for, she thought, was escape from her own limits, her own failures. And as she looked at the fortuneteller she could see all the moments of her own humiliation—the gypsy watching Bob couple with Helen on the floor, Peter returning only to tell her he was the father of Maggie's baby, Eliot's mocking whispers, the lackluster fight in the restaurant—all of them sideshows. Everything the gypsy touched turned cheap.

"A sideshow," Alyson murmured. "Hell must be a circus of some kind." She laughed lightly at herself.

The gypsy leaned closer. "All the world will know you. All the world will lay at your feet. Fireworks! Orchestras! Men who'll lick your toes!"

"Get thee behind me, Satan," Alyson said.

"Oh, *quotes*," the gypsy said dismissively.

Alyson laughed again. "Anything I got through you would be cheap. If you promised me gold, it would be painted brass. Everything you do crawls with spite, ripples with it like a centipede. I want nothing to do with you." She deliberately turned away.

Close by, Alyson heard a series of muffled shouts. A bulky figure that she first thought to be the devil's dog was coming at her through the trees. But it was paler, and bigger, and ran on four legs and then on two.

"I won't release you!" the gypsy cried spitefully.

Alyson's eyes were trained on the figure now hurtling straight at them. Yells and screams followed, only minutes away and approaching fast.

Alyson's heart was beating faster. The gypsy, red-faced and furious, began to sputter.

"I deny you," Alyson said.

"Beelzebub, Mephisto, Satan in all your glory, stand by me, lean to me, breathe through me," the fortuneteller began to intone, her eyes bulging, her arms flailing, and it was just at this moment that Alyson stepped back quickly as the rushing figure broke free of the trees. Its fur was silver, thin but plush, and at first she thought it was wearing a cape, for there seemed to be a drape between its arms and its back. But as it brushed by her, pushing at the gypsy in its way, she felt the air move like a breeze against her arms and she thought, "Some kind of wing." Taken unprepared by the sudden push, Madame Hope fell into the incline with a shocked gulp, rolling over and over again like a rock. The figure scrambled past her, lunging down the hill ahead of her and even leaping over her once or twice high into the air before disappearing at last into the woods. Madame Hope rolled to a stop at the foot of a tree, where she shook her head gently and gazed at the departing beast.

Two men and a woman came running up to Alyson. "Did you see it? Did you see it? I swear I almost touched it, I was that close. You got a picture, didn't you, Ellie?"

"I got two pictures," the one named Ellie swore. "I hope they're good, I had to focus so fast."

"But you saw it too?" one man asked Alyson.

Alyson nodded. "It ran right by me."

Three pairs of eyes looked at her carefully.

"Did you get a picture?" Ellie finally asked.

"I didn't even think of it," Alyson admitted. She looked down to where the gypsy was now standing up and dusting herself off. She looked very small. Ellie's eyes followed.

"And that one?" Ellie asked. "Do you know if she took a picture?"

"I don't think she even has a camera."

Everyone let out a sigh of relief. "Thank God for that," Ellie said triumphantly, "thank God for that."

Ellie and her friends won the competition. The pictures were out of focus, but they did show something big and blurry running, and measurements and calculations of the footprints as well put it all within the realm of possibility. Alyson looked carefully at the photos. They were too indistinct, and the creature's arms were at its side. She doubted, really, that there could have been wings.

Among the other entries that made it into the final round were a half-eaten cupcake with an unusual dental impression, a picture of the back of a furry head swimming in a pond (long-distance shot, blown up), and smudged fingerprints on a coffee pot left unattended outside camp. The hiker who owned the coffee pot swore he'd heard, but not seen, something large trampling off at his approach. The only thing that had been moved was the pot, which he promptly bagged and entered. The impression was quite human, but the poet considered it a fair possibility that could only be eliminated when and if Bigfoot was found and fingerprinted.

Two months after Alyson returned to New York, she was nominated to a local political board. She had looked uneasily around the crowded room, expecting to see Madame Hope's face. That night she walked to the gypsy's storefront, and found it boarded up. She stood in front of it for a long time, and then continued walking slowly with her dog Dingo down the street. There was a clean wind riding down the block and it lifted the hair off the back of her neck. She walked slowly, enjoying herself, feeling pleasantly light and still thin. It would be at least three months before she felt any added weight, she knew; three months before it would show, but she practiced walking big-bellied and sore.

She was pregnant, and there was every reason to believe the baby would be a girl who looked exactly the same as Alyson had as a baby.

Overhead, two sparrows sang to each other in the branches of a tree as Dingo pulled and sniffed and wagged his tail. She heard a sudden flutter of wings as the sparrows drove on, and she walked on with her eyes following them, certain that life would be marvelous indeed.

Author's photo: Tracy Sides Photography

Karen Heuler's stories have appeared in over 60 literary and speculative magazines and anthologies, from *Alaska Quarterly Review* to *Weird Tales*. She's published a short-story collection and two previous novels. She lives in NYC with her dog, Booker Prize, and her cat, Pulitzer.